Alf said nothing, but his blade flickered like a serpent's tongue. There was a wicked delight in this skill that seemed to grow from the muscles themselves, inborn, effortless. If he had known what he had when he was a boy, no one would ever have dared to torment him. If he had known what a wonder it was, he would have plunged gladly into the heart of Richard's battle. But he knew now, and he knew what he was. Kin to the great cats, the leopard, the panther, swift and strong and deadly dangerous.

The prey, baited, had become the hunter; and now at last Joscelin knew it. The blood had drained from his face. He glanced about, searching desperately for an opening. There was none. Cold steel wove a cage about him. With each pass it drew closer, until its edge flickered a hair's breadth from his body.

His blood would taste most sweet. But his terror was sweeter.

THE ISLE OF GLASS

VOLUME ONE OF

THE HOUND and THE FALCON TRILOGY

Look for all these Tor books by Judith Tarr

THE GOLDEN HORN
THE HOUNDS OF GOD
THE ISLE OF GLASS

JUDITH TARR

THE ISLE OF GLASS
VOLUME ONE OF

THE HOUND and THE FALCON TRILOGY

A TOM DOHERTY ASSOCIATES BOOK

THE ISLE OF GLASS

Copyright © 1985 by Judith Tarr

All rights reserved, including the right to reproduce this book or portions thereof in any form.

Reprinted by arrangement with Bluejay Books

First Tor printing: July 1986

A TOR Book

Published by Tom Doherty Associates
49 West 24 Street
New York, N.Y. 10010

Cover art by Kevin Eugene Johnson

ISBN: 0-812-55600-3
CAN. ED.: 0-812-55601-1

Library of Congress Catalog Card Number: 85-1295

Printed in the United States

0 9 8 7 6 5 4 3 2

For Meredith

"Quis est homo?"
"Mancipium mortis, transiens viator,
  loci hospes."
          —Alcuin of York

"What is a man?"
"The slave of death, the guest of an inn,
  a wayfarer passing."
          —Helen Waddell

1

"Brother Alf! Brother Alfred!"

It was meant to be a whisper, but it echoed through the library. Brother Alfred looked up from his book, smiling a little as the novice halted panting within an inch of the table. "What is it now, Jehan?" he asked. "A rescue? The King himself come to drag you off to the wars?"

Jehan groaned. "Heaven help us! I just spent an hour explaining to Dom Morwin why I want to stay here and take vows. Father wrote to him, you see, and said that if I had to be a monk, I'd join the Knights Templar and not disgrace him completely."

Brother Alfred's smile widened. "And what said our good Abbot?"

"That I'm a waste of good muscle." Jehan sighed and hunched his shoulders. It did little good; they were still as broad as the front gate. "Brother Alf, can't anybody but you see what's under it all?"

"Brother Osric says that you will make a tolerable theologian."

"Did he? Well. He told me today that I was a blockhead, and that I'd got to the point where he'd have to turn me over to you."

"In the same breath?"

"Almost. But I'm forgetting. Dom Morwin wants to see you."

Brother Alfred closed his book. "And we've kept him waiting. Someday, Jehan, we must both take vows of silence."

"I could use it. But you? Never. How could you teach?"

"There are ways." Just as Brother Alfred turned to go, he paused. "Tomorrow, don't go to the schoolroom. Meet me here."

Jehan's whoop made no pretense of restraint.

There was a fire in the Abbot's study, and the Abbot stood in front of it, warming his hands. He did not turn when Brother Alfred entered, but said, "The weather's wild today."

The other sat in a chair nearby. "Fitting," he remarked. "You know what the hill-folk say: On the Day of the Dead, demons ride."

The Abbot crossed himself quickly, with a wry smile. "Oh, it will be a night to conjure in." He sat stiffly and sighed. "My bones feel it. You know, Alf—suddenly I'm old."

There was a silence. Brother Alfred gazed into the fire, seeing a pair of young novices, one small and slight and red as a fox, the other tall and slender and very pale with hair like silver-gilt. They were very industriously stealing apples from the orchard. His lips twitched.

"What are you thinking of?" asked the Abbot.

"Apple-stealing."

"Is that all? I was thinking of the time we changed the labels on every bottle, jar, and box of medicine in the infirmary. We almost killed old Brother Anselm when he took one of Brother Herbal's clandestine aphrodisiacs instead of the medicine he needed for his indigestion."

Brother Alfred laughed. "I remember that very well indeed; after Dom Edwin's caning, I couldn't sit for a fortnight. And we had to change the labels back again. In the end we knew Brother Herbal's stores better than he did himself."

"I can still remember. First shelf: dittany, fennel, tansy, rue. . . . Was it really almost sixty years ago?"

"Really."

"*Tempus fugit*, with a vengeance." Morwin ran his hands through his hair. A little red still remained; the rest was rusty white. "I've had my threescore years and ten, with three more for good measure. Time to think of what I should have thought of all along if I'd been as good a monk as I liked to think I was."

"Good enough, Morwin. Good enough."

"I could have been much better. I could have refused to let them make me Abbot. You did."

"You know why."

"Foolishness. You could have been a cardinal if you'd cared to try."

"How could I have? You know what I am."

"I know what you think you are. You've had the story of your advent drummed into your head so often, you've come to believe it."

"It's the truth. How it was the winter solstice, and a very storm out of Hell. And in the middle of it, at midnight indeed, a novice, keeping vigil in the chapel, heard a baby's cry. He had the courage to go out, even into that storm, which should have out-howled anything living, and he found a prodigy. A babe of about a season's growth, lying naked in the snow. And yet he was not cold; even as the novice opened the postern, what had been warming him took flight. Three white owls. Our brave lad took a long look, snatched up the child, and bolted for the chapel. When holy water seemed to make no impression, except what one would expect from a baby plunged headlong into an ice-cold bath, he baptized his discovery, named him Alf—Alfred for the Church's sake—and proceeded to make a monk of him. But the novice always swore that the brat had come out of the hollow hills."

"Had he?"

"I don't know. I seem to remember, faint and far, like another's memory: fire and shouting, and a girl running with a baby in her arms. Then the girl, cold and dead, and a storm, and three white owls. No one ever found her." Brother Alfred breathed deep. "Maybe that's only a dream, and someone actually exposed me as a changeling. What better place for one? Here on Ynys Witrin, with all its legends and its old magic."

"Or else," said Morwin, "the Fair Folk have turned Christian. Though I've never heard that any of them could bear either holy water or cold iron."

"This one can." Brother Alfred flexed his long fingers and folded them tightly in his lap. "But to take a high place in the Church or in the world . . . no. Anywhere but here, I would have gone to the stake long ago. Even here, not all the Brothers are sure that I'm not some sort of superior devil."

Morwin bristled. "Who dares to think that?"

"None so bold that he voices his doubts, or even thinks them, often."

"He had better not!"

Alf smiled and shook his head. "You were always too fierce in my defense."

"And a good thing too. I've pulled you out of many a broil, from the first time I saw the other novices make a butt of you."

"So much trouble for a few harmless words."

"Harmless! It was getting down to sticks and stones when I came by."

"They were only trying to frighten me," Alf said. "But that's years past. We must truly be old if we can care so much for what happened so long ago."

"Don't be so kind. It's me, and you know it. I've always been one to bear a grudge—the worse for my soul." Morwin rose and stood with his hands clasped behind his back. "Alf. Someday sooner or later, I'm going to face my Maker. And when I do that, I want to be sure I've left St. Ruan's in good hands." Alf would have spoken, but he shook his head. "I know, Alf. You've refused every office anyone has tried to give you and turned down the abbacy three times. The more fool you; each time, the second choice has been far inferior. I don't want that to happen again."

"Morwin. You know it must."

"Why?"

Brother Alfred stood, paler even than usual, and spread his arms. "Look at me!"

Morwin's jaw set. "I'm looking," he said grimly. "I've looked nearly every day for sixty years."

"What do you see?"

"The one man I'd trust to take the abbacy and to keep it as it should be kept."

"Man, Morwin? Do you think I am a man? Come. You alone can see me as I truly am. If you will."

The Abbot found that he could not look away. His friend stood in front of him, very tall and very pale, his eyes wide with something close to despair. Strange eyes, palest gold like his hair and pupiled like a cat's.

"You see," said Alf. "Remember what else had the novices calling me devil and witch's get. My way with beasts and with men. My little conjuring tricks." He gathered a handful of fire and shadow, plaited it into a long strange-gleaming strand, and tossed it to Morwin. The other caught it reflexively, and it was solid, a length of cord at once shadow-cool and fire-hot. "And finally, Morwin, old friend, how old am I?"

"Two or three years younger than I."

"And how old do I look?"

Morwin scowled and twisted the cord in his hands, and said nothing.

"How old did Earl Rogier think I was when he brought Jehan to St. Ruan's? How old did Bishop Aylmer think I was, he who read my *Gloria Dei* thirty years ago and looked in vain for me all the while he guested here, only last year? How old did he think me, Morwin? And what was it he said to you? 'That lad has a great future, Dom Morwin. Send him along to me when he grows a little older, and I promise you'll not regret it.' He thought I was not eighteen!"

Still Morwin was silent, although the pain in his friend's face and voice had turned his scowl to an expression of old and bitter sorrow.

Alf dropped back into his seat and covered his face with his hands. "And you would make me swear to accept the election if it came to me again. Morwin, will you never understand that I cannot let myself take any title?"

The other's voice was rough. "There's a limit to humility, Alf. Even in a monk."

"It's not humility. Dear God, no! I have more pride than Lucifer. When I was as young as my body, I exulted in what I thought I was. There were Bishop Aylmers then, too, all too eager to flatter a young monk with a talent for both politics and theology. They told me I was brilliant, and I believed them. I knew I was an enchanter; I thought I might have been the son of an elven prince, or a lord at least, and I told myself tales of his love for my mortal mother and of her determination that I should be a Christian. And of three white owls." His head lifted. "I was even vain, God help me; the more so when I knew the world, and saw myself reflected in women's eyes. Not a one but sighed to see me a monk."

"And not a one managed to move you."

"Is that to my credit? I was proud that I never fell, nor ever even slipped. No, Morwin. What I have is not humility. It's fear. It was in me even when I was young, beneath the pride, fear that I was truly inhuman. It grew as the years passed. When I was thirty and was still mistaken for a boy, I turned my mind from it. At forty I began to recognize the fear. At fifty I knew it fully. At sixty it was open terror. And now, I can hardly bear it. Morwin—Morwin—what if I shall never die?"

Very gently Morwin said, "All things die, Alf."

"Then why do I not grow old? Why am I still exactly as I was the day I took my vows? And—what is immortal—what is elvish—is soulless. To be what I am and to lack a soul . . . it torments me even to think of it."

Morwin laid a light hand on his shoulder. "Alf. Whatever you are, whatever you become, I cannot believe that God would be so cruel, so unjust, so utterly vindictive, as to let you live without a soul and die with your body. Not after you've loved Him so long and so well."

"Have I? Or is all my worship a mockery? I've even dared to serve at His altar, to say His Mass—I, a shadow, a thing of air and darkness. And you would make me Abbot. Oh, sweet Jesu!"

"Stop it, Alf!" Morwin rapped. "That's the trouble with you. You bottle yourself up so well you get a name for serenity. And when you shatter, the whole world shakes. Spare us for once, will you?"

But Alf was beyond even that strong medicine. With a wordless cry he whirled and fled.

Morwin stared after him, paused, shook his head. Slowly, painfully, he lowered himself into his chair. The cord was still in his hand, fire and darkness, heat and cold. For a long while he sat staring at it, stroking it with trembling fingers. "Poor boy," he whispered. "Poor boy."

2

Jehan could not sleep. He lay on his hard pallet, listening to the night sounds of the novices' dormitory, snores and snuffles and an occasional dreamy murmur. It was cold under his thin blanket; wind worked its way through the shutters of the high narrow windows, and rain lashed against them, rattling them upon their iron hinges.

But he was used to that. The novices said that he could sleep soundly on an ice floe in the northern sea, with a smithy in full clamor beside him.

For the thousandth time he rolled into a new position, on his stomach with his head pillowed on his folded arms. He kept seeing Brother Alfred, now bent over a book in the library, now weaving upon his great loom, now singing in chapel with a voice like a tenor bell. All those serene faces flashed past and shattered, and he saw the tall slight form running from the Abbot's study, wearing such a look that even now Jehan trembled.

Stealthily he rose. No one seemed awake. He shook out the robe which had been his pillow; quickly he donned it. His heart was hammering. If anyone caught him, he would get a caning and a week of cleaning the privy.

Big though his body was, he was as soft-footed as a cat. He crept past the sleeping novices, laid his hand upon the door-latch. A prayer had formed and escaped before he saw the irony in it.

With utmost care he opened the door. Brother Owein the novice-master snored in his cell, a rhythm unbroken even by the creak of hinges and the scrape of the latch. Jehan flowed past his doorway, hardly daring to breathe, wavered in a turning, and bolted.

Brother Alf's cell was empty. So too was the Lady Chapel, where he had been all through Compline, prostrate upon the stones. St. Ruan's was large and Alf familiar with every inch of it. He might even be in the garderobe.

Jehan left the chapel, down the passage which led to the gateway. Brother Kyriell, the porter, slept the sleep of the just.

As Jehan paused, a shadow flickered past. It reached the small gate, slid back the bolt without a sound, and eased the heavy panel open. Wind howled through, armed with knives of sleet. It tore back the cowl from a familiar pale head that bowed against it and plunged forward.

By the time Jehan reached the gate, Alf had vanished into the storm. Without thought Jehan went after him.

Wind tore at him. Rain blinded him. Cold sliced through the thick wool of his robe.

But it was not quite pitch-dark. As sometimes happens in winter storms, the clouds seemed to catch the light of the drowned moon and to scatter it, glowing with their own phantom light. Jehan's eyes, already adapted to the dark, could discern the wet glimmer of the road, and far down upon it a blur which might have been Alf's bare white head.

Folly had taken him so far, and folly drove him on. The wind fought him, tried to drive him back to the shelter of the abbey. Alf was gaining—Jehan could hardly see him now, even in the lulls between torrents of rain. Yet he struggled onward.

Something loomed over him so suddenly that he recoiled.

It lived and breathed, a monstrous shape that stank like Hell's own midden.

A voice rose over the wind's howl, sounding almost in his ear. "Jehan—help me. Take the bridle."

Alf. And the shape was suddenly a soaked and trembling horse with its rider slumped over its neck. His numbed hands caught at the reins and gentled the long bony head that shied at first, then pushed against him. He hunted in his pocket and found the apple he had filched at supper, and there in the storm, with rain sluicing down the back of his neck, he fed it to the horse.

"Lead her up to the abbey," Alf said, again in his ear. The monk stood within reach, paying no heed to the wind or the rain. Warmth seemed to pour from him in delirious waves.

The wind that had fought Jehan now lent him all its aid, almost carrying him up the road to the gate.

In the lee of the wall, Alf took the reins. "Go in and open up."

Jehan did as he was told. Before he could heave the gate well open, Brother Kyriell peered out of his cell, rumpled and unwontedly surly. "What goes on here?" he demanded sharply.

Jehan shot him a wild glance. The gate swung open; the horse clattered over the threshold. On seeing Alf, Brother Kyriell swallowed what more he would have said and hastened forward.

"Jehan," Alf said, "stable the mare and see that she's fed." Even as he spoke he eased the rider from her back. More than rain glistened in the light of Brother Kyriell's lamp: blood, lurid scarlet and rust-brown, both fresh and dried. "Kyriell—help me carry him."

They bore him on his own cloak through the court and down the passage to the infirmary. Even when they laid him in a cell, he did not move save for the rattle and catch of tormented breathing.

Brother Kyriell left with many glances over his shoulder. Alf paid him no heed. For a moment he paused, buffeted by wave on wave of pain. With an effort that made him gasp, he shielded his mind against it. His shaking hands folded back the cloak, caressing its rich dark fabric, drawing strength from the contact.

The body beneath was bare but for a coarse smock like a serf's, and terrible to see: brutally beaten and flogged; marked with deep oozing burns; crusted with mud and blood and other, less mentionable stains. Three ribs were cracked, the right leg broken in two places, and the left hand crushed; it looked as if it had been trampled. Sore wounds, roughly tied up with strips of the same cloth as the smock, torn and filthy and too long neglected.

Carefully he began to cleanse the battered flesh, catching his breath at the depth and raggedness of some of the wounds. They were filthy and far from fresh; yet they had suffered no infection at all.

Alf came last to the face. A long cut on the forehead had bled and dried and bled again, and made the damage seem worse than it was. One side was badly bruised and swollen, but nothing was broken; the rest had taken no more than a cut and a bruise or two.

Beneath it all, he was young, lean as a panther, with skin as white as Alf's own. A youth, just come to manhood and very good to look on. Almost too much so. Even with all his hurts, that was plain to see.

Alf tore his eyes from that face. But the features haunted him. Eagle-proud, finely drawn beneath beard and bruises. The cast of them was uncanny: eldritch.

Resolutely Alf focused upon the tormented body. He closed his eyes, seeking in his mind for the stillness, the core of cool fire which made him what he was. There was peace there, and healing.

Nothing. Only turmoil and a roiling mass of pain. His own turmoil, the other's agony, together raised a barrier he could not cross. He tried. He beat upon it. He strained until the sweat ran scalding down his sides.

Nothing.

He must have groaned aloud. Jehan was standing beside him, eyes dark with anxiety. "Brother Alf? Are you all right?"

The novice's presence bolstered him. He nodded and breathed deep, shuddering.

Jehan was not convinced. "Brother Alf, you're sick. You ought to be in bed yourself."

"It's not that kind of sickness." He reached for a splint, a roll of bandages. His hands were almost steady. "You'll have to help me with this. Here; so."

There was peace of a sort in that slow labor. Jehan had a feeling for it; his hands were big but gentle, and they needed little direction.

After a long while, it was done. Alf knelt by the bed, staring at his handiwork, calm at last—a blank calm.

Jehan set something on the bed. Wet leather, redolent of horses: a set of saddlebags. "These were on the mare's saddle," he said. "And the mare . . . she's splendid! She's no vagabond's nag. Unless," he added with a doubtful glance at the stranger, "he stole her."

"Does he look like a thief?"

"He looks as if he's been tortured."

"He has." Alf opened the saddlebags. They were full; one held a change of clothing, plain yet rich. The other bore a flask, empty but holding still a ghost of wine, and a crust of bread and an apple or two, and odds and ends of metal and leather.

Amid this was a leather pouch, heavy for its size. Alf poured its contents into his hand: a few coins and a ring, a signet of silver and sapphire. The stone bore a proud device: a seabird in flight surmounted by a crown.

Jehan leaned close to see, and looked up startled. "Rhiyana!"

"Yes. The coins are Rhiyanan, too." Alf turned the ring to catch the light. "See how the stone's carved. *Guidion rex et imperator.* It's the King's own seal."

Jehan stared at the wounded man. "That's not Gwydion. Gwydion must be over eighty. And what's his ring doing here? Rhiyana is across the Narrow Sea, and we're the breadth of Anglia away from even that."

"But we're only two days' ride from Gwynedd, whose King had his fostering at Gwydion's hands. Look here: a penny from Gwynedd."

"Is he a spy?"

"With his King's own seal to betray him?"

"An envoy, then." Jehan regarded him, as fascinated by his face as Alf had been. "He looks like the elf-folk. You know that story, don't you, Brother Alf? My nurse used to tell it to me. She was Rhiyanan, you see, like my mother. She called the King the Elvenking."

"I've heard the tales," Alf said. "Some of them. Pretty fancies for a nursery."

Jehan bridled. "Not all of them, Brother Alf! She said that the King was so fair of face, he looked like an elven lord. He used to ride through the kingdom, and he brought joy wherever he went; though he was no coward, he'd never fight if there was any way at all to win peace. That's why Rhiyana never fights wars."

"But it never refuses to intervene in other kingdoms' troubles."

"Maybe that's what this man has been doing. There's been fighting on the border between Gwynedd and Anglia. He might have been trying to stop it."

"Little luck he's had, from the look of him."

"The King should have come himself. Nurse said no one could keep up a quarrel when he was about. Though maybe he's getting too feeble to travel. He's terribly old."

"There are the tales."

"Oh," Jehan snorted. "That's the pretty part. About how he has a court of elvish folk and never grows old. His court is passing fair by all I've ever heard, but I can't believe he isn't a creaking wreck. I'll wager he dyes his hair and keeps the oglers at a distance."

Alf smiled faintly. "I hope you aren't betting too high." He yawned and stretched. "I'll spend the night here. You, my lad, had better get back to your own bed before Brother Owein misses you."

"Brother Owein sleeps like the dead. If the dead could snore."
"We know they'll rise again. Quick, before Owein proves it."

Jehan had kindled a fire in the room's hearth; Alf lay in front of it, wrapped in his habit. Even yet the stranger had not moved, but he was alive, his pain gnawing at the edge of Alf's shield. But worse still was the knowledge that Alf could have healed what the other suffered, but for his own, inner confusion. How could he master another's bodily pain, if he could not master that of his own mind?

If I must be what I am, he cried into the darkness, *then let me be so. Don't weigh me down with human weakness!*

The walls remained, stronger than ever.

3

As Alf slept, he dreamed. He was no longer in St. Ruan's, no longer a cloistered monk, but a young knight with an eagle's face, riding through hills that rose black under the low sky. His gray mare ran lightly, with sure feet, along a steep stony track. Before them, tall on a crag, loomed a castle. After the long wild journey, broken by nights in hillmen's huts or under the open sky, it should have been a welcome sight. It was ominous.

But he had a man to meet there. He drew himself up and shortened the reins; the mare lifted her head and quickened her step.

The walls took them and wrapped them in darkness.

Within, torchlight was dim. Men met them, men-at-arms, seven of them. As the rider dismounted, they closed around him. The mare's ears flattened; she sidled, threatening.

He gentled her with a touch and said, "I'll stable her myself."

None of the men responded. The rider led the mare forward, and they parted, falling into step behind.

The stable was full, but a man led a horse out of its stall to make room for the mare. The rider unsaddled her and rubbed her down, and fed her with his own hands; when she had eaten her fill, he threw his cloak over her and left her with a few soft words.

Alone now, he walked within a circle of armed men, pacing easily as if it were an honor guard. But the back of his neck prickled. With an effort he kept his hand away from his sword. Fara was safe, warding his possessions, among them the precious signet. He could defend himself. There was no need to fear.

The shadows mocked his courage. Cold hostility walled him in.

It boded ill for his embassy. Yet Lord Rhydderch had summoned him, and although the baron had a name for capricious cruelty, the envoy had not expected to fail. He never had.

They ascended a steep narrow stair and gathered in a guardroom. There the men-at-arms halted. Without a word they turned on their captive.

His sword was out, a baleful glitter, but there was no room to wield it. Nor would he shed blood if he could help it. One contemptuous blow sent the blade flying.

Hands seized him. That touched his pride. His fist struck flesh, bone. Another blow met metal; a sixfold weight bore him to the floor, onto the body of the man he had felled.

Rare anger sparked, but he quenched it. They had not harmed him yet. He lay still, though they spat upon him and called him coward; though they stripped him and touched his body in ways that made his lips tighten and his eyes flicker dangerously; even though they bound him with chains, rusted iron, cruelly tight.

They hauled him to his feet, looped the end of the chain through a ring in the ceiling, stretched his arms taut above his head. His toes barely touched the floor; all his weight hung suspended from his wrists.

When he was well-secured, a stranger entered, a man in mail. He was not a tall man, but thickset, with the dark weathered features of a hillman, and eyes so pale they seemed to have no color at all. When he pushed back his mail-coif, his hair was as black as the bristle of his brows and shot with gray.

He stood in front of the prisoner, hands on hips. "So," he said. "The rabbit came to the trap."

The other kept his head up, his voice quiet. "Lord Rhydderch, I presume? Alun of Caer Gwent, at your service."

"Pretty speech, in faith, and a fine mincing way he has about it." Rhydderch prodded him as if he had been a bullock at market. "And a long stretch of limb to add to it. Your King must be fond of outsize beauties."

"The King of Rhiyana," Alun said carefully, "has sent me as his personal envoy. Any harm done to me is as harm to the royal person. Will you not let me go?"

Rhydderch laughed, a harsh bark with no mirth in it. "The Dotard of Caer Gwent? What can he do if I mess up his fancy-boy a little?"

"I bear the royal favor. Does that mean nothing to you?"

"Your King's no king of mine, boy."

"I came in good faith, seeking peace between Gwynedd and Anglia. Would you threaten that peace?"

"My King," said Rhydderch, "will pay well for word of Rhiyana's plotting with Gwynedd. And Anglia between, in the pincers."

"That has never been our intent."

Rhydderch looked him over slowly. "What will your old pander pay to have you back?"

"Peace," replied Alun, "and forgiveness of this insult."

Rhydderch sneered. "Richard pays in gold. How much will Gwydion give for his minion? Or maybe Kilhwch would be more forthcoming. Gwynedd is a little kingdom and Kilhwch is a little king, a morsel for our Lion's dinner."

"Let me go, and I will ask."

"Oh, no," said Rhydderch. "I'm not a fool. I'll set a price, and I'll demand it. And amuse myself with you while I wait for it."

There was no dealing with that mind. It was like a wild boar's, black, feral, and entirely intent upon its own course.

Alun pitched his voice low, level, and very, very calm. "Rhydderch, I know what you plan. You will break me beyond all mending and cast me at my King's feet, a gauntlet for your war. And while you challenge Rhiyana, you prick Gwynedd to fury with your incessant driving of the hill-folk to raid beyond the border. Soon Anglia's great Lion must come, lured into the war you have made; you will set the kings upon one another and let them destroy themselves, while you take the spoils."

While he spoke, he watched the man's face. First Rhydderch reddened, then he paled, and his eyes went deadly cold. Alun smiled. "So you plan, Rhydderch. You think, with your men-at-arms and your hill-folk and all your secret allies, that you are strong enough to take a throne and wise enough to keep it. Have you failed to consider the forces with which you play? Kilhwch is young, granted, and more than a bit of a hellion, but he is the son of Bran Dhu, and blood kin to Gwydion of Rhiyana. He may prove a stronger man than you reckon on. And Gwydion will support him."

"Gwydion!" Rhydderch spat. "The coward King, the royal fool. He wobbles on his throne, powdered and painted like an old whore, and brags of his miraculous youth. His so-called knights win their spurs on the dancing floor and their titles in bed. And not with women, either."

Alun's smile did not waver. "If that is so, then why do you waste time in provoking him to war?"

A vein was pulsing in Rhydderch's temple, but he grinned ferally. "Why not? It's the safest of all my bets."

"Is it? Then Richard must be the most perilous of all, for he is a lion in battle—quite unlike my poor Gwydion. How will he look on this plot of yours, Rhydderch? Rebellion in the north and a brother who would poison him at a word and the dregs of his Crusade, all these he has to face. And now you bring him this folly."

"Richard can never resist a good fight. He won't touch me. More likely he'll reward me."

"Ah. A child, a warmonger, and a dotard. Three witless kings, and three kingdoms ripe for the plucking by a man with strength

and skill." Alun shook his head. "Rhydderch, has it ever occurred
to you that you are a fool?"

A mailed fist lashed out. Alun's head rocked with the force
of the blow. "You vain young cockerel," Rhydderch snarled.
"Strung up in my own castle, and you crow like a dunghill king.
I'll teach you to sing a new song."

The fist struck again in the same place. Alun choked back
a cry. Rhydderch laughed and held out his hand. One of his
men placed a dark shape in it.

In spite of himself, Alun shrank. Rhydderch shook out a whip
of thongs knotted with pellets of lead. Alun made one last,
desperate effort to penetrate that opaque brain.

No use. It was mad. The worst kind of madness, which passes
for sanity, because it knows itself and glories in its own twisted
power. Alun's gentle strength was futile against it.

He felt as if he were tangled in the coils of a snake, its venom
coursing through his veins, waking the passion which was as
deep as his serenity. As many-headed pain lashed his body, his
wrath stirred and kindled. He forgot even torment in his desperate struggle for control. He forgot the world itself. All his
consciousness focused upon the single battle, the great tide of
his calmness against the fire of rage.

The world within became the world without. All his body
was a fiery agony, and his mind was a flame. Rhydderch stood
before him, face glistening with sweat, whip slack in his hand.
He sneered at his prisoner. "Beautiful as a girl, and weak as one
besides. You're Rhiyanan to the core."

Alun drew a deep shuddering breath. The rage stood at bay,
but it touched his face, his eyes. "If you release me now, I shall
forgive this infamy, although I shall never forget it."

"Let you go?" Rhydderch laughed. "I've hardly begun."

"Do you count it honorable to flog a man in chains, captured
by treachery?"

"A man, no. You, I hardly count as a villein's brat; and you'll
be less when I'm done with you."

"Whatever you do to me, I remain a Knight of the Crown of Rhiyana. Gwydion is far from the weakling you deem him; and he shall not forget what you have done to him."

"From fainting lass to royal lord in two breaths. You awe me." Rhydderch tossed the whip aside. "Some of my lads here like to play a little before they get down to business. Maybe I should let them, while you're still able to enjoy it."

The rage lunged for the opening. Alun's eyes blazed green; he bared his teeth. But his voice was velvet-soft. "Let them try, Rhydderch. Let them boast of it afterward. They shall need the consolation, for they shall never touch another: man, woman, or boy." His eyes flashed round the half-circle of men. "Who ventures it? You, Huw? Owein? Dafydd, great bull and vaunter?"

Each one started at his name and crossed himself.

Rhydderch glared under his black brows. "You there, get him down and hold him. He can't do a thing to you."

"Can I not?" asked Alun. "Have you not heard of what befalls mortals who make shift to force elf-blood?"

The baron snarled. "Get him down, I say! He's trying to scare us off."

One man made bold to speak. "But—but—my lord, his eyes!"

"A trick of the light. Get him down!"

Alun lowered his arms. "No need. See. I am down."

Eyes rolled; voices muttered.

"Damn you sons of curs! You forgot to fasten the chain!" Rhydderch snatched at it. Alun dropped to his knees. He was still feral-eyed. A blow, aimed at his head, missed.

He tossed back his hair and said, "Nay, I was firm-bound. Think you that the Elvenking would risk a mortal on such a venture as this?"

"You're no less mortal than I am." Rhydderch hurled Alun full-length upon the floor. Swift as a striking snake, his boot came down.

Someone screamed.

Pain had roused wrath; pain slew it. In red-rimmed clarity, Alun saw all his pride and folly. He had come to lull Rhydderch into making peace, and fallen instead into his enemy's own madness. And now he paid.

That clarity was his undoing; for he did not move then to stop what he had begun. Even as he paused, they were upon him, fear turned to bitter scorn.

After an eternity came blessed nothingness.

He woke in the midst of a choking stench. Oddly, he found that harder to bear than the agony of his body. Pain had some pretense to nobility, even such pain as this, but that monumental stink was beyond all endurance.

Gasping, gagging, he lifted his head. He had lain face down in it. Walls of stone hemmed him in—a midden with but one barred exit. The iron bars were forged in the shape of a cross. Rhydderch was taking no chances.

A convulsion seized him, bringing new agony: the spasming of an empty stomach, the knife-sharp pain of cracked ribs. For a long while he had to lie as he was. Then, with infinite caution, he drew one knee under him. The right leg would not bear his weight; he swayed, threw out a hand, cried out in agony as the outraged flesh struck the wall. His other, the right hand, caught wildly at stone and held. Through a scarlet haze he saw what first he had extended. It no longer looked even remotely like a hand.

His sword hand.

He closed his eyes and sought inward for strength. It came slowly, driving back the pain until he could almost bear it. But the cost to his broken body was high. Swiftly, while he could still see, he swept his eyes about.

One corner was almost clean. Inch by inch, hating the sounds of pain his movements wrenched from him, he made his way to it. Two steps upright, the rest crawling upon his face.

Gradually his senses cleared. He hurt—oh, he hurt. And one pain, less than the rest, made him burn with shame. After all his threats—and empty, they had not been—still—still—

He found that he was weeping: he who had not wept even

as a child. Helpless, child's tears, born of pain and shame and disgust at his own massive folly. All this horror was no one's fault but his own.

Even Kilhwch had warned him. Wild young Kilhwch, with his father's face but his mother's gray eyes, and a little of the family wisdom. "The border lords on both sides make a fine nest of adders, but Rhydderch is the worst of them. He'd flay his own mother if it would buy him an extra acre. Work your magic with the others as much as you like; I could use a little quiet there. But stay away from Rhydderch."

Kilhwch had not known of the baron's invitation to a parley. If he had, he would have flown into one of his rages. Yet that would not have stopped Alun.

His shield was failing. One last effort; then he could rest. He arranged his body as best he might, broken as it was, and extended his mind.

The normal rhythm of a border castle flowed through him, overlaid with the blackness that was Rhydderch and with a tension born of men gathering for war. Rhydderch himself was gone; a steward's mind murmured of a rendezvous with a hill-chieftain.

Alun could do nothing until dark, and it was barely past noon. Thirst burned him; hunger was a dull ache. Yet nowhere in that heap of offal could he find food or drink.

He would not weaken again into tears. His mind withdrew fully into itself, a deep trance yet with a hint of awareness which marked the passing of time.

Darkness roused him, and brought with it full awareness of agony. For a long blood-red while he could not move at all. By degrees he dragged himself up. As he had reached the corner, so he reached the gate. It opened before him.

How he came to the stable, unseen and unnoticed, he never knew. There was mist the color of torment, and grinding pain, and the tension of power stretched to the fullest; and at last, warm sweet breath upon his cheek and sleek horseflesh under his hand. With all the strength that remained to him, he saddled and bridled his mare, wrapping himself in the cloak which had covered her. She knelt for him; he half-climbed, half-fell into the saddle. She paced forward.

The courtyard was dark in starlight. The gate yawned open; the sentry stood like a shape of stone. Fara froze. He stirred upon her back. He could not speak through swollen lips, but his words rang in his brain: *Now, while I can hold the man and the pain — run, my beauty. Run!*

She sprang into a gallop, wind-smooth, wind-swift. Her rider clung to her, not caring where she went. She turned her head to the south and lengthened her stride.

Only when the castle was long gone, hidden in a fold of the hills, did she slow to a running walk. She kept that pace hour after hour, until Alun was like to fall from her back. At last she found a stream and knelt, so that he had but little distance to fall; he drank in long desperate gulps, dragged himself a foot or two from the water, and let darkness roll over him.

Voices sounded, low and lilting, speaking a tongue as old as those dark hills. While they spoke he understood, but when they were done, he could not remember what they had said.

Hands touched him, waking pain. Through it he saw a black boar, ravening. He cried out against it. The hands started away and returned. There were tightnesses: bandages, roughly bound; visions of the herb healer, who must see this tortured creature; Rhuawn's tunic to cover his nakedness. And again the black boar looming huge, every bristle distinct, an ember-light in its eyes and the scarlet of blood upon its tusks. He called the lightnings down upon it.

The voices cried out. One word held in his memory: *Dewin*, that was *wizard*. And then all the voices were gone. Only Fara remained, and the pain, and what healing and clothing the hill-folk had given.

Healing. He must have healing. Again he mounted, again he rode through the crowding shadows. At the far extremity of his inner sight, there was a light. He pursued it, and Fara bore him through the wild hills, over a broad and turbulent water, and on into darkness.

The fire burned low. Soon the bell would ring for Matins. Alf rose, stiff with the memory of torment, and looked down upon the wounded man. No human being could have endured what he had endured, not only torture but five full days after, without healing, without food, riding by day and by night.

Alf touched the white fine face. No, it was not human. Power throbbed behind it, low now and slow, but palpably present. It had brought the stranger here to ancient Ynys Witrin, and to the one being like him in all of Gwynedd or Anglia, the one alone who might have healed him.

Who could not, save as humans do, with splint and bandage and simple waiting. He had set each shattered bone with all the skill he had and tended the outraged flesh as best he knew how. The life that had ebbed low was rising slowly with tenacity that must be of elf-kind, that had kept death at bay throughout that grim ride.

He slept now, a sleep that healed. Alf envied him that despite its cost. His dreams were none of pain; only of peace, and of piercing sweetness.

4

Consciousness was like dawn, slow in growing, swift in its completion. Alun lay for a time, arranging his memories around his hurts. In all of it, he could not see himself upon a bed, his body tightly bandaged, warm and almost comfortable. Nor could he place that stillness, that scent of stone and coolness and something faint, sweet—apples, incense.

He opened his eyes. Stone, yes, all about: a small room, very plain yet with a hearth and a fire, burning applewood, and a single hanging which seemed woven of sunlight on leaves.

Near the fire was a chair, and in it a figure. Brown cowl, tonsure haloed by pale hair—a monk, intent upon a book. His face in profile was very young and very fair.

The monk looked up. Their gazes met, sea-gray and silver-gilt; warp and woof, and the shuttle flashing between. Alf's image; the flicker of amusement was the other's, whose knightly hands had never plied a loom.

As swiftly as fencers in a match, they disengaged. Alf was on his feet, holding white-knuckled to the back of his chair. With an effort he unclenched his fingers and advanced to the bed.

Alun's eyes followed him. His face was quiet, betraying none of his pain. "How long since I came here?" he asked.

"Three days," Alf answered, "and five before that of riding."

"Eight days." Alun closed his eyes. "I was an utter and unpardonable fool."

Alf poured well-watered mead from the beaker by the bed and held the cup to Alun's lips. The draught brought a ghost of color to the wan cheeks, but did not distract the mind behind them. "Is there news? Have you heard—"

Alf crumbled a bit of bread and fed it to him. "No news. Though there's a tale in the villages of a mighty wizard who rode over the hills in a trail of shooting stars and passed away into the West. Opinions are divided as to the meaning of the portent, whether it presages war or peace, feast or famine. Or maybe it was only one of the Fair Folk in a fire of haste."

A glint of mirth touched the gray eyes. "Maybe it was. You've heard no word of war?"

"Not hereabouts. I think you've put the fear of Annwn into too many people."

"That will never last," Alun murmured. "The black boar will rise, and soon. And I . . ." His good hand moved down his body. "I pay for my folly. How soon before I ride?"

"Better to ask, 'How soon before I walk?'"

He shook his head slightly. "I'll ride before then. How soon?"

Alf touched his splinted leg, his bound hand. Shattered bone had begun to knit, torn muscle to mend itself, with inhuman speed, but slowly still. "A month," he said. "No sooner."

"Brother," Alun said softly, "I am not human."

"If you were, I'd tell you to get used to your bed, for you'd never leave it."

Alun's lips thinned. "I'm not so badly hurt. Once my leg knits, I can ride."

"You rode with it broken for five days. It will take six times that, and a minor miracle, to undo the damage. Unless you'd prefer to live a cripple."

"I could live lame if there was peace in Gwynedd and Anglia

and Rhiyana, and three kings safe on their thrones, and Rhydderch rendered powerless."

"Lame and twisted and racked with pain, and bereft of your sword hand. A cause for war even if you put down Rhydderch, if knights in Rhiyana are as mindful of their honor as those in Anglia."

Alun drew a breath, ragged with pain. "Knights in Rhiyana pay heed to their King. Who will let no war begin over one man's folly. I will need a horse-litter, Brother, and perhaps an escort, for as soon as may be. Will you pass my request to your Abbot?"

"I can give you his answer now," Alf replied. "No. The Church frowns on suicide."

"I won't die. Tell your Abbot, Brother. The storm is about to break. I must go before it destroys us all."

Dom Morwin was in the orchard under a gray sky, among trees as old as the abbey itself. As Alf came to walk with him, he stooped stiffly, found two sound windfalls, and tossed one to his friend.

Alf caught it and polished it on his sleeve. As he bit into it, Morwin asked, "How is your nurseling?"

"Lively," Alf answered. "He came to this morning, looked about, and ordered a horse-litter."

The Abbot lifted an eyebrow. "I would have thought that he was on his deathbed. He certainly looked it yesterevening when I glanced in."

"He won't die. He won't be riding about for a while yet, either. Whatever he may think."

"He sounds imperious for a foundling."

"That, he's not. Look." Alf reached into the depths of his habit and drew out the signet in its pouch.

Morwin examined the ring for a long moment. "It's his?"

"He carried it. He wanted you to see it."

The other turned it in his hands. "So—he's one of Gwydion's elven-folk. I'd wondered if the tales were true."

"Truer than you thought before, at least."

Morwin's glance was sharp. "Doubts, Alf?"

"No." Alf sat on a fallen trunk. "We're alike. When he woke, we met, eye, mind. It was painful to draw back and to talk as humans talk. He was . . . very calm about it."

"How did he get here, as he was, with his King's signet in his pocket?"

"He rode. He was peacemaking for Gwydion, but he ran afoul of a lord he couldn't bewitch. He escaped toward the only help his mind could see. He wasn't looking for human help by then. I was the closest one of his kind. And St. Ruan's is . . . St. Ruan's."

"He's failed in his errand, then. Unless war will wait for the winter to end and for him to heal."

"He says it won't. I know it won't. That's why he ordered the horse-litter. I refused, in your name. He wanted something more direct."

"Imperious." The Abbot contemplated his half-eaten apple. "The border of Gwynedd is dry tinder waiting for a spark. There are barons on both sides who'd be delighted to strike one. And Richard would egg them on."

"Exactly. Gwydion, through Alun, was trying to prevent that."

"*Was?* Your Alun's lost, then?"

"For Gwydion's purposes. Though he'd have me think otherwise."

"Exactly how bad is it?"

"Bad," Alf answered. "Not deadly, but bad. If he's careful, he'll ride again, even walk. I don't know if he'll ever wield a sword. And that is if he does exactly as I tell him. If he gets up and tries to run his King's errands, he'll end a cripple. I told him so. He told me to get a litter."

"Does he think he can do any better now than he did before?"

"I don't know what he thinks!" Alf took a deep breath. More quietly he said, "Maybe you can talk to him. I'm only a monk. You're the Lord Abbot."

Morwin's eyes narrowed. "Alf. How urgent is this? Is it just a loyal man and a foster father looking out for his ward, and a general desire for peace? Or does it go deeper? What will happen if Alun does nothing?"

When they were boys together, they had played a game. Morwin would name a name, and Alf would look inside, and that name would appear as a thread weaving through the world-web; and he would tell his friend where it went. It had been a game then, with a touch of the forbidden in it, for it was witchery. As they grew older they had stopped it.

The tapestry was there. He could see it, feel it: the shape, the pattern. He lived in it and through it, a part of it and yet also an observer. Like a god, he had thought once; strangling the thought, for it was blasphemy.

Gwydion, he thought. *Alun. Gwynedd.* In his mind he stood before the vast loom with its edges lost in infinity, and his finger followed a skein of threads, deep blue and blood-red and fire-gold. Blood and fire, a wave of peace, a red tide of war. A pattern, shifting, elusive, yet clear enough. If this happened, and this did not; *if . . .*

Gray sky lowered over him; Morwin's face hovered close. Old—it was so old. He covered his eyes.

When he could bear to see again, Morwin was waiting, frowning. "What was it? What did you see?"

"War," Alf muttered. "Peace. Gwydion—Alun—He can't leave this place. He'll fail again, and this time he'll die. And he knows it. I told him what the Church thinks of suicide."

"What will happen?"

"War," Alf said again. "As he saw it. Richard will ride to Gwynedd and Kilhwch will come to meet him; Rhiyana will join the war for Kilhwch's sake. Richard wounded, Kilhwch dead, Gwydion broken beyond all mending; and lords of three king-doms tearing at each other like jackals when the lions have gone."

"There's no hope?"

Alf shivered. It was cold, and the effort of seeing left him weak. "There may be. I see the darkest colors because they're strongest. Maybe there can be peace. Another Alun . . . Rhydderch's death . . . a Crusade to divert Richard: who knows what can happen?"

"It will have to happen soon."

"Before spring."

Morwin began to walk aimlessly, head bent, hands clasped behind him. Alf followed. He did not slip into the other's mind. That pact they had made, long ago.

They came to the orchard's wall and walked along it, circling the enclosure.

"It's not for us to meddle in the affairs of kings," Morwin said at last. "Our part is to pray, and to let the world go as it will." His eyes upon Alf were bright and wicked. "But the world has gone its way into our abbey. I'm minded to heed it. Prayer won't avert a war."

"Won't it?"

"The Lord often appreciates a helping hand," the Abbot said. "Our King is seldom without his loyal Bishop Aylmer, even on the battlefield. And the Bishop might be kindly disposed toward a messenger of mine bringing word of the troubles on the border."

"And?"

"Peace. Maybe. If an alliance could be made firm between Gwynedd and Anglia . . ."

"My lord Abbot! It's corrupted you to have a worldling in your infirmary."

"I was always corrupt. Tell Sir Alun that I'll speak to him tonight before Compline."

Alun would have none of it. "I will not place one of your Brothers in danger," he said. "For there is danger for a monk of Anglia on Rhiyana's errand. Please, my lord, a litter is all I ask."

The Abbot regarded him as he lay propped up with pillows, haggard and hollow-eyed and lordly-proud. "We will not quarrel, sir. You may not leave until you are judged well enough to leave.

Which will not be soon enough to complete your embassy. My messenger will go in your stead."

For a long moment Alun was silent. At length he asked, "Whom will you send?"

Morwin glanced sidewise at the monk who knelt, tending the fire. "Brother Alfred," he answered.

The flames roared. Alf drew back from the blistering heat and turned.

"Yes," Morwin said as if he had not been there. "The Bishop asked for him. I'll send him, and give him your errand besides."

"Morwin," Alf whispered. "Domne."

Neither heeded him. Alun nodded slowly. "If it is he, then I cannot object. He shall have my mare. She frets in her stall; and no other horse is as swift or as tireless as she."

"That's a princely gift."

"He has need of all speed. How soon may he go?"

"He'll need a night to rest and prepare. Tomorrow."

Alf stood, trembling uncontrollably. They did not look at him. Alun's eyes were closed; Morwin stared at his sandaled feet. "Domne," he said. "Domne, you can't send me. You know what I am."

The Abbot raised his eyes. They were very bright and very sad. "Yes, I know what you are. That's why I'm sending you."

"Morwin—"

"You swore three vows, Brother. And one of them was obedience."

Alf bowed his head. "I will go because you command me to go, but not because I wish to. The world will not be kind to such a creature as I am."

"Maybe you need a little unkindness." Morwin turned his back on Alf, nodded to Alun, and left.

The Rhiyanan gazed quietly at the ceiling. "It hurts him to do this, but he thinks it is best."

"I know," Alf said. He had begun to tremble again. "I'm a coward. I haven't left St. Ruan's since—since—God help me! I can't remember. These walls have grown up round my bones."

"Time then to hew your way out of them."

"It frightens me. Three kingdoms in the balance; and only my hand to steady them."

Alun turned his head toward Alf. "If you will let me go, you can stay here."

The other laughed without mirth. "Oh, no, my lord! I'll do as my Abbot bids me. You will do as I bid you, which is to stay here and heal, and pray for me."

"You ask a great deal, Brother."

"So does the Abbot," Alf said. "Good night, my lord of Rhiyana."

5

"'She' that is, the Soul of the World—'woven throughout heaven from its center to its outermost limits, and enfolding it without in a circle, and herself revolving within herself, began a divine beginning of ceaseless and rational life for all time.' So, Plato. Now the Christian doctors say—"

Jehan was not listening. He was not even trying to listen, who ordinarily was the best of students. Alf broke off and closed the book softly, and folded his hands upon it. "What's the trouble, Jehan?"

The novice looked up from the precious vellum, on which he had been scribbling without heed or pattern. His eyes were wide and a little wild. "You look awful, Brother Alf. Brother Rowan says you were praying in the chapel all night."

"I do that now and again," Alf said.

"But—" Jehan said. "But they say you're leaving!"

Alf sighed. He was tired, and his body ached from a night upon cold stones. Jehan's pain only added to the burden of his troubles. He answered shortly, flatly. "Yes. I'm leaving."

"Why? What's happened?"

"I've been here too long. Dom Morwin is sending me to Bishop Aylmer."

"Just like that?"

"Just like that," Alf replied. "Don't worry. You won't go back to Brother Osric. You'll take care of Alun for me; and he has a rare store of learning. He'll keep on with your Greek, and if you behave, he'll let you try a little Arabic."

The hurt in Jehan's eyes had turned to fire. "So I'm to turn paynim while you run at the Bishop's heel. It's not so easy to get rid of me, Brother Alf. Take me with you."

"You know that's not my decision to make."

"Take me with you."

"No." It was curt, final. "With reference to Plato's doctrine, Chalcidius observes—"

"Brother Alf!"

"Chalcidius observes—"

Jehan bit back what more he would have said. There was no opposing that quiet persistence. Yet he was ready to cry, and would not, for pride.

It was the first lesson with Alf which had ever gone sour, and it was the last Jehan would ever have. When he was let go, having disgraced all his vaunted scholarship, he wanted to hide like a whipped pup. For pride and for anger, he went where his duties bade him go.

Alun was awake and alone. Jehan stood over him. "Brother Alf is going away," he said. "He's been sent to Bishop Aylmer. Bishop Aylmer is with the King. And it's the King you want to get to. What did you make him go for?"

Jehan's rude words did not seem to trouble Alun. "I didn't make him go. It was your Abbot's choice. A wise one in his reckoning, and well for your Brother. He was stifling here."

"He doesn't want to go. He hates the thought of it."

"Of course he does. He's afraid. But he has to go, Jehan. For his vows' sake and for his own."

Jehan glared at him. "Alone, sir? Do his vows say he has to

travel the length and breadth of Anglia by himself, a monk who looks like a boy, who doesn't even know how to hold a knife?"

"His vows, no. But he will have my mare and such aid as I can give him, and he has more defenses than you know of."

"Not enough." Jehan tossed his head, lion-fierce. "I came here for him. If he goes, I'll go."

"And what of your Abbot? What of your God?"

"My God knows that I can serve Him as well with the Bishop as at St. Ruan's. The Abbot can think what he likes."

"Proud words for one who would be a monk."

"I was a monk because Alf was!"

Jehan fell silent, startled by his own outburst. Slowly he sank down, drawing into a knot on the floor. "I was a monk because Alf was," he repeated. "I never meant to be one. I wanted to be a warrior-priest like Bishop Aylmer, but I wanted to be a scholar too. People laughed at me. 'A scholar!' my father yelled at me. 'God's teeth! you're not built for it.' Then I rode hell-for-leather down a road near St. Ruan's, with a hawk on my wrist and a wild colt under me and my men-at-arms long lost, and I nigh rode down a monk who was walking down the middle.

"I stopped to apologize, and we talked, and somehow we got onto Aristotle. I'd read what I could find, without really knowing what I was reading and with no one to tell me. And this person *knew*. More: he could read Greek. There in the middle of the road, we disputed like philosophers, though he really was one and I was a young cock-a-whoop who'd got into his tutor's books.

"Then and there, I decided I had to be what he was, or as close as I could come, since he was brilliant and I was only too clever for my own good. I fought and I pleaded and I threatened, and my father finally let me come here. And now Brother Alf if going away and taking the heart out of St. Ruan's."

Alun shifted painfully, waving away Jehan's swift offer of help. "I think, were I your Abbot, I would question your vocation."

"It's there," Jehan said with certainty. "God is there, and my books. But not—not St. Ruan's. Not without Brother Alf."

"Jehan." Alun spoke slowly, gently. "You're startled and hurt.

Think beyond yourself now. Alfred is much older than he looks, and much less placid. He has troubles which life here cannot heal. He has to leave."

"I know that. I'm not trying to stop him. I want to go with him."

"What can you do for him?"

"Love him," Jehan answered simply.

Alun's eyes closed. He looked exhausted and drawn with pain. His voice when he spoke was a sigh. "You can serve him best now by accepting what your Abbot says must be. Can you do that?"

"And leave him to go alone?"

"If such is the Abbot's will. Can you do it, Jehan?"

Very slowly the other responded, "I . . . for him. If it's right. And only if."

"Go then. Be strong for him. He needs that more than anything else you can do for him."

Alf regarded Alun with sternness overlying concern. "You've been overexerting yourself."

The Rhiyanan's eyes glinted. "In bed, Brother? Oh, come!"

"Staying awake," Alf said. "Moving about. Trying your muscles." He touched the bandaged mass of Alun's sword hand. "The setting of this is very delicate. If you jar it, you'll cripple it. Perhaps permanently."

"It is not so already?" There was a touch of bitterness in the quiet voice.

"Maybe not." Alf continued his examination, which was less of hand and eye than of the mind behind them. "Your ribs are healing well. Your leg, too, *Deo gratias*. If you behave yourself and trust to the care in which I leave you, you'll prosper."

He folded back the coverlet and began to bathe as much of the battered body as was bare of bandages. Alun's eyes followed his hands. When Alf would have turned him onto his face, there was no weight in him; he floated face down a palm's width above the bed.

The monk faltered only for a moment. "Thank you," he said.

After a moment he added, "If you take care not to let yourself be caught at it, you might do this as much as you can. It will spare your flesh."

Alun was on his back again; Alf could have passed his palm between body and sheet. "I've been this way a little. There's more comfort in it."

"My lord." Alf's compassion was as palpable as a touch. "I'll do all your errand for you as best I can. That I swear to you."

"I'll miss you, Brother." The way he said it, it was more than a title. "And I've had thoughts. It will look odd for a monk to ride abroad on what is patently a blooded horse. With her I give you all that I have. My clothing is plain enough for a cleric, but secular enough to avert suspicion. Come; fetch it, and try it for size."

"My lord," Alf said carefully, "you're most kind. But I have no dispensation. I can't—"

"You can if I say you can." Morwin shut the door behind him. "Do what he tells you, Alf."

Slowly, under their eyes, he brought out Alun's belongings. The ring in its pouch he laid in the lord's lap. The rest he kept. It had been cleaned where it needed to be and treated with care. Indeed the garments were plain, deep blue, snow white. When the others turned away to spare his modesty, he hesitated.

With a sudden movement he shed his coarse brown habit. There was nothing beneath but his body. He shivered as he covered it with Alun's fine linen. In all his life, he had never known such softness so close to his skin. It felt like a sin.

The outer clothes were easier to bear, though he fumbled with them, uncertain of their fastenings. Alun helped him with words and Morwin with hands, until he stood up in the riding clothes of a knight.

"It fits well," Alun said. "And looks most well, my brother."

He could see himself in the other's mind, a tall youth, sword-slender, with a light proud carriage that belied the brown habit crumpled at his feet.

As soon as he saw, he tried to kill the pride that rose in him.

He looked like a prince. An elven-prince, swift and strong, and beautiful. Yes; he was that. The rest might be a sham, a creation of cloth and stance, but beauty he had.

It would be a hindrance, and perhaps a danger. His pride died with the thought. "I don't think this is wise. I look too . . . rich. Better that I seem to be what I am, a monk without money or weapons."

Both the Abbot and the knight shook their heads. "No," Morwin said. "Not with the horse you'll be riding. This way, you fit her."

"I don't fit myself!"

Morwin's face twisted. A moment only; then he controlled it. "You'll learn. It isn't the clothes that make the monk, Alf."

"Isn't it?" Alf picked up his habit and held it to him. "Each move I make is another cord severed."

"If all you've ever been is a robe and a tonsure," snapped Morwin, "God help us both."

The other stiffened. "Maybe that is all I've been."

"Don't start that," Morwin said with weary annoyance. "You're not the first man of God who's ever set aside his habit for a while, and you won't be the last. Take what's left of the day to get used to your clothes, and spend tonight in bed. Asleep. That's an order, Brother Alfred."

"Yes, Domne."

"And don't look so sulky. One obeys with a glad heart, the Rule says. Or at least, one tries to. Start trying. That's an order, too."

"Yes, Domne." Alf was not quite able to keep his lips from twitching. "Immediately, Domne. Gladly, Domne."

"Don't add lying to the rest of your sins." But Morwin's glare lacked force. "See me tonight before you go to bed. There are messages I want to give to Aylmer."

In spite of his promise to Alun, Jehan dragged himself through that long day. No one seemed to know that Brother Alf was leaving, nor to care. Monks came and went often enough in so large an abbey.

But never so far alone, through unknown country, and against their will besides.

At last he could bear it no longer. He gathered his courage and sought the lion in his den.

By good fortune, Abbot Morwin was alone, bent over the rolls of the abbey. He straightened as Jehan entered. "This is stiff work for old bones," he said.

Jehan drew a deep breath. The Abbot did not seem annoyed to see him. Nor did he look surprised. "Domne," he said, "you're sending Brother Alf away."

Morwin nodded neutrally. That, in the volatile Abbot, was ominous.

"Please, Domne. I know he has to go. But must he go alone?"

"What makes you think that?"

Jehan found that he could not breathe properly. "Then— then—he'll have company?"

"I've been considering it." Morwin indicated a chair. "Here, boy. Stop shaking and sit down." He leaned back himself, toying with the simple silver cross he always wore. Jehan stared, half-mesmerized by the glitter of it. "It's as well you came when you did; I was about to send for you. I've been thinking about that last letter from your father."

The novice almost groaned aloud. The last thing he wanted to hear now was his father's opinion of his life in St. Ruan's.

But Morwin had no mercy. "Remember what Earl Rogier said. That your life was your own, and you could ruin it by taking vows here if that was what you wanted. But he asked you first to try something else. He suggested the Templars. That's extreme; still, the more I think, the better his advice seems to be. I've decided to take it in my own way. I'm sending you to Bishop Aylmer."

Bishop Aylmer . . . Bishop Aylmer. "I'm going with Brother Alf!" It was a strangled shout.

"Well now," Morwin said, "that would make sense, wouldn't it?"

Jehan hardly heard him. "I'm going with Brother Alf. He told me I couldn't. He's going to be surprised."

"I doubt it. I told him a little while ago. He was angry."

"*Angry*, Domne?"

Morwin smiled. "He said I was hanging for the sheep instead of for the lamb—and brought you these to travel in."

On the table among the heavy codices was a bundle. Jehan's fingers remembered the weight and the feel of it—leather, cloth, the long hardness of a sword. "My old clothes . . . but I've grown!"

"Try them. And afterward, find Alf. He'll tell you what you need to do."

Miraculously everything fit, though the garments had been made for him just before he met Brother Alf upon the road, over a year ago, and he had grown half a head since. But Alf's skill with the needle was legendary. The boots alone seemed new, of good leather, with room enough to grow in.

It felt strange to be dressed like a nobleman again. He wished there were a mirror in the dormitory, and said a prayer to banish vanity. "Not," he added, "that my face is anything to brag of."

"Amen."

He whipped about, hand to sword hilt. A stranger stood there, a tall young fellow who carried himself like a prince. He smiled wryly as Jehan stared, and said, "Good day, my lord."

"Brother Alf!" Jehan took him in and laughed for wonder. "You look splendid."

"*Vanitas vanitatum*," Alf intoned dolefully. "'Vanity of vanities, all is vanity!' Though you look as if you can use that sword."

Jehan let his hand fall from the hilt. "You know I've had practice with Brother Ulf. 'Ulf for the body and Alf for the brain; that's how a monk is made.'"

"So you're the one who committed that bit of doggerel. I should have known."

Although Alf's voice was light, Jehan frowned. "What's the matter, Brother Alf?"

"Why, nothing. I'm perfectly content. After all, misery loves company."

"It won't be misery. It will be splendid. You'll see. We'll take Bishop Aylmer by storm and astound the King; and then we'll conquer the world."

The hour after Compline found Alf in none of his usual places: not in his cell where he should have been sleeping; not in the chapel where he might have kept vigil even against Morwin's command; and certainly not in the study where the Abbot had gone to wait for him. He had sung the last Office—no one could miss that voice, man-deep yet heartrendingly clear, rising above the mere human beauty of the choir—and he had sung with gentle rebellion in his brown habit. But then he had gone, and no one knew where.

It was intuition more than either logic or a careful search that brought Morwin to a small courtyard near the chapel. There in a patch of sere and frostbitten grass grew a thorn tree. Ancient, twisted, stripped of its leaves, it raised its branches to the moon. Under it crouched a still and shadowed figure.

With much creaking of bones, Morwin sat beside him. The ground was cold; frost crackled as the Abbot settled upon it.

"I've never liked this place," Alf said, "or this tree. Though they say it grew from the staff of a saint, of the Arimathean himself . . . when I was very small I used to be afraid of it. It always seemed to be reaching for me. As if St. Ruan's were not for the likes of me; as if I were alien and the Thorn knew it, and it would drag me away, back to my own people."

"The people under the Tor?" Morwin asked.

The cowled head shifted. From here one could see the Tor clearly, a steep rounded hill wreathed in frost, rising behind the abbey like a bulwark of stone. "The Tor," murmured Alf. "That never frightened me. There was power in it, and wonder, and mystery. But no danger. No beckoning; no rejection. It simply was. Do you remember when we climbed it, for bravado, to see if the tales were true?"

"Madness or great blessings to him who mounts the Tor of Ynys Witrin on the eve of Midsummer. I remember. I don't think either of us came down mad."

"Nor blessed." Alf's voice held the glimmer of a smile. "We did penance for a solid fortnight, and all we'd found was a broken chapel and beds even harder than the ones we'd slipped away from." His arm circled Morwin's shoulders, bringing warmth like an open fire. The Abbot leaned into it. "But no; that wasn't all we found. I felt as if I could see the whole world under the Midsummer moon, and below us Ynys Witrin, mystic as all the songs would have it, an island floating in a sea of glass. *There* was the mystery. Not on the windy hill. Below it, in the abbey, where by Christmas we'd be consecrated priests, servants of the Light that had come to rule the world.

"But the Thorn always knew. I was—I am—no mortal man."

"So now you come to make your peace with it."

"After a fashion. I wanted to see if it was glad to be rid of me."

"Is it?"

Alf's free hand moved to touch the trunk, white fingers glimmering on shadow-black. "I think . . . It's never hated me. It's just known a painful truth. Maybe it even wishes me well."

"So do we all."

Alf shivered violently, but not with the air's cold. "I'm going away," he said as if he had only come to realize it. "And I can't . . . Even if I come back, it won't be the same. I'll have to grow, change—" His voice faded.

Morwin was silent.

"I know," Alf said with unwonted bitterness. "Everyone grows and changes. Even the likes of me. Already I feel it beginning, with Alun's fine clothes waiting for me to put them on again and the memory of all the Brothers at supper, staring and wondering, and some not even knowing who I was. Even Jehan, when he first saw me, took me for a stranger. What if I change so much I don't even recognize myself?"

"Better that sort of pain than the one that's been tearing you apart for so long."

"That was a familiar pain."

"Yes. Plain old shackle-gall. I'm chasing you out of your prison, Alfred—throwing you into the sky. Because even if you're blind and senseless, everyone else can see that you have wings."

The moon came down into the cup of Alf's hand, a globe of light, perfect, all its blemishes scoured away. Its white glow caressed his face; Morwin blinked and swallowed. Familiar as those features were, the shock of them blunted by long use; sometimes still, with deadly suddenness, their beauty could strike him to the heart.

Alf's hand closed. The light shrank with it, snuffing out like a candle flame; taking away Morwin's vision, but not his remembrance of it. Slowly, wearily, Alf said, "I won't fight you any longer, Morwin. Not on that account. But must you send Jehan with me?"

"He has no more place here than you do."

"I know that. I also know that I may be riding into danger. The message I'll carry is not precisely harmless. I could be killed for bearing it, Alun for passing it to me—"

"And St. Ruan's could suffer for taking him in. Don't you think I'm aware of all the consequences?"

"Jehan isn't. To him it's a lark, a chance to be free."

"Is it, Alf?"

"He's a child still for all his size. He doesn't know what this errand might mean or how he may be forced to pay for it. The game we play, the stakes we raise—"

"He knows," Morwin said with a touch of sharpness. "So he's glad enough about it to sing—that's not blissful ignorance, it's simply youth. When the time comes, if it comes, he'll be well able to take care of himself."

"And also of me," said Alf.

"Why not?" the Abbot demanded. "He's only been cloistered for half a year; and he grew up in the world—in courts, in castles." His eyes sharpened to match his tone; he peered into the shadow of Alf's hood, at the hint of a face. "Maybe you're not concerned for a young lad's welfare—pupil of yours though he is, and friend too. Maybe you don't want to be looked after by a mere boy."

Alf would not dignify that with an answer.

Nor would Morwin offer any apology. "I've done as I thought wisest," he said. "I trust you to abide by it. In the end you may even be glad of it."

The voice in the shadow was soft, more inhumanly beautiful than ever, but its words were tinged with irony. "Morwin my oldest friend, sometimes I wonder if, after all, I'm the witch of us two."

"This isn't witchcraft. It's common sense. Now stop nattering and help me up. Didn't I give you strict orders to get some sleep tonight?"

Morwin could feel Alf's wry smile, distinct as the clasp of his hand.

"Yes, grin at the old fool, so long as you do what I tell you."

"I am always your servant, Domne."

Morwin cuffed him, not entirely in play, and thrust him away. "Go to bed, you, before I lose my temper!"

Alf bowed deeply, the picture of humility; evaded a second blow with supernatural ease; and left his Abbot alone with the moon and the Tor and the ancient Thorn, and an anger that dissipated as swiftly as it had risen.

It was a very long while before Morwin moved, and longer still before he took the way Alf had taken, back into the warmth of St. Ruan's.

6

They left before dawn. Only Morwin was there to see them off. Morwin, and Alun's consciousness, a brightness in Alf's brain. They stood under the arch of the gate, Jehan holding the bridles of the two horses: Fara like a wraith in the gloom, and the abbey's old gelding standing black and solid beside her. He shivered, half with cold, half with excitement, and shifted from foot to foot. The others simply stood, Alf staring rigidly through the gate, Morwin frowning at his feet.

At last the Abbot spoke. "You'd best be going."

Swiftly Jehan sprang astride. Alf moved more slowly; as he gathered up the reins, Morwin touched his knee. "Here. Take this."

Light flashed between them, Morwin's silver cross. Alf hesitated as if to protest. But Morwin's eyes were fierce. He took the gift and slipped the chain over his head, concealing it under his tunic. It lay cold against his skin, warming slowly. He clasped the hand that had given it, met the eyes behind. "Go with God," Morwin said.

The gate was open, the road clear before them, starlit, aglitter with frost. Only once did Alf glance back. Already they had come far enough to see the whole looming bulk of the Tor, and the abbey against the wall of it, and mist rising with the dawn, turning the Isle to an isle indeed. Small and dark upon it, nearly lost beneath the great arch, the Abbot stood alone.

A wind stirred the mist, raising it like a curtain. Gray glass and silver and a last, faint flicker of moonlight, and of St. Ruan's, nothing at all save the shadow of a tower.

Fara danced, eager to be gone. Alf bent over her neck and urged her onward.

From St. Ruan's they rode northward, with the sun on their left hands and the morning brightening about them. Jehan sang, testing his voice that was settling into a strong baritone; when it cracked, he laughed. "I'm putting the ravens to shame," he said.

Alf did not respond. Here where the road was wide, they rode side by side; Jehan turned to look at him. His face was white and set. Part of that could be discomfort, for he had not ridden in a long while, yet he sat his mount with ease and grace.

Jehan opened his mouth and closed it again. For some time after, he rode as decorously as befit a novice of St. Ruan's, although he gazed about him with eager eyes.

At noon they halted. Alf would not have troubled, but Jehan's gelding was tiring. Already they were a good four leagues from the abbey, in a wide green country scattered with villages. People there looked without surprise on two lordly riders, squires from some noble house from the look of them, going about their business.

They had stopped on the edge of a field where a stream wound along the road. Jehan brought out bread and cheese, but Alf would have none.

The other frowned. "Dom Morwin told me you'd be like this. He also told me not to put up with it. So—will you eat, or do I have to make you?"

Alf had been loosening Fara's girths. He turned at that. "I'm not hungry."

"I know you're not. Eat."

They faced each other stiffly. Alf was taller, but Jehan had easily twice his breadth, and no fear of him at all.

Alf yielded. He ate, and drank from the stream where it settled into a pool. When the water had calmed from his drinking, he paused, staring at the face reflected there. It looked even younger than he had thought.

A wind ruffled the water and shattered the image. He turned away from it.

Jehan was busy with the horses, yet Alf could feel his awareness. Jehan finished and said, "Brother Alf. I've been thinking. We're riding like squires, but I'm the only one with a sword. I know you don't want one, but maybe you'd better know how to use it in case of trouble."

Alf tried to smile. "I'd probably cut off my own foot if I tried."

"You wouldn't either." He unhooked the scabbard from his belt. "Try it."

"No," Alf said. "If it comes to a fight, you're the one who knows what to do with it. Best that you keep it by you. I can manage as I am."

"That's foolish, Brother Alf." Jehan drew the good steel blade and held it out.

Alf would not take it. "Jehan," he said. "It's enough for me now that I dress as a worldling. Don't try to make me more of one. If you do, God alone knows where it will end."

"In a safer journey for us, maybe."

"Maybe not. You don't know what I am, Jehan."

"Do you?"

"I know enough. Put up your sword and ride with me."

Jehan sheathed the weapon, but did not move to mount. "Dom Morwin talked to me last night. He told me about you."

"He did?"

"Don't go cold on me, Brother Alf! I'd guessed most of it

already. People talk, you know. And it was obvious early on that you had to be the one who wrote the *Gloria Dei*. You knew too much, and thought too much, to be as young as your face."

"How old am I, then?"

"As old as Dom Morwin," Jehan answered calmly.

"And you scoff at the tales of Gwydion of Rhiyana?"

"That's hearsay. You're fact."

"Poor logic, student. I should send you back to Brother Osric."

"You can't," Jehan said. "Dom Morwin won't let you."

"Probably not." Alf rose into the high saddle, wincing at his muscles' protest. Before Jehan was well mounted, he had touched the mare into a trot.

They rode at a soft pace to spare their aching bodies. After some little time Jehan said, "You don't have to be afraid of me. I won't betray you."

"I know," Alf murmured as if to himself. "You and Morwin: fools of a feather. I could be a devil, sent to tempt you both to your destruction."

"*You*, Brother Alf?" Jehan laughed. "You may be a changeling as people say, or an elf-man, but a devil? Never."

For the first time Jehan saw the other's eyes, direct and unblurred. It was more than a bit of a shock.

He faced that bright unhuman stare, firm and unafraid. "Never," he repeated. "I'd stake my soul on that."

Alf clapped heels to Fara's sides. She sprang into a gallop.

They raced down a long level stretch. At the end, where the road bent round a barrow, Alf slowed to a canter and then to a walk. Jehan pounded to a halt beside him. "There," he panted. "Feel better?"

Alf bit his lip. "I'm being foolish, aren't I?" He essayed a smile. It was feeble, but it would do. "Yes, I do feel better. My body is glad to be under the open sky. I'll train my mind to follow suit."

By night they had traversed close on eight leagues, fair going for riders out of training. They slept in an old byre, empty and musty but still sturdy, with ample space for themselves and their horses.

Tired though he was, Jehan did not go to sleep at once. He prayed for a while, then lay down with his cloak for a blanket. Alf knelt close by him, praying still. Moonlight seemed to have come through a chink in the walls, for though it was pitch-dark in the barn, Jehan could see Alf's face limned in light, his hair a silver halo about his head.

But there was no moon. Clouds had come with the sun's setting; even as Jehan lay motionless, he heard the first drops of rain upon the roof.

He swallowed hard. In daylight he could accept anything. But darkness bred fear. He was alone here with one who was not human, who shone where there was no light and stared into infinity with eyes that flared ember-red.

They turned to him, set in a face he no longer knew, a moonlit mask white as death. But the soft voice was Alf's own. "Why are you afraid, Jehan?"

"I—" Jehan began. "You—"

Alf raised his hands that shone as did his face. The mask cracked a little into a frown. "This happens sometimes. I can't always control it. Though it's been years . . ." He closed his eyes.

The light flickered and went out.

Jehan sat bolt upright. "Brother Alf!"

Hands touched him. He started violently and seized them. They were warm and solid. Keeping his grip on one, he reached into blackness, finding an arm, a shoulder. Like a blind man he searched upward, tracing the face, the smooth cheek, the flutter of lids over eyes, the fringe of hair round the tonsured crown.

"Bring back the light," he said.

It grew slowly, without heat. He stared into the strange eyes. "I'm not afraid anymore."

"Why?"

Jehan paused a moment. "You're still yourself. For a while I was afraid you weren't. You looked so different."

Alf leaned close. They were almost nose to nose; their eyes met and locked. It seemed to Jehan that he could see through Alf's as if through glass, into an infinity the color of rubies.

"Jehan."

He rose to full awareness, as from water into air, and sat staring. He still held Alf's hand; it tightened, holding him fast.

He shivered convulsively. "How? How could I see like that? I've never—"

Alf looked away. "I did it. I'm sorry. I was looking at the mettle of you; you saw behind my looking."

"Has—has it ever happened before?"

Already Jehan had regained most of his self-possession. "Pure gold," Alf murmured. And, louder: "A few times. I think . . . some humans have in them the seeds of what I am."

Jehan's eyes went wide. "I? Brother Alf, I'm no enchanter!"

The other almost smiled. "Not as I am, no. But something in you responded to my touch. Don't worry; I won't wake it again."

"Of course you will. I said I wasn't afraid, and I'm not. Show me what you can do, Brother Alf!"

Most of it was bravado, and they both knew it. Yet enough was true desire that Alf said, "I can do many things, which probably will damn me, if I can die, and if I have a soul to give over to perdition."

"Dom Morwin said that you can do what saints do. That you can heal hurts, and walk on air, and talk to people far away."

"I can do those things. Though by them I may defy the Scripture which commands that you shall not suffer a witch to live."

"He also said that you could never use your powers for evil."

"*Would*, Jehan. Not *could*. I can heal, but I can also kill."

There was a silence. Jehan searched the pale face, although the eyes would not meet his. "*I* can heal, Brother Alf. And I can kill." He lifted his hand. "This can stitch up a wound or make one, wrap a bandage or wield a sword. Is it any different from your power?"

"Other men have hands, Jehan."

"And others have power."

Alf cuffed Jehan lightly. "Out upon you, boy! You're death to my self-pity. Though it's true I'd no more threaten the powerless than you would attack a handless man. There'd be no fairness in it."

He drew back, and his light died. His voice was soft in the darkness. "Go to sleep now. We've talked enough for one night."

Jehan delayed for a moment. "Brother Alf?"

The other paused in lying down. "What?"

"I'm really not afraid of you."

"I know. I can feel it in you."

"So that's how you'd get around vows of silence."

"Good night, Jehan," Alf said firmly.

The novice wrapped his cloak about him and grinned into the night. "Good night, Brother Alf."

On the second day the travelers could barely move, let alone ride. Yet ride they did, for obstinacy; with time and determination, their bodies hardened. By the fourth day Jehan had remembered his old sturdiness. Even Alf was beginning to take a strange, painful joy in that ride, even to sing as he rode, to Jehan's delight. Hymns at first; then other songs, songs he had learned a lifetime ago, that rose to the surface of his memory and clung there. The first time or two, he stopped guiltily, as if he had been caught singing them in chapel; then, with Jehan's encouragement, he let his voice have its way.

Sometimes they met people on their road, peasants afoot or in wagons, who looked stolidly upon their passing. Once there was a pilgrim, who called for alms and blessed Alf for what he gave, not seeing the tonsure under the hood. And once there was a lord with his meinie, inviting the strangers to spend the night in his castle. Since it was early still, Alf refused, but courteously. Their camp that night seemed rough and cold, even with a fire; and it had begun to rain.

* * * * *

Open land gave way to forest, dark and cheerless. More than ever Alf regretted his refusal of the lord's hospitality; though Jehan laughed and said, "Don't be sorry. If someone had known me there, there'd have been a huge to-do and we'd never have got away."

"Maybe," Alf said. "But our food is running low, and we won't find any here. More likely, what we have will be stolen."

"Do you want to go around?"

"It would add two days to our journey. But maybe we'd better."

"Not I!" Jehan cried. "I'm no coward. Come on; I'll race you to that tree."

He was already off. After an instant, Alf sent the mare after him.

It was quiet under the trees, all sounds muted, lost in the mist of rain. Leaves lay thick upon the track; the horses' passing was almost silent to human ears. The travelers rode as swiftly as they might, yet warily, all their senses alert. Nothing menaced them, though once they started a deer, to Fara's dismay. Only the high saddle and Alf's own skill kept him astride then.

The farther they rode, the older the forest seemed. The trees were immense, heavy with the memory of old gods. Elf-country, Alf thought. But the cross on his breast made him alien.

Wild beasts moved within the reach of his perception, numerous small creatures, deer, a boar going about its dark business; even the flicker of consciousness that was a wolf. Nothing to fear.

Night fell, early and complete. They found a camp, a cluster of trees by a stream, that afforded water and shelter and fuel for a fire.

When they had tended the horses and eaten a little, they huddled together in the circle of light.

"I wonder how Alun is," Jehan said after a while.

Alf glanced at him, a flicker in firelight. "Well enough," he answered. "Brother Herbal has had him up and hobbling about a little. And he's had Morwin bring him treasures from the library."

"You talk to him?"

"Yes."

Jehan tried to laugh. "What's he wearing? You've got his clothes!"

"He borrows mine. Though he says he looks a poor excuse for a monk."

"Does he fret?"

Alf shook his head. "Alun never frets. He simply follows me with his mind."

"Is he watching now?"

"No. He's asleep."

Jehan glanced about uneasily at the whispering dark. "Are you sure?"

"Fairly." Alf smiled. "Come, lad! He can't see any secrets. He's a man of honor."

"But he *follows* us!"

"Me, to be more precise. Sometimes he borrows my eyes."

Jehan's had gone wild. When Alf touched him, he started like a deer. Those were Alf's eyes upon him: Alf's own, strange, familiar eyes. No one else lived behind them.

They flicked aside before he could drown. He swayed; Alf held him. "Jehan. Alun is like me. My own kind. As you and I share speech, so we share our minds. It comforts him. He gave me all he had; should I refuse to let him be with me?"

The other battled for control. "It's not that. It's . . . it's . . . I can't *see* him!"

"Would you like me to tell you when he's here?"

"Please. I'd rather know."

"Then you will. Sleep, Jehan. I'll keep the first watch."

He would have argued, but suddenly he could not keep his eyes open. Even as suspicion stirred, he slid into oblivion.

The road wound deeper into the forest, growing narrower as it proceeded, and growing worse, until often the travelers were slowed to a walk. Jehan rode with hand close to sword hilt; Alf's every sense was alert, although he said once, "No robber, unless he's desperate, will touch us: two strong men, well-mounted, and one big enough for two."

Jehan laughed at that, but he did not relax his guard. Nor, he noticed, did Alf. Even as that disturbed him, it brought comfort.

The second night under the trees, they camped in a place they could defend, a clearing which rose into a low hill, and at the top a standing stone. Jehan would not have chosen to stop here; but he glanced at his companion and grimaced. Here he was, riding with an elf-man, a proven enchanter, and he was afraid to sleep on an old barrow.

It did not seem to trouble Alf. He made camp quietly and ate as much as he would ever eat, and sat afterward, silent, fixing the fire with a blank, inward stare.

When he spoke, Jehan started. "Alun is here."

The novice shuddered and closed his eyes. For a moment in the fire he had seen a narrow hawk-face, a glint of gray eyes, staring full into his own.

Alf's voice murmured in his ear. "Alun sends greetings."

Jehan opened his eyes. There was no face in the fire. "Is he still . . ."

"No." Alf rose and stretched, arching his back, turning his face to the stars. Below, in the clearing about the mound, the horses grazed quietly.

He laid his hand upon the standing stone. It was cold, yet in the core of it he sensed a strange warmth. So it was in certain parts of St. Ruan's: cold stone, warm heart, and power that sang in his blood. The power hummed here, faint yet steady. It had eased the contact with Alun, brought them mind to mind almost without their willing it.

Yet there was something . . .

Jehan; the horses; a hunting owl; a wolf.

He called in all the threads of his power, and looked into Jehan's wide eyes. The moon was very bright, turning toward the full; even the novice could see almost as well as if it had been day.

Alf cupped his hands. The cold light filled them and overflowed. Slowly he opened his fingers and let it drain away.

"What does it feel like?" Jehan's voice was very low.

He let his hands fill again and held them out to Jehan. The other reached out a hand that tried not to tremble. "It—I can feel it!"

Again Alf let the light go. It poured like water over Jehan's fingers, but he could not hold it. "I could make it solid, weave a fabric of it. I tried that once. Moonlight and snowlight for an altar cloth. It was beautiful. The Abbot wanted to send it to Rome. But then he realized that it was made with sorcery."

"What did he do with it?"

"Exactly what he did with me. Blessed it, consecrated it, and put it away." Alf lay down, propped up on his elbow. "But now I'm out. I wonder what will happen to the cloth."

"Maybe," said Jehan, "Dom Morwin should send it to Rhiyana. The Pope wouldn't appreciate it, but the Elvenking would."

Alf considered that. "Maybe he would."

"He'd certainly appreciate you."

For answer Jehan received only a swift ember-glance. They did not speak again that night.

7

The third day in the forest dawned bleak and cold. They ate and broke camp in silence, shivering. Jehan's fingers were numb, his gelding's trappings stiff and unmanageable; he cursed softly.

Alf moved him gently aside and managed the recalcitrant straps with ease. Jehan glanced at him. "You're never cold, are you?"

"Not often," Alf said. The task was done; he took Jehan's hands in both his own. His flesh felt burning hot.

Startled, Jehan tried to pull away. Alf held him easily. "You don't need to add frostbite to your ills."

Jehan submitted. The warmth no longer hurt; it was blissful. "You're a marvel, Brother Alf."

"Or a monster." Alf let him go. "Come, mount up. We've a long way to go."

The cold did not grow less with the day's rising. Jehan thought the air smelled of snow.

Alf rode warily, eyes flicking from side to side. More than once he paused, every sense alert.

"What is it?" Jehan asked. "Bandits?"

The other shook his head.

"Then why do you keep stopping?"

"I don't know," Alf said. "Nothing stalks us. But the pattern isn't . . . quite . . . right. As if something were concealing itself." His eyes went strange, blind.

Jehan looked away. When he looked back, Alf was blinking, shaking his head. "I can't find anything." He shrugged as if to shake off a burden. "We're safe enough. I'd know if we weren't."

That was not particularly comforting. But they rode on in peace, disturbed only by a pair of ravens that followed them for a while, calling to them. Alf called back in a raven's voice.

"What did they say?" Jehan wondered aloud when they had flapped away.

"That we make enough noise to rouse every hunter but a human one." Alf bent under a low branch. The way was clear beyond; he touched the mare into a canter. Over his shoulder he added, "We should leave the trees by tomorrow. There's a village beyond; we'll sleep tomorrow night under a roof."

"Is that a solemn promise?"

"On my soul," Alf replied.

Which could be ironic, Jehan reflected darkly. His gelding stumbled over a tree root; he steadied it with legs and hands. Ahead of him, Alf rode lightly on a mount which never stumbled or even seemed to tire. Elf-man, elf-horse. Maybe this was all part of a spell, and he was doomed to ride under trees forever and never see the open fields again.

He was dreaming awake. His hands were numb; the sun hung low, and it was growing dark under the trees. He would be glad to stop.

Alf had begun to sing softly. *"Nudam fovet Floram lectus; Caro candet tenera . . ."*

He stopped, as he often did when he caught himself singing something secular. And that one, Jehan thought, was more secular than most. "Naked Flora lies a-sleeping; whitely shines her tender body . . ."

When he began again, it was another melody altogether, a hymn to the Virgin.

That night, as before, Alf took the first watch. The air was cold and still; no stars shone. Nothing moved save the flames of the fire.

He huddled into his cloak. He heard nothing, sensed nothing. Perhaps he was a fool; perhaps he was going mad, to watch so when no danger threatened.

Sleep stole over him. He had had little since he left St. Ruan's, and his body was beginning to rebel. He should wake Jehan, set him to watch. If anything came upon them—

Alf started out of a dim dream. It was dark, quiet.

Very close to him, something breathed. Not Jehan, across the long-dead fire. Not the horses. A presence stood over him.

He blinked.

It remained. A white wolf, sitting on its haunches, glaring at him with burning bronze-gold eyes.

A white girl, all bare, glaring through a curtain of bronze-gold hair.

"What," she demanded in a cold clear voice, "are you doing here?"

He sat up, his hood falling back from a startled face. Her eyes ran over him; her thought was as clear as her voice, and as cold. *God's bones! a monk's cub. Who gave him leave to play at knights and squires?*

His cheeks burned. Unclasping his cloak, he held it out to her. She ignored it. "What are you doing here?" she repeated.

Suddenly he wanted to laugh. It was impossible, to be sitting here in the icy dark with a girl who wore nothing but her hair. And who was most certainly of his own kind.

"I was sleeping," he answered her, "until you woke me." Again he held out his cloak. "Will you please put this on?"

She took the garment blindly and flung it over her shoulders.

It did not cover much of consequence. "This is his cloak. His mare. His very undertunic. Damn you, where is he?"

Alf stared at her. "Alun?"

"Alun," she repeated as if the name meant nothing to her. Her mind touched his, a swift stabbing probe. "Yes. Alun. *Where is he?*"

"Who are you?" he countered.

She looked as if she would strike him. "Thea," she snapped. "Where—"

"I'm called Alf."

She seized him. Her hands were slender and strong, not at all as he had thought a woman's must be. Her body—

The night had been cold, but now he burned. Abruptly, fiercely, he pulled away. "Cover yourself," he commanded in his coldest voice.

His tone touched her beneath her anger. Somewhat more carefully, she wrapped the cloak about her. "Brother, if that indeed you are, I'll ask only once more. Then I'll force you to tell me. Where is my lord?"

"Safe," Alf replied, "and no prisoner."

Thea was not satisfied. "Where is he?"

"I can't tell you."

She sat on her heels. Without warning, without movement, she thrust at his mind.

Instinctively he parried. She paled and swayed. "You're strong!" she gasped.

He did not answer. A third presence tugged at his consciousness, one for which he could let down his barriers. Slowly he retreated into a corner of his mind, as that new awareness flowed into him, filling him as water fills an empty cup.

Thea cried a name, but it was not Alun's.

Alf's voice spoke without his willing it in a tone deeper and quieter than his own. "Althea. Who gave you leave to come here?"

She lifted her chin, although she was very pale. "Prince Aidan," she answered.

Alf sensed Alun's prick of alarm, although his response was quiet, unperturbed. "My brother? Is there trouble?"

"Of course there's trouble. He's not had an honest communication from you in almost a month. And I'm not getting one now. What's wrong? What are you hiding?"

"Why, nothing," Alun said without a tremor. "If he is so urgent, where is he?"

"Home, playing the part you set him and growing heartily sick of it. He would have come, but your lady put a binding on him. Which he will break, as well you know, unless you give him some satisfaction."

"I'm safe and in comfort. So I've told him. So you can tell him."

Thea glowered at the man behind the stranger's face. "You're a good liar, but not good enough." Suddenly her face softened, and her voice with it. "My lord. Aidan is wild with worry. Maura has been ill, and—"

For an instant, Alun lost control of the borrowed body. It wavered; he steadied it. "Maura? Ill?"

"Yes. For no visible cause. And speaking of it to no one. So Aidan rages in secret and Maura drifts like a ghost of herself; I follow your mare and your belongings, under shield lest you find me out, and come upon a stranger. Why? What's happened?"

Alf watched his own hands smooth her tousled hair and stroke her soft cheek. "Thea, child, I'm in no danger. But what I do here is my own affair, and secret."

She did not yield to his gentleness. She was proud, Alf thought in his far corner, and wild. "Tell me where you are."

"Inside this body now," he answered her.

"And where is yours? What is this shaveling doing with all your belongings? Have you taken up his?"

He nodded.

"*Why?*" she cried.

"Hush, Thea. You'll wake Jehan."

She paid no heed to the oblivious hulk by the fire with its reek of humanity. "Tell me why," she persisted.

"Someday." He touched her cheek again, this time in farewell, and kissed her brow. "The bells are ringing for Matins. Good night, Althea. And good morning."

Alf reeled dizzily. His hands fell from Thea's shoulders; he gasped, battling sickness. For a brief, horrible moment, his body was not *his:* strange, ill-fitting, aprickle with sundry small pains.

She fixed him with a fierce, feral stare. But it was not he whom she saw. "You dare—even you, you dare, to bind me so . . . Let me go!"

His eyes held no comprehension. She raised her hand as if to strike, and with a visible effort, lowered it. "He bound me. I cannot follow him or find him. Oh, damn him!"

In a moment Alf was going to be ill. He had done—freely done—what he had never dreamed of, not even when he let Alun use his eyes. Given his body over to another consciousness. Possession . . .

He was lying on the ground, and Thea was bending over him. She had forgotten the cloak again. He groaned and turned his face away.

"Poor little Brother," she said. "I see he's bound you, too. I'd pity you if I could." Her warm fingers turned his head back toward her. His eyes would not open. Something very light brushed the lids. "I'm covered again," she told him.

She was. He looked at her, simply looked, without thought.

Thea stared back. She was the first person, apart from Alun, who had seen no strangeness in him at all. His own kind. Were they all so proud?

"Most of us," she said. "It's our besetting sin. We're also stubborn. Horribly so. As you'll come to know."

"Will I?" He was surprised that he could speak at all, let alone with such control. "Since you can't approach Alun, surely you want to go back to his brother."

She shook her head vehemently. "Go back to Aidan? *Kyrie eleison!* I'm not as mad as all that. No; I'm staying with you. Either Alun will slip and let his secret out, or at least I'll be safe out of reach of Aidan's wrath."

"You can't!" His voice cracked like a boy's.

"I can," she shot back. "And will, whatever you say, little Brother."

He rose unsteadily. He was nearly a head taller than she. "You can't," he repeated, coldly now, as he would have spoken to an upstart novice. "I'm on an errand from my Abbot to the Bishop Aylmer. I cannot be encumbered with a woman."

To his utter discomfiture, she laughed. Her laughter was like shaken silver. "What, little Brother! Do I threaten your vows?"

"You threaten my errand. Go back to Rhiyana and leave me to it."

For answer, she yawned and lay where he had lain. "It's late, don't you think? We'd best sleep while we can. We've a long way still to go."

No power of his could move her. She was not human, and her strength was trained and honed as his was not. Almost he regretted his reluctance to use power. She had no such scruples.

Like a fool, he tried to reason with her. "You can't come with us. You have no horse, no weapons, not even a garment for your body."

She smiled, and melted, and changed; and a white wolf lay at his feet. And again: a sleek black cat. And yet again: a white hound with red ears, laughing at him with bright elf-eyes.

He breathed deep, calming himself, remembering what he was. In the shock of her presence, he had forgotten. He picked up his cloak and stepped over her, setting Jehan and the fire between them, and lay down.

He did not sleep. He did not think that she did, either. With infinite slowness the sky paled into dawn.

Jehan had strange dreams, elf-voices speaking in the night, and shapes of light moving to and fro about the camp; and once a white woman-shape, born of Alf's song and his own waking manhood. When he woke, he burned to think of her. He sat up groggily and stared.

A hound stared back. Her eyes were level, more gold than brown, and utterly disconcerting.

Alf came to stand beside her, brittle-calm as ever. "What—" Jehan began, his tongue still thick with sleep. "Whose hound is that?"

"Alun's," Alf answered.

The novice gaped at her. "But how—"

"Never mind," said Alf. "She's attached herself to us whether we will or no."

Jehan held out his hand. The hound sniffed it delicately, and permitted him to touch her head, then her sensitive ears. "She's very beautiful," he said.

Alf smiled tightly. "Her name is Thea."

"It fits her," Jehan said. Something in Alf's manner felt odd; he looked hard at the other, and then at the hound, and frowned. "Is she what's been following us?"

"Yes." Alf knelt to rekindle the fire.

Jehan fondled the soft ears. She was sleek, splendid, born for the hunt, yet she did not look dangerous. She looked what surely she was, a high lord's treasure, bred to run before kings.

He laughed suddenly. "You're almost a proper knight now, Brother Alf! All you need is a sword."

"Thank you," Alf said, "but no." The fire had caught; he brought out what remained of their provisions, and sighed. "What will you have? Moldy bread, or half a crumb of cheese?"

8

The trees were thinning. Jehan was sure of it. The road had widened; he and Alf could ride side by side for short stretches with Thea running ahead. Like Fara, she seemed tireless, taking joy in her own swift strength.

By noon a gray drizzle had begun to fall. They pressed on as hard as they might, following the white shape of the elf-hound.

At last they surmounted a hill, and the trees dwindled away before them. Jehan whooped for delight, for there below them in a wide circle of fields stood a village.

It was splendid to ride under the sky again, with no dark ranks of trees to hem them in and the wind blowing free upon their faces. Jehan's gelding moved of its own accord into a heavy canter; the gray mare fretted against the bit. Alf let her have her head.

They did not run far. A few furlongs down the road, Alf eased Fara into a walk. He smiled as Jehan came up, and stroked the mare's damp neck. "We'll sleep warm tonight," he said.

The village was called Woodby Cross: a gathering of houses about an ancient church. Its priest took the travelers in, gave them dry clothes to wear after they had bathed, and fed them from his own larder. He was rough-spoken and he had little enough Latin, and the woman who cooked for him had at her skirts a child or two who bore him an uncanny resemblance. But he received his guests with as much courtesy as any lord in his hall.

"It's not often we see people of quality hereabouts," he told them after they had eaten and drunk. "Mostly those go eastaway round Bowland, to one of the lords or Abbots there. Here we get the sweepings, woodsfolk and wanderers and the like."

"People don't go through the forest?" Jehan asked.

He shook his head. "It's a shorter way, if you don't lose yourself. But there's bad folk in it. They're known to go after anybody who goes by."

"They didn't bother us."

The priest scratched the stubble of his tonsure. "So they didn't. But you're two strong men, and you've got good horses and yon fine hound."

Thea raised her head from her paws and wagged her tail. Her amusement brushed the edges of Alf's mind.

He ignored her. He had been ignoring her since he had turned in his bathing and found her watching him with most unhound-like interest.

"The King," Father Wulfric was saying. "Now there's someone who could sweep the outlaws out of Bowland, if he'd take the trouble. But he's away north, chasing those rebels who broke out while he was on Crusade. You'll have a fine time finding him."

"Actually," said Jehan, "we're looking for Bishop Aylmer; but that means we have to look for the King. They're always together. Two of a kind, people say. Fighters."

"That's certain. But I think my lord Bishop ought to pay a little more attention to his Christian vows and a little less to unholy bloodletting."

Jehan carefully avoided saying anything. The woman and the children had left, ostensibly to return to their own house. The children had looked surprised and fretful; one had started toward

the curtain that hid the priest's bed from public view, before
her mother dragged her away.

He shrugged a little. Alf had not spoken, either. He was gazing
into the fire, eyes half-closed. Something in his face spoke to
Jehan of Alun's presence.

The novice yawned. "Whoosh! I'm tired. It's a long ride from
the Marches."

"And a fair way to go yet," said Father Wulfric. "Me, I'm a
lazy man. I stay at home and mind my flock, and leave the
traveling to you young folk." He rose from his seat by the hearth,
opening his mouth to say more.

He never began. Alf stirred, drawing upright, taut as a bow-
string. Firelight blazed upon his face; the flames filled his eyes.
"Kilhwch," he whispered. "Rhydderch." It was a serpent's hiss.
"He rends the web and casts it to the winds of Hell."

Thea growled. His eyes blazed upon her. "War, that means.
War. I can delay no longer. I must go to the King."

"Tomorrow." Jehan's voice was quiet, and trembled only a
little.

"Tonight." Alf reached for his cloak, his boots. "War comes.
I must stop it."

Jehan held his cloak out of his reach. "Tomorrow," he
repeated, "we ride like the wrath of God. Tonight we rest."

The wide eyes scarcely knew him. "I see, Jehan. I *see*."

"I know you do. But you're not leaving tonight. Go to bed
now, Brother Alf. Sleep."

The priest backed away from them, crossing himself, muttering a prayer. He remembered tales, demons in monks' guise,
servants of the Devil, elf-creatures who snatched men's souls
and fled away before the sunrise. Even solidly human Jehan
alarmed him: soul-snatched already, maybe, or a changeling
mocking man's shape.

They signed themselves properly and prayed before they went
to bed, Latin, a murmur of holy names. He was not comforted.

They slept to all appearances as men slept. He knew; he
watched them. The novice did not move all night. The other,

the pale one with the face like an elf-lord, dreamed nightlong, murmuring and tossing. But Wulfric could not understand his words, save that some of them were Latin and some might have been names: Morwin, Alun, Gwydion; and often, that name he seemed to hate. Rhydderch.

When they roused before dawn, he had their horses ready. They acted human enough; stumbling, blear-eyed, yawning and stretching and drawing water to wash in though they had bathed all over only the night before. They helped with breakfast, and ate hungrily, even Alf, who looked pale and ill. Nor did they vanish at cockcrow. In fact it was closer to sunrise when they left, with a blessing from the monk and a wave from the novice. Well before they were out of sight, the priest had turned his back on their strangeness and gone to his work.

9

Alf rode now for three kingdoms. Jehan had caught his
urgency, but the old gelding, for all its valiant heart, could not
sustain the pace they set. In a village with a name Jehan never
knew, Alf exchanged the struggling beast for a rawboned rake
of a horse with iron lungs and a startling gift of speed—a trans-
action that smacked of witchery. But it all smacked of witchery,
that wild ride from the borders of Bowland, errand-riding for
the Elvenking.

Three days past their guesting in Wulfric's house, they paused
at the summit of a hill. Fara snorted, scarcely winded by the
long climb, and tossed her proud head. Almost absently Alf
quieted her.

This was a brutal country, empty even of the curlew's cry:
a tumbled, trackless waste, where only armies would be mad
enough to go. An army in rebellion and an army to break the
rebellion—hunter and hunted pursued and fled under winter's
shadow. Rumor told of a hidden stronghold, a fortress looming
over a dark lake somewhere among the fells; the rebels sought
it or fought in it or had been driven out of it, always with the

King's troops pressing close behind them. Fifty on either side, people had whispered in the last village, no more; or Richard had a hundred, the enemy twice that; or the rebels fought with a staggering few against the King's full might.

Truth trod a narrow path through all the tales. The rebels had taken and held the town of Ellesmere, and the King had laid siege to them there; driven forth, they had fled away southward, pursued by four hundred of Richard's men. Neither force could have gone far, for this was no land to feed an army. The enemy were starved and desperate, ready to turn at bay, the King eager to bring the chase to its end.

Alf gazed over the sweep and tumble of the moor, casting his other-sight ahead even of his keen eyes. "They're close now," he said: "to us, and to each other."

Jehan's nostrils flared, scenting battle. "Do you think they'll fight before we get to them?"

"More likely we'll arrive in the middle of it."

The novice loosed a great shout. "*Out! Out!*" The echoes rolled back upon him in hollow Saxon. *Out! Out! Out! Out!* He laughed and sent his mount careening down the steep slope.

Before he reached the bottom, Fara had passed him, bearing Alf as its wings bear the hawk, with Thea her white shadow. The rangy chestnut flattened its ears and plunged after.

In a fold of the hills lay a long lake, gray now under a gray sky. Steel clashed on steel there; men cried out in anger and in pain; voices sang a deep war chant.

A jut of crag hid the struggle until the riders were almost upon it. There where the lake sent an arm into a steep vale, men fought fiercely in the sedge, hand to hand. Those who were lean and ragged as wolves in winter would be the rebels, nearly all of them on foot. The King's men, well-fed and -armed, wore royal badges, and mailed knights led them, making short work of the enemy.

Alf found the King easily enough. Richard had adopted a new fashion of the Crusader knights, a long light surcoat over his mail; royal leopards ramped upon it, and on his helm he wore a crown. He of cross and keys in the King's company, wielding a mace, would be Bishop Aylmer.

A hiss of steel close by made Alf turn. Jehan had drawn his sword; there was a fierce light in his eyes.

Battle sang in his own blood, gentle monk though he was, with no skill in weapons. It was a poison; he fought it and quelled it. "No," he said. "No fighting, Jehan."

For a moment he thought Jehan would break free and gallop to his death. But the novice sighed and sheathed his sword. Reluctantly he followed Alf round the clash of armies, evading stray flights of arrows, seeking the King's camp.

When they had almost reached it, a roar went up behind them. The rebels' leader had fallen.

Alf crossed himself, prayed briefly, rode on.

Richard had camped on a low hill above the lake, open on all sides and most well-guarded. But no one stopped a pair of youths on hard-ridden horses, errand-riders surely, trotting purposefully toward the center of the camp.

They sought the horse-lines first and saw to their mounts. There again, no one questioned them.

Folly, Thea decreed, watching Alf rub Fara down. *A thief could walk in, take every valuable object here, and walk out again as peaceful as you please.*

Alf glanced at her. *What thief would come out here?*

Who knows? She inspected a bucket, found it full of water, drank delicately. *What are you going to do now?*

Jehan asked the same question aloud at nearly the same time. "Wait for Bishop Aylmer," Alf answered them both. He shouldered his saddlebags, laden with books and with Morwin's letter to the Bishop, and slapped the mare's neck in farewell.

They walked through the camp. It was nearly deserted, except for a servant or two, but one large tent seemed occupied. As they neared it, they heard screams and cries, and Alf caught a scent that made his nose wrinkle. Pain stabbed at him, multiplied tenfold, the anguish of men wounded in battle.

He had meant to wait by the Bishop's tent, but his body turned itself toward the field hospital. Even as he approached, a pair of battered and bloody men brought another on a cloak.

There were not so many wounded, he discovered later. Thirty in all, and only five dead. But thirty men in agony, with but a surgeon and two apprentices to tend them, tore at all his defenses.

"Jehan," he said. "Find water and bandages, and anything else you can." Even as he spoke, he knelt by a groaning man and set to work.

He was aware, once, of the master-surgeon's presence, of eyes that took him in from crown to toe, and marked his youth and his strangeness and his skillful hands. After a little the man left him alone. One did not question a godsend. Not when it was easing an arrow out of a man's lung.

The power that had forsaken him utterly with Alun rose in him now like a flood-tide. He fought to hold it back, for he dared work no miracles here. But some escaped in spite of his efforts, easing pain, stanching the flow of blood from an axe-hewn shoulder. He probed the wound with sensitive fingers, seeing in his mind the path of the axe through the flesh, knowing the way to mend it—so.

He raised his hands. Blood covered them and the man beneath them—young, no more than a boy, wide-eyed and white-faced. There was no wound upon him.

Thea touched Alf's mind. *You'd better make him forget, little Brother, or one of two things will happen. You'll be canonized, or you'll be burned at the stake.*

"No," Alf said aloud. He forced himself to smile down at the stunned face. "Rest a while. When you feel able, you can get up and go."

The boy did not answer. Alf left him there.

Little Brother—

He slammed down all his barriers. Thea yelped in pain, but he did not look at her. The shield not only kept her out; it kept his power in. There were no more miracles.

Somewhere in the long task of healing, word came. The battle was over. The last few men who came, grinned beneath blood and dust and told proud tales while their wounds were tended.

Alf caught Jehan's eye. The novice finished binding a sword-cut and joined Alf near the tent wall. They washed off the stains of their labors and slipped away.

Weary though the King's men were, they prepared to consume the night in wine and song and bragging of their victory. Even the King drank deep in his tent and listened as one of his knights sang his triumph: a mere hundred against a thousand rebels, and the King slew them by the ten thousands. Legends bred swiftly about Richard.

Bishop Aylmer did not join in the carousing. When he had seen to the dead and dying, he sought his tent, close by the King's and but little smaller. His priest-esquire disarmed him and helped him to scour away the marks of battle, while his monks waited upon his pleasure. That was to pray and then to eat, and afterward, to rest alone.

Alf waited until the Bishop was comfortable, half-dreaming over his breviary but still awake, with the lamp flickering low. There was no guard in front of his tent, for trust or for arrogance. Alf raised the flap and walked in, with Jehan and Thea behind.

The Bishop looked up. They were a strange apparition in the gloom, two tall lads and a white hound, yet he showed no surprise at all. "Well?" he asked, cocking a shaggy brow. "What brings strangers here so late?"

Alf knelt and kissed his ring. "A message from the Abbot of St. Ruan's, my lord," he answered.

Aylmer looked him over carefully. "I know you. Brother . . . Alfred, was it? And you there, would you be a Sevigny?"

Jehan bowed. "The second son, my lord."

"Ah. I'd heard you'd turned monk. Not to your father's liking, was it?"

Something in the Bishop's eye made Jehan swallow a grin. "Not really, my lord."

"It doesn't seem to have hurt you," Aylmer observed.

Alf held out Morwin's letter. "From the Abbot, my lord," he said.

The Bishop took it and motioned them both to sit. "No, no, don't object. Humility's all very well, but it wears on the exalted."

As they obeyed, he broke the seal and began to read. "'To my dear brother in Christ'—he's smoother on parchment than he is in the flesh, that's certain. Sent to me . . . plainly . . . What's this? You have urgent business with the King?"

Alf began to reply, but Aylmer held up a hand. "Never mind. Yet. I've inherited you two, it seems; I'm to treat you with all Christian kindness and further your cause with His Majesty, 'as much as my office and my conscience permit.'" He looked up sharply. His eyes were small, almost lost beneath the heavy brows, but piercingly bright. "Your Abbot plays interesting games, Brothers."

"Of necessity," said Alf. "He didn't dare write the full tale in case the letter fell into the wrong hands. But there's no treason in this. That I swear."

"By what, Brother? The hollows of the hills?"

"The cross on my breast will do, my lord."

Aylmer marked his coolness, but it did not abash him. "So—what couldn't be written that needs Morwin's best young minds and such haste that even a war can't interfere?"

For a moment Alf was silent. Jehan's tension was palpable. Aylmer sat unmoving, dark and strong and still as a standing stone.

Alf drew a breath, released it. "It's true that Jehan and I have been . . . given . . . to you. You asked for me. Jehan was never made to live in the cloister. But our haste rises from another cause. Some while ago, on All Hallows' Eve, a rider came to the Abbey. He was badly hurt; and we tended him, and discovered that he was the envoy of the King of Rhiyana."

The Bishop's expression did not change, but Alf sensed his start of interest.

"This knight," Alf went on, "had been in Gwynedd with the young King, and had ridden into Anglia to speak with a lord there, seeking peace among the kingdoms. The lord with whom he spoke was preparing war; he meant to use our knight as a gauntlet to cast in Rhiyana's face. The knight escaped to us, though in such a state that even yet he can't leave his bed, and the Abbot took it on himself to send us with his messages to the King."

"What sort of messages?"

"Kilhwch has no desire to go to war with Anglia. But a lord of Anglia has begun to raid in Gwynedd. If our King will refuse to join in the war and will take steps to punish his vassal, there can be peace between the kingdoms."

Aylmer sat for a long while, pondering Alf's words. At last he spoke. "But your man is from Rhiyana. Why is this struggle any concern of his?"

"Gwydion of Rhiyana fostered Kilhwch in the White Keep; he still takes care for his foster son's well-being."

Again Aylmer considered, turning his ring on his hand, frowning at it. "I think you'd better talk to the King. But not tonight. He's celebrating his victory; he won't want to hear about anything else. Tomorrow, though, he'll be sober and in a mood to listen to you. Though peace is never a good sermon to preach to Coeur-de-Lion."

"I can try," Alf murmured.

"I was right about you, I think. You were wasted in the cloister."

"I was happy there. And I was serving God."

"And here you aren't?"

"I never said that, my lord."

"No. You just meant it."

"One may serve God wherever one is. Even in battle."

"Would you do that?"

Alf shook his head, eyes lowered. "No. No, my lord. Today, I watched for a moment. That was enough."

The Bishop nodded. "It takes a strong stomach."

Jehan stirred beside Alf. "My lord," he said with some heat, "Brother Alf is no coward. He spent the whole day with the wounded. And it takes a good deal more courage to mend hurts than it does to make them."

Aylmer looked from one to the other, and his dark weathered face warmed into a smile. "I see that you two are somewhat more than traveling companions." He rose. "You'll sleep here tonight. Tomorrow you'll see His Majesty. I'll make sure of that. But I'm warning you now: Don't hope for too much. War is Richard's life's blood, and he's had his eye on Gwynedd for a long time. One man isn't going to sway him."

"We'll see," said Alf. "My lord."

10

Alf was up before the sun. The Bishop had not yet stirred; Jehan lay on the rug with Alf, curled about Thea's slumbering body. It was very cold.

He rose, gathered his cloak about him, and peered through the tent flap. The camp was silent, wrapped in an effluvium of wine and blood, the aftermath of battle. A mist lay like a gray curtain over the tents.

The horses were well content, with feed and water in plenty. Alf left them after a moment or two and went down to the lake.

The wide water stretched before him, half-veiled in fog. There was no one near to see him; he stripped and plunged in, gasping, for the water was icy. But he had bathed in colder in the dead of winter in St. Ruan's.

When he was almost done, the water turned warm so suddenly that it burned.

He whipped about. Thea stood on the bank in her own shape, wearing his shirt. It needed a washing, he noticed.

She walked toward him, her soles barely touching the surface of the lake. A yard or two away from him, she sat cross-legged on air. "What are you scowling for?" she asked him. "Hurry and finish your bath. I can't keep the water warm forever."

"If anyone sees you," he said, "there will be trouble."

"Don't worry. I'm not easily raped. Even by King Richard's soldiers."

Alf flushed. That was not what he had meant, and she knew it.

"You do blush prettily," Thea remarked. Still wearing his shirt, she let herself sink. "Ah—wonderful. Somehow a bath feels much better on skin than on fur." She wriggled out of the shirt, inspected it critically, rolled it up and tossed it shoreward before Alf could stop her. She was chest-deep, as he was; he averted his eyes and waded past her.

Between one step and the next, the water turned from blood-warm to icy cold. He ran to the bank and fumbled for his clothes. His shirt was warm, dry, and clean, as were the rest. Thea's gift.

Once safely clad, he should have returned to the camp. He stayed where he was, not looking at Thea but very much aware of her.

She emerged at length and accepted his cloak. "Thank you," she said, not entirely ironically. "I suppose I should turn into a hound again and give you some peace."

He glanced at her. She was very fair, wrapped in the dark blue cloak. He remembered what lay beneath; the memory burned. His body kindled in its fire.

So this is what it is, he thought in the small part of him which could still think.

Thea stared. Beautiful eyes, golden bronze, burning. "You mean you've never—"

He turned and fled.

Once he had left her, he cooled swiftly enough. But he could not still his trembling. So long, so long— Other novices had groaned and tossed in their beds or crept to secret shameful trysts with girls from the village, even with each other. Monks had confessed to daylight musings, to burning dreams, to outright sin; accepted their penances; and come back soon after with the same confessions. Alfred had lived untroubled, novice, monk, and priest; had pitied his brothers' frailty, but granted it no mercy. A man of God should master his body. Had not he himself done so?

He had been a fool. A child. A babe in arms.

Was he now to become a man?

He drew himself up. A man was his own master. He faced what he must face and overcame it boldly. Even this, torment that it was, but sweet—honey-fire-sweet, like her eyes, like her—

"*No!*"

His mind fell silent. His body stilled, conquered.

But he did not go back. Nor did she follow him, as a woman or as a hound.

He was calm when he returned to the Bishop's tent, to find Aylmer awake and dressed and surrounded by his monks. Jehan stood among them, conspicuous for his lordly clothes though not for his size; one or two of Aylmer's warrior-priests easily overtopped him.

There were curious glances as Alf entered. One man in particular fixed him with a hard stare, a small dark man in a strange habit, gray cowl over white robe. Something about him made Alf's skin prickle.

"Brother Alfred," Aylmer greeted him. "I'm getting ready to say Mass. Will you serve me?"

Alf forgot the stranger, forgot even the lingering shame of his encounter with Thea. He had not gone up to the altar in years. Ten years, nine months, four days. Not since he had found himself unable completely to reconcile his face with his years; when he had ceased to doubt that he would not grow old.

But Aylmer had not asked him to say Mass, did not know that he had taken priest's vows. Surely he could serve at the altar. That was no worse than singing in the choir.

Aylmer was waiting, growing impatient. Alf willed himself to speak. "I'll do it, my lord."

Aylmer nodded. "Brother Bernard, show Brother Alfred where everything is. We'll start as soon as the King is ready."

Dressed in alb and dalmatic and moving through the familiar ritual, Alf found that his fear had vanished. In its place had come a sort of exaltation. This, he was made for. Strange, half-human, elvish creature that he was, he belonged here at this altar, taking part in the shaping of the Mass.

He was preternaturally aware of everything, not only the priest and the rite, but the Bishop's tent about him, the high lords kneeling and standing as the ritual bade them, and the King.

Richard was difficult to pass by: a tall man, well-made, with a face he was proud of and a mane of gold-red hair. He heard the Mass with apparent devotion, but the swift fierce mind leaped from thought to thought, seldom pausing to meditate upon the Sacrament. His eyes kept returning to Alf, caught by the fair strange face, as Aylmer had known they would be.

When the Mass was ended, the celebrants disrobed swiftly. Alf paused with Alun's knightly garments in his hands. "My lord," he said to Aylmer, who watched him, "if you would allow me a moment to fetch my habit—"

The Bishop shook his head. "No. It's better this way." A monk settled his cloak about his shoulders; he fastened the clasp. "Alfred, Jehan, come with me."

Richard sat in his tent, attended by several squires and a knight or two. "Aylmer!" he called out as the Bishop entered. "Late for breakfast, as usual."

"Of course, Sire," the Bishop said calmly. "Should I endanger my reputation by coming early?"

The King laughed and held out a cup. "Here, drink. You've taken unfair advantage already by going to bed sober last night."

As Aylmer took the cup and sat by the King, Richard noticed the two attendants. "What, sir, have you been recruiting squires in this wilderness?"

"They've been recruiting me, Sire. Brother Alfred, Brother Jehan, late of St. Ruan's."

One of the knights stirred. "Jehan de Sevigny! They've thrown you out of the cloister?"

"Alas," Jehan replied, "yes. I outgrew it, you see."

"Like Bran the Blessed," Alf said, "he grows so great that no house will hold him."

The King's golden lion-eyes had turned to him and held, as they had during Mass. The others laughed at the jest, Jehan among them; the King was silent, although he smiled. "And you, Sir Monk-in-knight's-clothing? Wouldn't the house hold you?"

"No, Sire," Alf responded.

They were all staring now, at him, at the King. Their thoughts made him clench his fists. Richard had found another pretty lad, the prettiest one yet.

That was not what Richard was thinking of. He had been trying since Mass to put a name to that cast of features, but none would come.

"Alfred," he said, "of St. Ruan's on Ynys Witrin. Are you a clerk?"

"Of sorts, Sire."

"Pity. You look as if you'd make a swordsman in the Eastern fashion. Light and fast." With an abrupt gesture, Richard pointed to a seat. "Sit down, both of you. While we eat, you can tell us a tale or two we haven't heard before."

It was the first time Alf had sat at table with a King, though he had waited upon royalty once or twice, long ago. Those high feasts had been not at all like this breaking of bread upon the battlefield. Richard was at ease, standing little upon ceremony; no one paid much heed to rank.

Afterward, as they all rose to go, Richard gestured to Alf. "Sir monk. Stay."

Aylmer's satisfaction was palpable; as was the sudden interest of the others. Jehan frowned and wavered. But the Bishop's cold eye held him; he retreated.

One was not precisely alone with a King. Squires cleared away the table; another sat in a corner, polishing a helm. But those in Richard's mind were nonentities. He relaxed in his chair, eyes half-closed, saying nothing.

Alf was used to silence. He settled into it and wrapped himself in it.

The King's voice wove its way into the pattern of his thoughts. "Brother Alfred. Alf. What are you?"

He regarded Richard calmly. His God, a white elf-woman, himself—those he feared. A King troubled him not at all. "I'm a monk of St. Ruan's Abbey, Sire."

"Noble born?"

He shrugged slightly. "I doubt it."

The King's eyes narrowed. "Don't you know?"

"I was a foundling, Sire."

"A changeling?"

"Some people think so."

"I can see why," Richard said. And, abruptly: "What does Aylmer want?"

"Aylmer, Sire?" Alf asked, puzzled.

"Aylmer. Why is he thrusting you at me? What's he up to?"

This King was no fool. Alf smiled without thinking. "The Bishop is up to nothing, Sire."

"So now he's corrupting his monks in the cradle."

Alf's smile widened. Richard's eyes were glinting. "Don't blame him for this, Sire. I asked him for an audience with you."

Richard frowned; then he laughed. "And he didn't even ask. He simply placed you where I'd fall over you. Well, Brother Obstacle, what do you want?"

The mirth faded from Alf's face. He spoke quietly, carefully. "I've been sent to serve the Bishop. But I've also been entrusted with another errand."

"By whom?"

"The King of Rhiyana, on behalf of Kilhwch of Gwynedd."

The drowsing lion tensed. "One monk, with only a boy for company. Are they trying to insult me?"

"No, Sire. They honor you with their trust."

"Or taunt me with it. I know what Gwydion is like. He lairs in his White Keep and spins webs to trap kings in. How did I stumble into this one?"

"You didn't. One of your vassals did. A baron of the Marches, named Rhydderch."

The King stroked his beard and pretended a calm he did not feel. "Rhydderch. What has he done?"

"You know that there's been trouble on the Marches."

There was a dangerous glint in Richard's eye. "I know it," he said.

"Rhydderch is behind it. He's sent forces into Gwynedd and is ravaging the lands along the border."

"Are you implying that I don't keep my lords in hand?"

"I'm implying nothing, Majesty," Alf said.

If Richard had had a tail, it would have been lashing his sides. "You tell me that one of my barons foments a major war, and that the King of Rhiyana will concern himself with it. Gwydion's a meddler, but even so, in this he's going far afield."

"Of course he's concerned. Kilhwch is his foster son. A war with you would end in disaster."

"For one side. Kilhwch is a boy, and Gwydion's no soldier."

"For both sides, Sire. Kilhwch is nineteen, which isn't so very young, and he takes after his father. And Gwydion, I think, would surprise you. Isn't his brother said to be the best knight in the world?"

"His brother is as old as he is. Which is ancient."

Alf shook his head. "The Flame-bearer has no equal, nor ever shall have. Not even Coeur-de-Lion."

That barb had sunk deep. Richard's eyes blazed. His voice was too quiet, almost a purr. "You're very sure of that, little monk. Do you even know which end of a sword to hold onto?"

"I can guess, Sire."

"And you guess at the prince's prowess?"

"The world knows it. I believe it." Calmly, boldly, Alf sat on a stool near the King, his long legs drawn up.

The other did not react to this small insolence in the face

of the greater one. "Do you know how to convince me that I ought to go to war? Aylmer could have told you. Anyone could. It's ludicrously simple. Tell the brawn-brained fool the other man is a better fighter than he is."

To Richard's utter amazement, Alf laughed. It was a light free sound, with nothing in it but mirth. "You, Sire? Brawn-brained? Far from it. But you have an alarming passion for fighting, and you want Gwynedd. Unwise, that. You'd do better to send ambassadors to Kilhwch and tell him you want peace. Else you'll have Gwynedd on your left and Rhiyana on your right, and all Hell between."

"A small kingdom whose King is barely in control of his vassals, and a greater one which hasn't fought a war since before I was born. But Anglia is strong, tempered in the Crusade."

"And tired of fighting, though you may not be, Sire. Surely it will be adventure enough to quell Rhydderch."

Richard looked him over again, slowly this time, musing. "Why are you doing this? Are you Rhiyanan?"

"No, Sire. It was entrusted to me by someone else. A knight of Rhiyana who fell afoul of Rhydderch."

"Dead?"

"No, though not for Rhydderch's lack of trying."

"So Gwydion already has a reason to be my enemy."

"Rhiyana doesn't know yet. And won't, if you help us, Sire. Send word to Rhydderch. Order him to withdraw from Gwynedd on pain of death. And let Kilhwch know what you're doing."

The King was silent. Alf clasped his knees, doing his utmost not to reveal his tension. Richard hung in the balance, debating within himself. War, and winter coming, and troops to deal with who fretted already at campaigning so late in the year. To stop Rhydderch, to beg Kilhwch's kind pardon—no. But a truce now, and in the spring . . .

He nodded abruptly and stood. "I'm bound to ride now for Carlisle. By the time I get there I'll have an answer for you."

Alf rose as the King had and bowed, slightly, gracefully. "As you will, Sire."

The lion-eyes glinted upon him. "But it's not as *you* will, is it?"

"I don't matter, Majesty."

Richard snorted. "Stop pretending to be so humble. You're as proud as Lucifer."

Alf nodded. "Yes, I am. But I try. That's worth something."

"A brass farthing." Richard tossed him something that glittered; reflexively he caught it. "I have work to do if we're to ride out of here by night. You'll wait on Aylmer. But I may steal you now and again. You're interesting, sir monk."

Alf bowed low without speaking. Metal warmed in his hand, the shape of a ring, the sense of silver, moonstone.

A simple monk had no business with such things. He knew he should return it with courtesy; half-raised his hand, opened his mouth to speak.

When he left, he had not spoken. The ring was still clenched in his fist.

11

The King broke camp shortly after noon and turned his face toward Carlisle. His men, recovered from the ravages of battle and of drink, set forth in high spirits, singing as they went, songs that made no concessions to the small somber-clad party about the Bishop. The more pious of those pretended not to listen; the rest beat time on thigh or pommel and at length joined in.

Alf rode in silence. He had been silent since he returned from the King's tent.

Jehan frowned. He had hoped that, once Alf had delivered his message and given himself over to Bishop Aylmer, he would be his old self again. But he seemed more moody than ever. He did not even answer when Jehan, looking about, asked, "Where's Thea?"

A little after that, Alf left his place behind the Bishop. Others were riding apart from the line, young knights impatient with the slow pace, bidden by their commanders to patrol the army's edges. He did not belong with them, unarmed and unarmored as he was, but no one rebuked him. He had an air about him, Jehan thought, like a prince in exile.

"An interesting young man," a voice said.

Someone had ridden up beside him, the man in the gray cowl
on a bony mule. Jehan swallowed a sharp retort. He did not
like this Brother Reynaud—not his face, not his eyes, and not
at all his high nasal voice.

The monk did not seem to notice Jehan's silence. He was
watching Alf with a peculiar, almost avid stare. "Very interesting,"
he repeated. "I understand that he's a churchman?"

Jehan had his temper in hand. "Yes, Brother," he said easily
enough. "He has a dispensation to wear secular clothes. So do
I. We thought it would be less dangerous to travel this way."

"Oh, yes. Yes. It might be. Certainly he looks most well in
that guise. Though one so fair would look well even in sack-
cloth." Brother Reynaud smiled a narrow, ice-edged smile. "Does
he come of a princely family?"

"Not that anyone knows of. But he doesn't need to be a lord's
get. He's princely enough as he is."

"That," said the monk, "is clear to see. His parents must be
very proud of such a son."

"He's an orphan. He was raised in the abbey."

"Oh? How sad." Brother Reynaud's eyes did not match his
words; they glittered, eager. Like a hound on the scent, Jehan
thought.

Hound. Gray cowl, white robe. Jehan remembered dimly a
name he had overheard, a word or two describing a habit and
an Order. Hounds. *Canes. Canes Dei.* Hounds of God.

He went cold. His fingers clenched upon the reins; the
chestnut jibbed, protesting.

He made himself speak calmly. "Tell me, Brother. I can't seem
to place your habit. Is it a new Order?"

Reynaud glanced at him and smiled again. "New enough. The
Order of Saint Paul."

The Paulines. They were the hunting-hounds of Rome,
seekers and destroyers of aught that imperiled the Church.
Heretics. Unbelievers. Witches and sorcerers.

Alf rode unheeding, his white head bare, the gray mare dancing
beneath him. Someone called out to him, admiring his mount;

he replied, his voice clear and strong and inhumanly beautiful. No one could see his eyes as they were—those, he blurred, by subtle witchery—but that was a small thing to the totality of him. He looked what he was, elf-born, alien.

The King had summoned him. The mare wheeled and fell in beside the red charger. They rode on so, horses and men matched in height, but the King heavier, slower, earthbound.

"The King has taken to him," Reynaud observed.

Jehan's heart hammered against his ribs. He could smell the danger in this man, a reek of blood and fire. "I'm not surprised," he said. "He was quite the most brilliant monk in our abbey. And the most saintly."

Reynaud did not react at all to that thrust. "Your Abbot must have been sorry to see him go."

"He was. But Bishop Aylmer asked for Brother Alfred, and it was best for him to leave. He needed to stretch his wings a little."

"Strong wings they must be to attain a King in their first flight."

"That's what the Abbot thought. And Dom Morwin's right about most things."

"Was it your Dom Morwin who admitted this paragon to the abbey?"

"Oh, no. Dom Morwin's only been Abbot for five years. Brother Alf came when he was a baby."

The gleam in Reynaud's eye had brightened. "Alf, you call him?"

Jehan swallowed and tried to smile. "There are a lot of Saxons in our abbey. And of course there's the great scholar, the one who wrote the *Gloria Dei*. With two Alfreds in the place, one had to have his name shortened."

"Ah, yes. Alfred of St. Ruan's. I hadn't noticed the coincidence. Is he still alive?"

"Still. Though he doesn't go out anymore, nor write much. He's getting quite old, and his health isn't very good."

"That's a pity. Your young Brother is named after him, then?"

Jehan nodded. "Takes after his scholarship, too. He hated

to see Brother Alf go. But the Abbot insisted. There are other teachers, he said, and one of them is the world."

"True enough," Alf said.

Jehan drew his breath in sharply. Intent upon the fabric of truth and falsehood, he had not heard the approaching hoofs.

Alf's eyes looked darker than usual, more gray than silver. He smiled at Jehan and said, "I heard you talking about me. Base flattery, all of it. I'm really quite an ordinary young nuisance; my Abbot decided he'd had enough of me and inflicted me on the poor Bishop."

"Both of us," Jehan put in. "What did the King say, Brother Alf?"

Alf shrugged. "A word or two. He wanted to buy Fara." He smoothed the mare's wind-ruffled mane.

"Did you say yes?"

"Of course not. I said she was only lent to me; he said that he understood; we both agreed that she's the most beautiful creature afoot." She arched her neck; he stroked it and laughed a little. "Aye, you are, and well you know it."

Reynaud had withdrawn in silence. But his presence remained, like a faint hint of corruption; surely he strained to hear what they said. Jehan wanted to shout a warning, but he dared not.

Their horses moved together; knee brushed knee. Alf gripped Jehan's shoulder for an instant, as a friend will, saying something meaningless. But Jehan caught the thought behind, the surge of comfort. Alf knew. He was on guard. And the Hounds of God, for all their fire and slaughter, had never caught one of the true elf-blood. That he was sure of, with Alun's surety.

Alf started awake. It was very late, with a scent of dawn in the air. Jehan's warm body lay against him, dreaming boy-dreams. His own had been far less gentle, a wild confusion of fire and darkness, Alun's black boar and a pack of ghost-white hounds, and a lion transfixed with a flaming sword.

He lay still as the cold sweat dried from his body. He had not cried out; no one had awakened.

Thea crouched close in hound-shape, glaring as she had glared on that first night.

"Thea," he breathed. "I thought you'd gone back to Rhiyana."

Her lip curled in a snarl. She was exhausted and in a foul temper. *I set out for St. Ruan's, and traveled all this black day and half the night, and found myself outside this tent. With Alun in my mind all the while, telling me about the book he read today and chanting the Offices.*

You knew it would happen, Alf said in his mind.

Her hackles rose; she bared her teeth. *I put up every barrier I had. I went down to the very bottom of my power. And I hunted a trail that led me in a long arc back to you.*

Alf sighed. *I hoped you'd be wise enough to go home.*

No!

He winced. Her anger was piercing. *I'm sorry*, he said.

Don't pity me!

I don't. He drew the blanket up to his chin.

She lay down beside him. He went rigid. Her body was beast-warm. But her mind was a woman's.

Her annoyance pricked him, less painful than her anger but more shameful. *Don't be so ridiculous. You never minded it when I slept with Jehan.*

But he doesn't know —

No more do you. She rested her chin on his chest and closed her eyes. All her barriers had firmed against him.

A test, Brother, he told himself. *Think of it as a test.*

By infinite degrees he relaxed. She was only a hound. A sleeping hound, worn out with her long fruitless chase.

Boldly he stroked her ears. She did not respond. With the air of a man plunging into deadly peril, he laid his arm over her flank. It was sleek-furred, wholly canine; her heart beat as a hound's will, swift, slow, swift, slow, in time with her breathing.

He loosed his breath in a long sigh. He had done it. He had mastered her, and himself.

Perhaps.

12

Alf rode most of the way to Carlisle at the King's side. It was not the place he would have chosen, but Richard would not let him ride in obscurity behind the Bishop. "You interest me," the King would say when he protested. "Tell me another tale, Brother!"

And Alf would obey. Or Richard would tell tales of his own: accounts of his travels and of his many battles, of the sea, and of the lands of the East. "Have you ever traveled?" he asked.

"A little," Alf replied. "I went to Canterbury once, and to Paris to the schools."

"Paris! Why, you've never been out of the dooryard. When I get these troubles out of the way, I'm going Crusading again. This damp, dripping land—pah!" He spat. "I'm hungry for the hot sun and the dust and the bare hills of Outremer."

Alf could see them in his eyes, a fierce pitiless country, yet beautiful. He yearned after it as a man yearns after a woman.

"Jerusalem!" he said. "They kept me out of it, those fools and cowards who called themselves my allies; and I had to take a craven's peace, and smile, and bow to the Infidel. But I'll take the city yet. I told him that, the Emir Saladin. He's a black heathen, but he's a knight and a gentleman. He laughed and said that I could try, and then we'd know who was the better general."

"I'd like to see Jerusalem," murmured Alf. "And Byzantium."

"That city I never saw. The Great City they call it, because its proper name is so much of a mouthful."

"Constantinopolis. Constantine's City, Jewel of the East. I've always wanted to see the dome of Hagia Sophia and the Golden Horn; the caravans coming in from Cathay, and the ships sailing west with the wealth of the Indies."

"Why, Brother! you're a dreamer, too."

Alf laughed a little, surprised. "I suppose I am. That's why I learned Greek, to read about the East."

"You know Greek?"

"Yes, Sire. A little."

"And Arabic?"

"A few words. Maybe."

"God's bones! I've found myself a wonder. When I go back to Outremer, my friend, I'll take you with me. We'll take Jerusalem, and we'll visit the Emperor in Constantinople, and we'll be lords of the East."

When Richard was delighted, he reminded Alf of Jehan. Alf smiled, and blinked. For a moment he had seen a strange thing, the flash of sun on blue water; and scented an air that had never known the gray chill of Anglia. Then the image was gone. Richard had looked back, inspecting the line of march; their speech thereafter turned to other things.

They reached Carlisle in the evening after a day of bitter rain. To Alf it seemed a grim city, walled about with dark red stone, dripping with wet. Its people had come out to greet the King, but their welcome was muted, the dour welcome of the North; they gave their liege-lord precisely his due, no more and no less.

The Earl of the city met them at the gate of the castle, with a sour smile; it little pleased him to play host to four hundred of the King's men, and many more besides, come from all about to attend Richard's court.

Richard's smile was wider and brighter, but with more than a hint of malice. "Hugo," he had told Alf, "has been paying me tribute with one hand and stroking my beloved brother with the other. One fine day I'll catch him between the jaws of the trap he's made. But meanwhile, I'll clean out his larder and use up his hoard, and make him thank me for the privilege."

Yet to all appearances the Earl received his King with proper courtesy, and the army dispersed itself about the town. Aylmer lodged in the Bishop's palace near the cathedral. Bishop Foulques loved Aylmer no better than the Earl loved the King, but he had had the grace to withdraw to the abbey near the walls; his dwelling was somewhat more spacious than the castle and considerably more comfortable. Aylmer's attendants, Alf among them, were not forced like the King's to settle as best they could about the great hall; rooms were allotted them, and beds.

Alf shared a cell with Jehan and with a tongue-tied young priest, and with the Pauline monk. Reynaud's doing, Alf was certain. There were others of his Order about, pale shapes in gray cowls, with watchful eyes.

I feel like a cat in a kennel, Alf thought.

Thea made herself comfortable on one of the cell's two beds, to Father Amaury's great discomfiture. *Hounds have only teeth,* she pointed out. *You have teeth and claws.*

If I dare to use them, said Alf.

Reynaud approached her. She showed her teeth; he retreated hastily. She laughed.

They did not keep monastic hours here. But Alf's body, attuned to waking in deep night for Matins, could not lie sluggishly abed until dawn. In the black dark before it, he slipped carefully from the bed he shared with Jehan, gathered up a small bundle, glided out of the cell.

Only the cooks were awake, baking the new day's bread. The bath behind the kitchen was deserted. Alf lit the lamp over the nearest wooden tub and took up the yoked buckets by it, passing through the warm rich-scented kitchen to the well. He was seen but not remarked, a monk in cloak and hood indulging in the eccentricity of a bath.

It was not Thea alone who could warm water without fire, though this was far easier, a mere tubful. He folded himself into it, sighing with pleasure. Let the saints have their holy filth; this ill-made monk would be clean.

He washed swiftly but with fastidious care, rose and dried himself, and took up the bundle he had brought. For a long moment he regarded it. The brown habit was his better one, almost new, yet the near-newness only made it the harsher to the touch.

Slowly Alf drew it on. Without tunic or trews to cushion it, it was nigh as galling as a hair-shirt; and his skin, once inured to it, yearned for the caress of princely linen.

He bound the cincture tightly, settled the cowl over his shoulders, let the hood fall back. On the floor lay the last of the bundle's contents, a fine sharp razor. A stroke or six, and Brother Alfred would have returned wholly from bare feet to bare crown.

He did not know he sighed until he had done it, and then he did not know why. Kneeling by the tub, he groped for the razor.

It eluded his hand. At length, piqued, he turned to look for it. He had gained a companion, a slight figure in a habit like his own, but within the deep cowl shone a smile he knew all too well, full of dancing mockery. "Returning to the womb, little Brother?" asked Thea.

He held out his hand, tight-lipped.

She folded her arms. The razor glittered in her hand, close to the merest suggestion of a curve.

Alf's breath hissed between his teeth.

Her head tilted; her smile retreated to the corner of her mouth. "It's a pity, you know. To make yourself ugly for God—as if He could care for such trifles."

"It's done, as you say, for God, whether He heeds it or no; and to mark me as the Church's own."

"A slave of Rome. How dramatic. It's still ridiculous, little Brother. Why not make a real sacrifice? Like the pagan priests— or like the monk, the one they all call a heretic—"

"Origen."

"Origen," she agreed lightly. "God's eunuch. Now that is an irrevocable choice."

Alf spoke with care. "I should like to finish what I have begun. If you please—"

"If you insist," she said, "I'll help you. Or are my hands too foul to perform so sacred a rite? Schismatic Greek that I am, unconsecrated by any vows, and—ah, horrors!—a female."

She would prick him into a rage, and only laugh the harder. He struck on his own account with all his native sweetness. "I should not touch a woman, nor she touch me. But in the circumstances, I hope you have a light hand."

Light as air, and as gentle as her tongue was cruel. "What lovely skin you have. Soft as a child's. And your hair—I know women who'd kill to have hair half so thick or half so fine."

"Including yourself?"

She could even mock his self-possession, won as it was through bitter battle. "Why, little Brother! My touch hasn't struck you speechless. You've even mustered a tiny bit of wit. If I were a proper woman, I'd swoon with astonishment."

"If I were a proper monk, I'd exorcise you as a devil."

She was done, the razor secreted somewhere within the pilfered habit. She laid her cool hands on his shaven crown, a touch light almost to intangibility, yet it held him rooted. "Believe me, Brother Alfred of Ynys Witrin, you are a very proper monk. Now you even look it, though I never needed the proof."

His head came up with the swiftness of temper. But she was

gone, vanished. There remained only a brown habit, crumpled on the floor.

"*I* need it!" he cried.

The air returned no answer.

Since that first morning in the camp, Alf had served Aylmer each day at Mass. The Bishop called upon him to do the same in Carlisle in the small chapel. Its walls were of that grim red stone which seemed to have been dyed with blood, but arras of eastern work concealed them, and the furnishings were rich, treasures from the first Crusade. Alf sensed both their age and their foreignness; the silver chalice with its graven Apostles held a flavor of old Rome.

As he aided Aylmer in disrobing, a very small page in royal livery slipped through the door. His eyes upon Alf were wide and rather frightened, though it was to the Bishop that he bowed and said, "My lord, His Majesty wishes to borrow Brother Alfred."

"His Majesty knows that he doesn't need to ask," said Aylmer. "Tell him Brother Alfred will be along directly."

The child bowed again, shot Alf a last glance, and fled.

Alf smiled a little, wryly, and laid the Bishop's alb in the press. Aylmer watched him with narrow eyes until he straightened and turned.

"Brother," the Bishop said, "what would you do if I gave you to the King?"

Alf stood still. "In what capacity, my lord?"

"As a clerk, to begin with. Richard needs a good secretary. And," Aylmer added, "a friend."

"Am I competent to be the King's friend?"

"You've been doing well enough at it. He likes you, Brother. Richard deals well with men and knows how to make them love him; but he seldom returns the favor."

"You know what people are saying."

Aylmer snorted. "Of course I know. And I'll be frank with

you; there's substance in it, as far as Richard is concerned. He has a weakness for a fair face. But he doesn't stoop to force. He'll do no more than you let him do."

"My lord," Alf said, "I've only felt desire once. And that . . . that was for a woman." His cheeks were flaming, but he kept his head up. "I don't think the King will endanger me. Not that way. But I had thought—I had hoped—I am a simple monk, cloister-bred. My Abbot sent me to be your servant. Not to become a King's favorite."

"You think so?" Aylmer asked. "I give Dom Morwin a shade more credit. He entrusted you with the Rhiyanan's message. I doubt he expected your errand to end with its delivery."

Alf bowed his head. No. Morwin would not have expected that, old fox that he was, knowing Richard's nature and the nature of the message.

And that of the messenger.

"With whip and spur he drives me into the world." Alf looked up. Aylmer's gaze was unsurprised, understanding. "He drives me straight into the lion's den."

A smile touched the Bishop's eye. "This Lion only devours the weak. And that, Brother, you are not. I'm not afraid for you. If you fear for yourself—" He lifted the silver cross from the other's breast and held it in the light. "This is stronger than armor. Trust in it." He let it fall. "You'll sleep here and you'll serve me at Mass, but you belong to the King. Stay with him. Serve him. Be his friend."

Alf knelt to kiss Aylmer's ring. "As my lord wishes."

Before he could leave, Aylmer stopped him. "Brother. Be wary. This isn't your cloister; people here can be dangerous, especially around the King. If you sense trouble, come to me at once. Do you understand?"

"I understand," Alf said very low.

Aylmer frowned. "Do you? You're not a spy, Brother. Nor are you a watchdog. But I'm the King's Chancellor and your protector. I don't want harm to come to either of you."

"Yes, my lord."

"Go then. The King's waiting."

Alf bowed. As he departed, he felt Aylmer's eyes and mind upon him and shivered. The Bishop saw far more than Alf wished him to see. And Alf did not trust him. Not yet, and not quite.

When Alf presented himself at the keep, the Earl's guards eyed his face and his habit and his newly tended tonsure, and sneered. Yet they let him pass, following him with leers and not-quite-inaudible remarks.

So too the King's own squires, though there was no mockery in their eyes and voices but black hostility. Alf dressed as their equal and mounted on a horse fit for a prince, and always in the company of the King or the Bishop or the outsize novice, had been hard enough to endure. But Alf alone and afoot and in monk's garb was unbearable. They glared as they admitted him to the solar, and one spat, although he was careful to miss.

The King was deep in converse with several men with the garb and the bearing of noblemen. Alf effaced himself, a silent figure in a brown cowl, settling by the wall. No one noticed him.

The audience was long and tedious. At last Richard brought it to a close, dismissing the barons with courtesy that was a thin veil over irritation. Even as the door closed upon the last, he stretched until his bones cracked, and grinned at Alf, a lion's grin with a gleam of sharp teeth. "Well, Brother. You took your time."

"I'm sorry, Sire," Alf murmured.

"Never mind." Richard looked him over, fingering the rough fabric of his habit. "Hideous stuff, this. Where are your other clothes?"

"They were only to travel in, Sire," said Alf.

"You should have kept to them. They suited you."

"This is my proper habit, my lord. And it's an excellent disguise. Who notices a monk in a cowl?"

Richard laughed with one of his sudden changes of mood. "Aye, who does? And monks hereabouts are ten for a ha'penny. Don't tell me you're about to vanish among them."

"No, Sire. Bishop Aylmer has set me at your disposal. He asks only that I sleep and serve Mass with his people."

"Does he feel that he needs a spy?" Though the King's tone jested, his eyes did not.

"You know my lord needs no such thing. You also know that you were about to ask him for me. So, he anticipated you. What will Your Majesty have of his servant?"

"First," answered Richard, "the truth."

"That is the truth, Sire."

The King pointed to a chair. "Sit." As Alf obeyed, he paced, restless. "I call Aylmer friend. We owe each other our lives many times over. But a King can never trust a friend. God's feet! He can't even trust his own family."

Richard stood in front of Alf, hands on hips. "When my older brother was as young as you are, he tried to throw my father down and make himself King. He died for it. And I learned something. Blood-ties mean nothing. Friendship means even less. All that matters is myself. And winning, Brother. And winning."

"I don't believe that."

"Tell me so when your beard has grown."

Alf did not know that he smiled, until Richard glared and said, "You laugh at me. What do you know that I'm so ignorant of?"

"That the world is a cruel place," Alf responded, "but that it's not as cruel as you think. Aylmer cares for you, as his King and as his friend; I'm his free gift. Even though I look as if I were about to deliver a sermon."

That won laughter; Richard relaxed visibly. "Ah, but you just have." He sat by a table laden with sheets of parchment. "There's a promise I made to you when you were playing at royal ambassador."

"Yes, Sire?"

"Yes, Brother." He shuffled the written sheets, frowning at them. "When I came here, there were messages waiting. You've told me the truth about Rhydderch's raids. Bitter ones they've been, too, for Gwynedd. And Rhydderch's neighbors are worried that he'll bring down reprisals upon them all, for there's word of resistance, and forces gathering along the Marches. There's a war in the making, and no small one either."

"So I told you, Sire."

"It's a bad time for it," Richard said. "Winter's begun and the harvest's in; everyone's laid his sword away and hung his shield on the wall. A sitting target for a man who's not only reckless but clever."

Alf watched the King steadily, with a sinking heart. Richard moved restlessly in his chair, tugging at his beard, contemplating a winter campaign: snow and cold and long grim nights, and the swift heat of battle. Perhaps there would be glory, a contest with Kilhwch, King against King, with a crown for the winning; or with the elven-prince, the Flame-bearer of Rhiyana, who had raised his scarlet shield in all the lands from the sunrise to the sunset.

The King turned his eyes to Alf, only half-seeing the white tense face. "As soon as I can escape, I'm riding south. But I'll do this much for you: I won't take my army with me. Only my own knights, and whoever else pleases to come. Rhydderch will learn that he can't start a war without involving his King in it."

"Sire," Alf said, "this is madness. To destroy three kingdoms for a few days' pleasure—Sire, you can't!"

The lion-eyes glared. "Do you gainsay your King?"

Alf opened his mouth, closed it again. He knew how Alun had felt before Rhydderch. Helpless, and raging. And he could not loose his sorceries upon this madman as Alun had upon Rhydderch.

His head drooped. He had failed. He would have to tell Alun.

If he closed his eyes, he could see the Rhiyanan knight hobbling down a passageway, aided by a crutch and by a sturdy monk – Brother Edgar, who was simple but strong. Alun was intent upon his body's struggle, only dimly aware of the mind-touch. Alf withdrew. Later would be soon enough.

"Come now, Brother! Don't look so grim."

For a moment Alf recognized neither the voice nor the face. His own face had gone cold; Richard checked a moment, then slapped his shoulder. "We've both had enough of this. Ride out with me."

Alf rose slowly. Richard grimaced at his habit. "You can sit astride a horse in that?"

"Try me," Alf said.

The King grinned. "So I will. But boots you'll have – you won't gainsay me there." He turned away, calling for his own riding gear. "And boots for the Brother, Giraut; and mind you bring a pair that will fit!"

After the riding there was work to do, a charter to copy and a letter to write; and after that, a feast in the Earl's great hall. Richard kept Alf by him, although there were stares and murmurs at this blatant display of a new favorite; and such a fair one, with so grim an expression, who ate little and drank less and spoke not at all.

The Earl feasted his guests well though unwillingly, and regaled them with all the wealth of the North. His triumph was a minstrel who knew not only the latest airs from Languedoc, but the old songs of Anglia in the old tongue. "For," said the jongleur, tossing back his yellow mane, "my father was a troubadour in the court of the Count of Poictesme, but my mother was a Saxon; and she swore by King Harold's beard, though he was dead a full hundred years. She told me tales of the old time and my father taught me the songs of the south, and between them they made a jongleur. What will you have, then, my lords? Sweet tales of love?" His fingers lilted upon the lutestrings. "Deeds of old heroes?" A stirring martial tune. "A call to the path of virtue?" Stern didactic chords. "A drinking song?" An irresistibly cheerful and slightly drunken air. "Only speak, and whatever you ask for you shall have."

"War," the King said promptly. "Sing about war."

The minstrel bowed and began to play.

Alf toyed with his wine-cup, half-listening. He knew that Richard watched him. As did many another: Aylmer farther down the high table, and Jehan below among the squires, and Thea forgetting to play the proper hungry hound. He looked at none of them. *War*, he thought, hating it and all it meant. *War. Blood. Three kings, three kingdoms. I have to stop it. I have to.*

But how, he did not know.

Richard's voice rang out suddenly, cutting off the singer. "Enough of that! Sing us something new, man. With a moral in it that a priest would like to hear." As he spoke, he caught Alf's eye; the monk looked away.

The singer bowed in his seat and said, "His Majesty commands; I obey. There's a tale my mother used to tell me that's so old, maybe it's new again." He struck a sudden ringing note and intoned, "*Hwæt!*"

The listeners started; he laughed. "That's the Saxon for *Oyez!* Once on a time, my lords and ladies, which was in the old Angla-land, there was an abbey. There lived a cowherd named Caedmon. He was a gentle man, was Caedmon, but rather slow in the wits; everyone loved him, but everyone laughed at him, too: for that is the way people are, as we all know, sieurs.

"It was the custom then when there was a feast for the revelers to pass the harp round, and for each person to sing a song. Poor Caedmon dreaded that harp's coming, for he couldn't sing a note and he had never learned a song. When the harp drew near to him, he would get up and slink away to his byre, and hide in the dark and the silence and the warmth of the cows.

"One night, when he had fled from the singing and gone to his bed in the hayloft, he dreamed that a man came and greeted him and said, 'Caedmon, sing me something.' Caedmon was bitterly ashamed and like to weep, and he said, '*Ne con ic noht singan*'–'I don't know how to sing.' But the man, who was an angel of the Lord, insisted that Caedmon sing. Then Caedmon stood up, and lo! music came pouring out of him, the most beautiful song in the world. This is what he sang:

    '*Nu sculon herigean heofonrices Weard,*
    Meotodes meahte ond his modgeþanc,
    weorc Wuldorfæder, swa he wundra gehwæs,
    ece Drihten, or onstealde.
    He ærest scop eorðan bearnum
    heofon to hrofe, halig Scyppend;
    þa middangeard moncynnes Weard,
    ece Drihten, æfter teode
    firum foldan, Frea ælmihtig.'

And that in our feeble tongue is to say: 'Now must we praise the Guardian of heaven's kingdom, the might of the Measurer and His mind's thought, the work of the Father of glory, as He, eternal Lord, ordained the beginning of all wonders. First He shaped for the children of earth, heaven as a roof, a holy shaping; then afterward for men He created Middle-earth, the earth's surface–He, Guardian of Mankind, eternal Lord, almighty King.'"

The singer fell silent. There was a pause; then all at once the feasters began to applaud. He bowed and smiled and bowed again, and accepted a cup from the King's own hand. "Splendid!" Richard cried. "Wonderful! It's a pity we've let the old custom lapse. We ought to revive it." He paused, struck by his own words. "Well, and why not? Walter, fetch my harp! We'll all try our hand at it."

Several of the higher lords looked mildly appalled; their inferiors either feigned interest or answered sudden and urgent calls of nature. Alf saw one man's lips move as he struggled to recall a song.

By Richard's will they all tried the game, some well, some

badly, with the aid of a free flow of wine. One dour-faced elderly knight startled them all with a bawdy drinking-song; Bishop Aylmer countered it with an *Ave Maria*.

At last there was only one who had not sung. "Come now," said the King, holding out the harp. "Are you a Caedmon, Brother Alfred? Sing me something!"

Alf took the harp slowly and set it on his knee. It had been a long lifetime since he had learned to play such an instrument from old Brother Æthelstan, who had been a gleeman in his youth. He tightened a string which had gone out of tune three songs ago and met the King's stare, his own level, almost defiant. His head bent, his fingers flickering through a melody. Down the hall, he sensed Jehan's start of recognition.

"*'Ut quid iubes, pusiole,
quare mandas, filiole,
carmen dulce me cantare,
cum sim longe exsul valde
   intra mare?
O! cur iubes canere?'*"

"'Why do you bid, beloved child, why do you command, my dearest son, that I should sing a sweet song, when I am an exile afar upon the sea? O! why do you bid me sing?'"

Richard was no scholar, but he knew enough Latin to understand Alf's meaning. His expression darkened as the song went on; then little by little it lightened. For the lament turned to a soaring hymn, companion to that which had begun it all, and Alf's eyes above the harp were bright, challenging.

His own eyes began to dance, amused, admiring. Here at last was one who could both obey him and gainsay him, yet who bore no taint of treachery.

Alf silenced the harp and returned it to the King, and slowly smiled.

13

The rain which had buried the town in mire gave way to a heavy blanket of snow. Richard cursed it and his court, which held him back from his war, though he prepared with as much speed as he might. "I'll be King of Gwynedd by spring," he vowed to Alf, "or I'll have Rhydderch's head on a pike and your I-told-you-so's in my ears from dawn until sundown."

"King Winter may prove stronger than Richard of Anglia," Alf said. "Why not yield to him and spare yourself a struggle?"

"Am I to turn craven before a flake or two of snow? I'll ride south before the month is out, you and winter and all the rest of it be damned."

So might they well be, Alf thought as he made his way from the castle to the Bishop's palace. It was late, and dark, and it had begun to snow again; he huddled into the cloak Richard had given him.

All at once he realized that he had fallen into the midst of a small company, youths with the King's livery under their cloaks, three of Richard's squires escaped from their duties. He tensed and walked more quickly.

But they had seen and recognized him. "Hoi!" one called out. "It's Pretty-boy!"

They surrounded him, solid young men, battle-hardened. Their eyes glittered; they hemmed him in, wolves advancing upon tender prey.

He had averted his own eyes instinctively, lest they catch the light and flare ember-red. Wherever he turned stood a squire, grinning. He stopped. "Please, sieurs," he said. "It's late and I have no time to spare."

They laughed. "'Please, sieurs. Pretty please, sieurs. Oh, prithee, let me go home to my cold, cold bed!'" One took his arm, friendly-wise. "Poor little Brother. I'll wager you've never had a proper good time. We'll have to fix that, won't we, lads?"

The others chorused assent. Alf stood still. Perhaps, if he pretended to play their game, they would let him go.

They herded him toward an alehouse. The ringleader, a handsome dark-curled fellow whom the others called Joscelin, held still to his arm. "Come, little Brother," he said. "Join us in a mug or two. Or three. We all know how well a priest can hold his ale."

They reached the tavern's door and swarmed through it. The room was crowded; it reeked of smoke, of sour ale, and of unwashed bodies. The three squires and their unwilling guest elbowed their way to a table, put to flight the townsmen who had occupied it, and shouted for ale.

Joscelin clung close to Alf, stroking-close. The other two were content to laugh; he shot small barbs meant to draw blood. "It isn't sacramental wine we get here, but it's not refectory ale either. Drink up, pretty Brother. I'm paying."

Alf stared at a brimming mug. It was not clean, he noticed. Abruptly he swept it up and drained it in three long gulps.

Another appeared, and another. He felt nothing but a heaviness of the stomach, although his companions, having matched him mug for mug, were beginning to wax hilarious. He measured the distance to the door, considered all the obstacles between, and waited for his chance.

After the fourth round, as the serving girl withdrew, Joscelin seized her plump wrist and pulled her back. She came with but a token protest, giggling on a high note. "Here, Bess," he said. "What do you think of our clerkly friend?"

Her eyes flicked over Alf, once, twice. Cold clear eyes, shrill titter. "Oh, he's *handsome!*"

"Handsomer than I?"

She tittered. "Well, sir, I really couldn't—"

"Of course you could. Because he is. And do you know something?" Joscelin's voice lowered, but it was no less penetrating. "He's never been with a woman." He stressed the last word very slightly.

Again that swift appraisal. Alf kept his eyes lowered, but he heard her maddening giggle. "He *hasn't?*"

Suddenly she was in his lap. She was warm and soft, flowing out of her tight bodice; and she stank.

He shrank a little, fastidiously. She took it for shyness and pressed herself close, nuzzling his neck.

For all her squirmings, he felt nothing but disgust. Gently but firmly, with strength that made her stop and stare, he set her on her feet and handed her his mug. "May we have more ale, please?"

"Bravo, Brother!" Joscelin cried. "Another triumph for Holy Church. Or maybe we've made the wrong offer. Perkin! Perkin lad, where are you?"

Alf rose. "I have to go."

All three united in pulling him down. "Oh, no, Brother," Joscelin purred. "It must get monotonous to spend all your time with men. You need a change."

"All beds look alike," hiccoughed the youngest squire. "So do all backsides."

"Sirs," Alf said carefully, "I wish you a pleasant night. But I must go."

"He can wait, can't he?" Joscelin smiled at him, all sweetness. "He'll have to wait until we've made a man of you."

The others held him down, one on either side, grinning at

his white-lipped silence. At last he gritted, "You will tire of waiting before I will."

Joscelin shook his head. "We won't wait. Come on, lads. And hold tight."

Alf felt as if he were trapped in a nightmare. Memories flashed through his brain, a thin pale child set upon with stones and cudgels and cries of changeling and witch's get; a young novice baited by his fellows, mocked for his strangeness; a man with a boy's face, taunted in the schools of Paris for his beauty and his shyness, and made a butt of cruel pranks. And helpless, always helpless, until Morwin or another came to his rescue.

The room to which the squires led him was as fetid as the one below, and occupied. It was not fragrant Bess who lay on the bed there but a younger woman, thinner, almost pretty under the dirt. He could see that very well, as she had nothing to cover it. He looked away.

His captors laughed. He knew what they would do to him, but his struggles had no strength. They tore his habit from neck to navel, baring his upper body. Morwin's cross glittered on his breast; Joscelin snatched at it. There was a brief sharp pain; the squire held the broken chain and smiled. "Pretty," he said, slipping it into the purse he wore at his belt. "Let's see what the rest of you is like."

Alf lunged toward him. The squires tore at him, rending skin with cloth, stripping off his habit. He snatched in vain; they gripped him with iron fingers. He hung there gasping.

"Well." Joscelin whistled softly. "*Well.* Aren't you a beauty? Look, Molly; see what Rome and Sodom claim for themselves. A mortal shame, that."

There was a point beyond shame; a cold calm point, that was not numbness, nor ever acceptance. Seventy years, Alf thought. Seventy years, and he had never struck a blow. Such a good Christian monk he had been.

Deep within him, darkness stirred. *Enough*, it whispered. *Enough*.

He stood erect. A shrug: he was free. One of the squires wore a sword; swifter than human sight he swooped upon it. Cold steel gleamed in his hand.

They were not afraid. He had no skill with weapons—they all knew that. "My, my," warbled the youngest. "Look at the Church Militant. The cross is mightier than the sword, you know."

"And if that fails, take a Bible and throw it," the second added.

"Or at the last," Joscelin said, third in their chorus, "waggle your white behind."

He barely heard. His hand knew the sword; knew it as it knew its own fingers. His arm balanced easily with its weight of steel; his body crouched, ready for battle.

"Oh, come," Joscelin chided him. "*That's* not the sword you'll use. Put it down like a good lad and stop frightening poor Molly."

"Molly is not afraid." Alf's voice was cold. "Molly is excited. She thinks that she will have me when I am done with you. She is a fool. I do not fornicate with animals."

He felt her anger as a burning pinprick, and heeded it not at all. The squires had begun to tremble. His face was white and set; his sword flickered swiftly, darting toward each in turn. They had stripped a meek monkish boy and found a beast of prey.

But Joscelin, being clever, was slowest to understand. He laughed and drew his own sword. "Why, sir! You want to duel? It's a little cramped here, but I'll be happy to oblige you."

The others had scrambled out of the way. Alf measured the one who was left. They were nearly of a height and nearly of a weight, but the squire wielded a heavier weapon. His own blade was shorter and lighter, balanced for a single hand; a mere sliver against the great two-handed broadsword.

Joscelin circled; Alf followed. The door was at the squire's back; he backed through it, leaped and spun, and bolted down the stair.

Alf read him clearly. Either the priest would remember his nakedness and shrink from pursuit, or he would forget and run full into the laughter of the crowd below.

Alf snatched at shadows, fingers flying, and wrapped them about his body. They clung and grew and made a robe like dark velvet, girdled with a flare of sword-light.

Joscelin clattered still upon the stair. Alf sprang after him. They met at the bottom, dark eyes wide to see him so well and swiftly clad, pale eyes lit with a feral light. This game was not ending as Joscelin had planned it. He essayed a light, mocking smile, playing to the large and fascinated audience. "Come now, friend," he said. "I told you you could have her."

Alf said nothing, but his blade flickered like a serpent's tongue. There was a wicked delight in this skill that seemed to grow from the muscles themselves, inborn, effortless. If he had known what he had when he was a boy, no one would ever have dared to torment him. If he had known what a wonder it was, he would have plunged gladly into the heart of Richard's battle. But he knew now, and he knew what he was. Kin to the great cats, the leopard, the panther, swift and strong and deadly dangerous.

The prey, baited, had become the hunter; and now at last Joscelin knew it. The blood had drained from his face. He glanced about, searching desperately for an opening. There was none. Cold steel wove a cage about him. With each pass it drew closer, until its edge flickered a hair's breadth from his body.

His blood would taste most sweet. But his terror was sweeter. Alf smiled into his eyes, and neatly, with consummate skill, sent each of his long dark curls tumbling to the floor. He dared not even breathe lest his ears follow, or his nose, or his head itself.

When he was shorn from crown to nape—laughter erupting behind, and cheers, and wagers laid and paid—Alf leaned close. "Am I a man?" he asked, very softly.

The squire's eyes were rimmed with white. Yet some remnant of pride made him laugh, a hideous, hollow sound. "Not yet, Sir Priestling, though you're not an ill barber."

A panther, prodded, strikes without thought. Alf struck, but not, in some last glimmer of sanity, with the sword's edge. The flat of it caught Joscelin beneath the ear and felled him without a sound.

Slowly Alf turned. The cheering died. Someone offered him a mug, grinning.

Still gripping the sword, he ran from them all.

The snow had stopped; a bitter wind was blowing, scattering the clouds. Alf welcomed the cold upon his burning face. He stumbled against hard stone and vomited. Even after his stomach was empty, he crouched heaving, soul-sick. People passed with no pity to spare for a drunken soldier. At last he staggered erect. His robe was heavy with sorcery; he tore at it until it melted away, leaving him bare in the cold.

His fingers were numb, frozen about the sword hilt. He dragged it behind him, stopping again for illness, and yet again. He had hated and he had used sorcery and he had almost killed. He had given torment for torment and thirsted for blood.

What does it matter? a small voice taunted. *You'll never die. You have no soul. Nothing you do can damn you.*

"My conscience can!" he cried.

The voice laughed. *How can you have a conscience if you have no soul?*

"I do. It torments me." He fell into a heap of snow, and lay there. No owls would come to warm him now. If he was immortal, could he freeze to death?

Try and see. His second self sounded as if it already knew the answer. *You and your delusions*, it went on. *You think you have a conscience, because your teachers said you must have one. It's all delusion. You have no soul. You cannot sin.*

"*No!*" he shouted. "That's black heresy."

How can it be? You can be neither damned nor saved. Your mind is your only standard. Your mind and your body. You were a fool to refuse that woman and to let that boy live, for fear of what does not and cannot touch you.

"God is," he countered. "He can touch me."

How? And if He can, what sense is there in anything? He created you, if He exists, to live forever. He denied you the reward He dangles before humans. He gave you a body with beauty and strength and potent maleness; yet He would have you deny it all, and worship His arrogance, and thank Him for forbidding you to be what you were made to be.

Alf twisted, struggling to escape from that sweet deadly voice. "I serve Him as best I may, whatever the cost."

Do you? Look at you. Your face tempts humans away from virtue; your body incites even your own kind to active lust. If you would serve your paradox of a god, take that sword you clutch so tightly, and scar your face, and maim your body, and cut away your useless manhood.

He shuddered. "I can't destroy what God gave me."

Laughter rang, cold and scornful. *Can't, cant. Pick yourself up, and let your body do what it wants to do. The woman, the boy, even the King: take them all, and rule them. They're but human. They'll kiss your feet.*

"No," he gasped. "No."

The elf-maid, the voice purred. *She is yours for the asking. And she is no foul-scented animal. She is of your own kind, and most fair: and she yearns after you. Go. Take her.*

He clapped his hands over his ears, but it was useless. The voice was in his brain, teasing, tempting, luring him down into darkness. He was immortal, he was beautiful, he was powerful. He could be lord of the world, if he but stretched out his hand.

He raised his head. The sword lay beside him, half-hidden in snow. Death dwelt in it; death even for one who would not grow old. And after, nothing. Was he not soulless?

He set the hilt in the snow and turned the point toward his body, leaning forward until it pricked his breast above the hammering heart.

14

"Have you gone mad?"

Alf recoiled, dropping the sword. A swift hand snatched it up and hurled it away. He never knew where it fell, for Thea had seized him and held him with strength greater than any man's. Her face was white and her eyes were wild; she looked fully as uncanny as she was.

His hand moved to cover himself. She was clad, for once, in his own spare habit and Alun's cloak. "Even in that," he said, "you're far fairer than the other was."

She threw the cloak over him and made him walk with her, half-leading, half-dragging him.

"I didn't want her," he went on. "She disgusted me. She was an animal; and she stank. She made me realize something. I'm truly not human, and I have no tolerance for those who are."

She did not speak. She had drawn up the cowl; he could not see her face.

"No tolerance," he repeated. "I almost killed someone tonight. In the end I don't know why I didn't. I humiliated him terribly, but I let him live. I *let* him live. I had that power, Thea. And I wanted it. I delighted in it."

"That's no excuse to throw yourself on your sword."

He pulled away from her with sudden violence. "You don't understand."

"Unfortunately," she said, "I do."

She was speaking to his back. He had fled from her.

Jehan sat late in the Bishop's library, peering at a very old text by candlelight. It was in Greek, and strange, crabbed, difficult Greek at that; he wished that Brother Alf would come to help with it as he had promised. The candle had burned alarmingly low, and still there was no sign of him. The King had never kept him quite so late before.

Jehan rubbed his eyes and yawned. He would wait a little longer; then he would go to bed. He had Mass to serve in the morning and arms-practice after, and lessons with Father Michael, who had just come back from Paris.

The door opened upon a familiar brown habit. He half-rose, framing words, welcome, rebuke.

Alf looked pale, almost ill. When he spoke, cutting off what the other would have said, his voice was faint. "Come with me. Quickly."

Jehan rose fully. "What's wrong?"

"There's no time," Alf said. "Just come."

After a moment's hesitation, Jehan followed him. He moved swiftly and in silence, cowl drawn up. When they left the Bishop's palace for the outer darkness, Jehan could not see him; a thin strong hand gripped his wrist and drew him onward.

He knew where he was by scent more than by sight. Hay and horses and leather: a stable. A dim light glowed at the far end, shining upon a white shape. Fara. Alf led him to her.

There was something in the straw at her feet; from it came the light, welling through folds of dark fabric. Jehan discerned a human shape drawn into a knot, arms wrapped about its head.

He knelt. The figure was naked under the cloak, drawing tighter as he touched it; and he knew it. He turned to his guide, wild-eyed.

Alf's habit. But not his stance nor his height, nor ever his face, that pale oval within the cowl, with its frame of dark hair and its dark winged brows and its eyes gleaming green. Nor was that his voice. His was golden; this was shaken silver. "Yes, I tricked you; but I brought you here without a fuss."

"But how—" he began.

She cut him off. "Later. That really is your little Brother, and he needs a strong dose of common sense."

Jehan looked from her to Alf, seeing the likeness between them. "What's happened to him? Why is he like this?"

She told him, succinctly. His fists clenched and his face hardened. "You," he said when she was done, his voice level, controlled. "Are you the woman?"

She laughed aloud. Fara snorted at the sound. "Dear God, no! If I had been, he'd be there still, and the better for it too."

"Who are you then? What are you doing here?"

Her eyes danced, mocking him. "Don't you know me yet? I've run at your heels for close upon a fortnight."

He stared thunderstruck. "Thea?"

"Thea," she agreed with but little patience. She knelt beside Jehan and contemplated Alf's still body. "He's more than half-mad, you know. After a lifetime of self-delusion, he's had a very rude awakening; he doesn't want to face it."

"Why?" Jehan demanded harshly. "What has he awakened to?"

"The truth. Your monks raised him to think he was a gentle little ringdove, but he's grown into an eagle. And he's just discovered that he has talons."

"No wonder he's terrified." Jehan touched the tense shoulder gently. "Brother Alf. It's all right. I'm here."

There was no response. Thea frowned, but Jehan sensed concern beneath her impatience. "I couldn't do anything with him, either."

"Did you really try?" Again Jehan touched Alf's shoulder.

"Brother Alf, it's late, and I've been waiting for hours for you to help me with Dionysius. Won't you come back and go to bed?"

Alf was still for so long that Jehan feared he had failed again. Then the knot loosened, and Alf lay on his back, open-eyed, staring at nothing. "No," he said. "I can't go back. I've sinned mortally. I tried to kill a man, and I tried to kill myself."

"You were provoked," Jehan pointed out steadily, though he wanted to cry. "I'd have tried to kill that son of a sow too."

"It was still a sin. If I can sin. I may not have a soul, Jehan."

The other shook his head firmly. "I don't believe that."

Alf did not seem to have heard. "I wrote the *Gloria Dei*. Even in Rome they sang its praises: the jewel of theological works, the triumph of orthodoxy over heresy. I wrote it in a grand fire of arrogance, in utter certainty of its truth. It is true; I know that, and Rome knows it. But if I am a creature of darkness, a soulless one whose other self is a sword, then what does that make all my pretensions to piety?"

"Logic," said Thea, "is a wonderful thing. But you carry it too far. '*Mouse* is a syllable,' you say. 'A mouse eats cheese. Therefore, a syllable eats cheese.'"

In spite of himself, Jehan laughed. "She's right, Brother Alf. So you're different; so you've never got old. God made you, didn't He? He let you see enough of Him to write your *Gloria*."

Alf closed his eyes. "And people say that I was a changeling, a demon's get; and when I was anointed a priest, the oil cast a spell on me, holding me as I was then, a boy of seventeen."

"Nonsense," snapped Thea. "Get up and face the truth. You are wallowing. You have been wallowing for most of your life. And tonight you found out that you had a temper, by God and all His angels; as if the lowest human cur didn't have one too. Why, even the Christ got angry once and whipped the money-changers out of his Temple. Have you been trying to outdo him?"

He leaped up, eyes blazing. "How dare you speak so?"

"There now. A little honest anger—though your piety is false. You should get angry more often and less piously. Then you won't be tempted to barber brats of squires with a sword."

Alf sank down, head in hands. "Go away," he muttered. "Go away."

"Brother Alf," Jehan said. "She's right. You're taking this too hard. You had to leave St. Ruan's, and the King wouldn't listen when you asked for peace, and those idiots of squires treated you too foully for words. Of course you went a little wild. Come to bed now and get some sleep. In the morning you'll feel better."

Alf let Jehan draw him to his feet again, but he would not go. "The cross," he said. "Morwin's cross. Joscelin took it. And I—I forgot—"

"Poor little Brother." Thea held up a glimmer of silver. "This was much too precious to waste on the likes of him. I rescued it. Mended it, too." She slipped the chain over Alf's head and settled it on his breast.

His hand sought the cold silver as if for comfort. She smiled at him, half in mockery, half in something else, and melted. The white hound wriggled out of the habit under Jehan's wide eyes, and nosed it disdainfully. *Here's something to preserve your modesty. Put it on and go to bed.*

Alf fumbled into the robe, gathered up the cloak, and shook straw from them both. He paused to stroke Fara's neck and to quiet her concern for him; and followed the others.

Some moments after they had gone, a shadow slipped from a host of its fellows and glided after them.

15

Alf did not wake all at once as he usually did, but sluggishly, reluctantly. Long before he opened his eyes, he sensed that he was alone.

He sat up slowly. His hands stung; he stared at them. Each palm bore two thin, parallel cuts. He closed his fingers over them and rose.

The air tasted of full morning, with a touch of incense, and of bread for the day-meal, and of smoke from the kitchen fires. Mass was long since over; everyone had gone about his work. Even Thea was out, pursuing her own business; her mind-touch was sharp, swift, preoccupied.

He bathed with exaggerated care, as if water could wash away the memory of the night. When he dressed, it was in the garments Alun had lent him.

The King was looking for him. But something within him had broken when he took up the sword and had not yet mended. When he left, it was to the stable that he went.

He rode out alone by ways he knew from his riding with the King. The moors rolled away before him, lands that had been empty since the legions marched along the Wall of the Emperor, white now and still, dazzling in fitful sunlight. Away from the town in a hollow of the hills, a small glassy tarn reflected the changeful sky. There he halted, stripped off the mare's saddle and bridle, and hid them in the heather. She stood still, head up, breathing deep of the free air. "Go," he said to her. "Run as you will."

She bent her head and nuzzled his hands. Would he not go with her?

He smoothed her forelock. "I need to think," he said. "I can't do it back there. But you needn't linger with me. Go; be free."

His words made no sense to her. She turned and knelt, inviting him to mount.

He framed a protest, thought better of it. Even as he settled upon her back, she straightened and sprang into a gallop.

The sun hung low when they returned to the tarn. A white hound guarded the saddle, rising as a woman and inspecting them both with approval. "You look well," Thea said.

Alf slid from Fara's back and stood with his hand on her neck. "I've shirked all my duties."

Thea wrapped his cloak about her and helped him to saddle and bridle the mare. "The King is yelling for you," she said as he tightened the girths.

"Is he angry?"

"Upset. He's already heard about your adventure with his squires. The two boys are riding home as soon as he can spare escorts for them. He wasn't even going to do that, but Aylmer talked some sense into him. As for Master Joscelin, he's locked in a cell. He'll get his sentence as soon as Richard cools down enough to pass it. It will be dismissal at the very least; Richard can't decide whether to strike his head off or to condemn him to keep it as you've left it."

Alf turned to her, dismayed. "He can't do that! Those children have already suffered enough, between the fear I put into them and the ridicule they've won themselves. They don't need any more punishment."

"Except a good whipping."

"They didn't know what they were doing." He gathered up the reins. "I'd better go back and talk to the King."

Thea caught his arm. "Wait." He stopped. Her face was pale, and more serious than he had ever seen it. "Brother, Richard's not the only one who's upset. The tale has grown in the telling. You're the hero of it still in most places—but not in all. Some people are saying that you did more than prove your prowess with a sword. That you used sorcery."

"I did," Alf said.

She shook him hard. "Haven't you got your wits back yet? Reynaud and his Hounds have been closeted with Bishop Foulques. Who's no friend to either Aylmer or the King. And whose brother is assistant to the Pauline Father General."

Alf nodded calmly. "I know that. Will you let me go? I have to see the King."

"You *are* mad." But she released him. He mounted and turned the mare's head toward Carlisle.

Even as Fara moved forward, a weight settled on the crupper; arms circled his waist. "Now," Thea said in his ear. "Tell me what you know that I don't."

He looked back and started. It was still Thea, but Thea changed, dressed as a farm girl, with a brown freckled face. She laughed at him. "I had to give you a reason for being out all day, didn't I?"

"No," he answered. "You didn't. Get down and run as a hound."

"Oh, no. I won't give you the pleasure. I think I know what you're up to, little Brother, and it's rampant folly."

"What am I up to?"

"Self-sacrifice. Holy martyrdom. Giving your all to the cause of the Elvenking." He said nothing. "See how well I know you. You rode out in a great passion of despair; you cast that despair to the winds; you prayed and you meditated, and you

rediscovered serenity. And then, behold! a revelation. Fiends
and false prophets are plotting against you. What to do? Flight
is wisest. But wisdom has never been your great virtue. Why
not stand and face the consequences of your own foolishness?
You'll win the delay you've prayed for, bind Richard until spring
and give Gwydion time to plan another embassy. And last but
far from least, put an end to your dilemma. The Hounds will
burn you if you tell them the truth."

"Yes," he said. "They will."

"What did you tell Alun about suicide?"

"He had something to live for. His lady, his brother, all his
people. And I . . . I was an innocent. I didn't really understand
what I'm capable of. Nor was I sure that there wasn't some way
to reconcile the two halves of myself. Now I know better. I
can't be both monk and enchanter; I can't be only one of the
two. Even when I try to be a plain man, my power slips its chain
and betrays me. I'll destroy myself whatever I do. Why not to
some purpose?"

"Noble," she said. "Stupid. You may be as old as most humans
ever get, little Brother, but you're the merest child."

"Are you any more?"

"Probably not. But I didn't grow up in a cloister. I've been
hunted as these Hounds hunt you."

"You weren't caught."

"I didn't mean to be."

He was silent, his eyes fixed upon the walls of Carlisle. Yet
he was very much aware of Thea's presence. Strange, he
thought. The women in the tavern had roused only disgust; and
they had set themselves to seduce him. Thea, fully clothed and
decorously riding pillion, and calling to mind all his troubles,
made him want to abandon his vows.

Why not? his dark self asked in the deep cell to which he
had banished it. *You seek your own death. You know you cannot
be either damned or saved. What would it matter if you had your
way with her?*

And she would welcome it. But he could not. He was a fool, as she had said, and a coward. That would be his epitaph.

Just within the city's gate, the mare halted. Thea slid to the ground in full view of the guards. "Thanks to you, sir," she said in the broad accent of the North.

Alf flushed. People were staring; most knew who he was. He wheeled the mare about without speaking.

"Thank you for the ride!" she shrilled behind him. Somewhere, someone laughed.

16

Jehan was at arms-practice when a monk brought a summons from Bishop Aylmer. He had been tilting at the quintain with two or three of the younger warrior-priests; and he was more than a year out of practice. Mis-aimed strokes or over-slow reactions had brought the wooden Saracen spinning round more times than he could count, to return his own blows with ones at least as heavy. He ached all over; he was glad to stop.

Stripped of his heavily padded practice-armor and bathed and dressed, he presented himself at the door of the Bishop's library. Lamps glimmered there, for the high narrow windows let in little light; Aylmer stood near the far wall, listening as a secretary read from a charter. When Jehan entered, he dismissed the man and beckoned. "Ah, Jehan. How went it with the quintain?"

Jehan grinned ruefully. "Terrible," he answered. "I think my father's right. I've gone soft."

"Give yourself time," Aylmer said. "I hear you're doing somewhat better with the sword."

"A little, my lord."

Aylmer nodded toward a chair. He sat carefully to spare his

bruised muscles; the Bishop watched with amusement. "How old are you now?" he asked.

"Just sixteen, my lord."

"So?" Aylmer's brows rose. "You'll grow rather more, I think."

"My father's a big man. So is my brother Robert. The others are too young to tell, but they're all robust little monsters. Even my sister Alys."

The Bishop smiled a rare warm smile. "Yes: I've heard of the Sevignys. A proper pride of lions, those."

"We hold our own," said Jehan.

"You do," Aylmer agreed. "Father Michael speaks well of your scholarship. Very well, in fact."

Jehan rubbed a callus on his sword hand and sighed involuntarily. Father Michael had not been pleased to see his new pupil. Quite the contrary. Was he, who had sat at the feet of the greatest scholars in Christendom, to be condemned to teach grammar to this great ox of an Earl's son?

He had made no secret of his contempt. "Do you know Latin?" he had demanded in the vernacular.

"Yes," Jehan had answered in the same language.

"So." The priest had barely concealed his sneer. "Say in Latin: 'The boy sees the dog.'"

Jehan had obliged. And continued to oblige because it amused him, though his good humor had begun to wear thin. At last, as Father Michael framed yet another simple sentence, he had said in the Latin which Master Peter had taught him and Brother Osric refined and Brother Alf perfected, "Father, this is very pleasant, but isn't it rather dull? Could we do a little Vergil? Or maybe a bit of Martianus?"

He smiled even yet to remember Father Michael's face. Skeptical at first, but breaking into incredulity and then into joy. "God in heaven!" he had cried. "The ox has a brain!"

Aylmer had marked both sigh and smile. "Troubles, lad?"

"No," Jehan answered. "Not really. By now I should be used

to the way people react to me. I've got such a big body and such a stupid face. But actually, inside, I'm a skinny little rat with his nose in a book."

Aylmer laughed aloud. "Hoi, lad! you're good for me. Here, have an apple. They're from your own St. Ruan's, the Isle of Apples itself."

"Are they?" Jehan took one from the bowl on the table. "They call it Ynys Witrin, too, you know. Though I've heard that the real Isle isn't even in the world."

"The Land of Youth. Yes." While Jehan nibbled at the apple, Aylmer wandered down the line of books, pausing now and then to peer at a title. At the end, he turned. "Do you think there's such a place?"

"There's a lot in the world I don't know, and a lot out of it. Maybe there is a real Ynys Witrin, or Tir-na-n'Og, or Elysium. Or maybe they're all just other names for Heaven."

"Maybe," said Aylmer. He came to sit by Jehan across the table. "Some people say that the mystic realm is right across the water in Rhiyana."

"I've heard that."

"Your mother is Rhiyanan, isn't she?"

"Yes, my lord. She's the Earl's daughter of Caer Dhu."

"Kin to the King, I hear."

Jehan finished the apple and set the core upright on the table. "Distantly. She never went to court. She was fostered by a lord and lady in Poictesme, and married my father when she was barely out of childhood." His eyes upon Aylmer were wide, blue, and guileless. "Are you curious about Gwydion, my lord?"

The Bishop's cheek twitched. "Somewhat," he admitted. "When you were in St. Ruan's, did you talk much with the Rhiyanan knight?"

"I took care of him," answered Jehan. "He slept a lot. Sometimes he talked. He wasn't the talkative sort. He was very quiet, actually, unless he had something to say."

"What did he look like?"

Jehan shrugged. "Rhiyanan. Tall, black hair, gray eyes. Face like a falcon's."

"Young?"

"Rather. Old enough to be a knight, but not much older."

"Well-born?"

"Yes." Jehan tipped over the apple core, and rolled it from hand to hand.

"Was he one of the elven-folk?"

The apple core stopped. "Do they exist?" Jehan asked with a touch of surprise.

"So it's said." Aylmer shifted in his chair and sighed. "So it's said. Did you know that the Monks of St. Paul are forbidden to preach or to found abbeys in Rhiyana?"

"Are they? Why?"

"It's the King's command. The old Orders are sufficient, he says, and the Church in his kingdom is thriving. It needs no Hounds to hunt its heretics."

"Or its Fair Folk? If they exist," Jehan added.

"If they do," agreed Aylmer. "Tell me. Where was Brother Alfred born?"

Jehan went cold. Brother Reynaud he could deal with; for all his cleverness, the man was an idiot. But Bishop Aylmer was another matter altogether.

"He was born somewhere near St. Ruan's," he said. "I don't know where. He was one of the abbey's orphans. There are always a few about. Most grow up and take some sort of vows— by then they're used to the cloister, you see. They tend to forget exactly where they were from, and so does everybody else." He paused. "Brother Alf isn't Rhiyanan, if that's what you're wondering. I think maybe he's Saxon."

"You and he are close friends."

"I don't know about that," Jehan said. "I used to bother him to help me with my books. He was my teacher for a while. Then we came here."

"He taught you?"

"Well. Somebody had to."

Aylmer did not smile, but his eyes glinted. "Isn't it odd that he should have been teaching you? You must be almost of an age."

"Not really. He'd been there all along, and he's brilliant."

"Like his namesake, the other Alfred? I used to dream of sitting at the great scholar's feet and being his disciple. But I never had the chance; and when I was in St. Ruan's last year, he was ill and seeing no one."

"I remember," Jehan said. "I'd just come to the abbey."

"Had you? I never saw you. Though I saw young Brother Alfred. He struck me as a remarkable boy."

"And he doesn't now? Is that why you're asking about him?" Jehan's fists knotted. "That's not true, my lord! He's all you thought he was. But he's having troubles. He's not used to living in the world, and he never wanted or expected to be the King's friend, and people are cruel to him. They can't stand someone who's good and brilliant and handsome, all at once."

The Bishop's smile won free. "Now, lad, there's no need to shout at me. I like to think that I can judge a man by those who love him; and by that reckoning, he doesn't have many equals."

"He doesn't by any reckoning," Jehan muttered.

"I think not. But there's another side to this. Brother Alfred has friends of very high quality indeed. Unfortunately, his enemies are at least as powerful, and more numerous besides."

"The Hounds!"

Aylmer's eyes narrowed. "You know of them?"

"They've been after me about Brother Alf. Who is he, what is he, what do I know about him?"

"Last night," Aylmer said, watching him under heavy brows, "there was an uproar in one of the alehouses in the town. Brother Alfred, it's said, was in the middle of it."

Jehan sat still, his face blank.

"There were unusual circumstances," the Bishop continued. "Alarming ones, some think. Have you ever tried to shave a man with a sword?"

"Shave him? With a *sword?*" Jehan laughed. "It's hard enough to land a proper blow."

"According to the tales I've heard, our frail young Brother, who was raised from infancy in an abbey, barbered a man with a sword as well as any surgeon with a razor."

There was a long pause. "My lord," Jehan said slowly. "I saw Brother Alf last night. He was awfully sick. Not drunk. Just very sick. It was inside more than out. He wanted to die, my lord."

That caught Aylmer off guard. He leaned forward. "What!"

"He wanted to die. A—a friend found him. Stopped him, and came and got me."

Jehan thought he could decipher Aylmer's expression. Deeply shocked, and—concerned? "Why? What happened?"

"I'm not absolutely sure. I do think . . . the stories may be true. But he's no devil, my lord. Nor any devil's servant."

"God knows," Aylmer muttered, "I want to believe that."

"You're learning to love him," Jehan said. "The best people always do. But the rest hate him. It's that hate that makes the Hounds want to hunt him."

"It's more than that, lad."

"Not much more," Jehan said fiercely. "He's so much more God's creature than any of the rest of us. The world scares him witless. Last night he tried to run away from it. He still wants to. And now the hunt is up. He'll run right into the middle of it." He struck the heavy table with his fist, rocking it upon its legs. "Why can't people leave him alone?"

"Because," Aylmer answered, "he isn't like anyone else. I'll shield him if I can. But I may not be able to."

"No one will. And he'll die, and I—I'll kill the man who does it to him!" Jehan leaped up and ran blindly for the door.

The apple core had fallen to the floor. Aylmer set it on the table, carefully upright; and sat for a long while unmoving.

17

Alf paused in the doorway of the King's bedchamber. It was a small room, little more than a cell, dominated by a great carved and curtained bed; Richard had concealed the bare walls with several layers of hangings, and set in it a brazier from the East that did what it could to dispel the northern cold.

The King sat near the coals in hose and fur-lined cotte, playing at chess with Earl Hugo. A lamp hung above them, swinging slightly in the draft that lifted the heavy tapestries, casting its uncertain glow upon the board and the carven pieces. The white knights were warriors of Allah wielding curved scimitars, the black heavy and lumpen in chain mail upon Frankish chargers; the white king a Saracen sultan, the black a Christian with a crown of crosses and leaves.

Richard set a black castle before the ivory sultan. "Checkmate, my lord," he said.

Earl Hugo glowered at the board. "Checkmate," he agreed at last. "Sire."

The King smiled at him, a deceptively gentle smile. "A good game, sir. And," he added, "a good night."

Alf stepped aside to let Hugo pass. The Earl glanced at him and started, and crossed himself.

The poison was spreading rapidly. Alf entered the room, letting the door-curtain fall behind him.

Richard stood by the chessboard. His eyes were very bright. "Well, Brother," he said. "You're later than usual."

Alf bowed slightly and said nothing. His gaze rested upon the chessboard, where a mitered bishop stood beside the Frankish king.

"Sit," the King commanded him.

He obeyed, taking the chair the Earl had left. Richard took up the ebony king and turned it in his hands. "I'm fond of this," he said. "The Emir Saladin gave it to me, a token of our battles and our truce."

"Are you at war with me now?" Alf asked quietly.

Richard set the chessman in the center of the board and took from a cabinet a flask and two silver cups. He filled them both and gave one to Alf. "You were out all day," he said. "Why?"

"I needed to be alone."

"Longing for your cloister?"

Alf shook his head.

"Liar." Richard sat at his ease, sipping from his cup. "It's quieter there, isn't it? No wars. No kings. No drunken squires."

Under the King's keen eye, Alf sat very still. "They didn't know what they were doing."

Richard spat a curse. "They knew, plague take them. They knew exactly what they did."

Alf looked up, a startling, silver flare. "No," he said. "They didn't. Or they would never have dared."

The King paused. This was an Alf he had never seen, bright, brittle, dangerous. "They told me a fine tale," he said, "of swords and sorcery, and a monk turned demon. Are you an elven-knight in disguise?"

"No knight, I."

"But a master of the sword. Twenty men swear to that—and one is my own master-at-arms."

Alf's fingers clenched about the cup. "I . . . avoid weapons. They tempt me."

"Sweeter than women, aren't they? I wish I'd seen you. Thierry was almost crying. That sweet touch, that perfect control, wasted on a pious shavepate."

"Not wasted," Alf said very low. "Buried deep, and well buried. I think . . . I think I am a killer by nature."

"Aren't we all?"

With an effort Alf unlocked his fingers. They had bent the cup's rim into a narrow oval. He set it down and wiped his hands on his breeches. "All men may be," he said, "but I am worse than most. Or would be, if God's grace had not set me in St. Ruan's."

"God's grace." Richard snorted in derision. "God's japery. With ample help from Mother Church. Look what they've made of you—a butt for every snot-nosed brat who happens by. You who should be out in the lists, daring the Flame-bearer himself to throw you down."

"Whatever I should have been, this I am. And I regret that I ever let my temper destroy my reason. It was unpardonable."

"So was what caused it."

"No." Alf dropped to one knee. "Sire. Pardon the boys who mocked me. One night's hell-raising is not worth three noblemen's disgrace."

The King's brows drew together. "It isn't?"

"Never, Sire. They won't trouble me again. I can assure you of that."

"When they attacked you, they attacked me. They knew it. And they know that they're getting off lightly in only being sent home."

"In dishonor, my lord; and one is in fetters now. Would you make enemies of all his kin, simply because he failed to carry off a prank? Isn't it enough that all Carlisle is laughing at him?"

"By God, no!"

Alf stood. "Then, Sire, you are a fool."

As he reached the door, the King seized him and spun him about.

The hand on Alf's arm was cruelly tight. He glanced from it to the furious face. "Pardon them," he said.

Richard's jaw worked. His fingers tightened, and suddenly sprang free. He stood still, fists clenching and unclenching, battling to master his voice. "You," he said thickly. "You damned, pious, preaching priest."

Alf smiled faintly. "All of that," he agreed, "I may well be. Let the squires go."

"I'll sentence you as I sentenced them. They started the fight, but you brought steel into it."

Alf said nothing. They were eye to eye, almost body to body; he could feel the King's anger as a physical thing, a wave of white heat.

Abruptly Richard spun away, stalked back to the chessboard, began to set the pieces in their proper places. Alf watched him. He paused, balancing the king and his ebony bishop. "Two of them I'll give you. But not the worst of them."

"All three," said Alf. "Especially Joscelin."

Richard glanced over his shoulder, a swift, vicious, lion's glare. "Don't abuse my generosity, priest."

"All three," Alf repeated. "Pardon them."

The King ignored him, setting down a double rank of pawns, ebony men-at-arms, ivory Saracens. When all stood in their places, he regarded them, arms folded.

A long step brought Alf to stand beside him. "I take your gift of the two boys with gratitude. But give me Joscelin."

"No."

"What will you do with him?"

His gentle persistence drove Richard through rage to a quivering calm. "I'll keep the fool's head shaved and give him to a monastery." The King bared his teeth. "That ought to satisfy you."

"No," Alf said. "It does not. Set him free."

"Priest," purred Richard, "you've got as much as you'll get. Get out of my sight before I take it all back again."

Alf did not move. "Joscelin," he said. "Let Joscelin go."

The King's hand flew up, swifter than thought. Swifter still, Alf blocked it, held it. There was a moment of frozen stillness.

In Richard's eyes, a spark caught. With all his great strength he fought to break the other's grip.

Alf swayed slightly, but did not let go. Richard stopped, panting, staring at the thin white fingers. They looked as if they would break at a word. They held like bands of steel.

The spark grew. Richard looked from the hand to the body behind, and to the pale face. "Let me go," he said, neither commanding nor pleading.

Alf obeyed.

Richard rubbed his wrist, still staring, as if he had never seen Alf before. "Two go free," he said. "You've won that. But the third has to pay."

"How?"

"Either he humbly craves your pardon for his sins, and escapes; or he goes into the cloister."

Alf opened his mouth; Richard cut him off. "No more! That's as far as I'll go."

Slowly Alf bowed his head. "Yes, Sire," he murmured. "Do I have your leave to go?"

"Go, damn you. *Go!*"

The King's wrath had not confined Joscelin to the Earl's dungeon. The squire rested in relative comfort in a dark box of a room behind the kennels, with a straw pallet to sleep on and only a single ankle-chain to bind him.

He lay in a huddle upon the pallet, his cloak drawn over his shorn head, nor did he respond when his guard thrust a torch into a wall niche, flooding the cell with light. The man nudged him with an ungentle foot. "Wake up, handsome. You've got company."

"I'll speak with him alone," Alf said. Joscelin started a little at the sound of his voice, and peered through slitted eyes, seeing only a hooded shadow behind the smaller, broader shape of the guard.

The man withdrew with a coin in his hand and a blessing on his head, fair wages for the night's work.

Alf settled beside the pallet and waited for Joscelin to focus. The squire looked little like the elegant young man who had sought to torment a helpless monk, dirty and disheveled, his dark curls gone. Yet as his sight cleared, he knew the face within the hood; his lip curled. "Well, pretty Brother," he said. "Come to gloat over the victim before he goes to the block?"

"No," Alf said. "I've spoken to the King. He's promised to let you go. On one condition."

Hope leaped high in the dark eyes, though the voice was mocking. "Oh, yes. There's always a condition. What is it? Do I have to kiss your fundament?"

In spite of himself, Alf flushed. "You have to ask my pardon."

"Same thing," said Joscelin. "What if I won't?"

"You'll go into the cloister."

Joscelin yawned and stretched and rattled his ankle-chain. "Is that all? And here I was, saying Paternosters for the repose of my soul. His Majesty's getting soft."

"I don't think so."

"You wouldn't."

"If you fulfill the King's condition," Alf said, "you go free. Completely free."

"And back to my family in disgrace."

"No."

"He really has gone soft. Pity. There was a time when he'd have cropped my ears for getting into a fight with a lily maid, and losing."

"You choose the cloister, then?"

Joscelin lay back and closed his eyes. "Maybe," he said. "It's not a bad life. Wine and song and a woman here and there, and boys whenever I want them."

"Do you think it's like that?"

One eye opened, dark and scornful. And in its depths, a black fire of hate. "Pretty Brother. I *know* it's like that. Don't pretend to be so much holier-than-thou."

"If you only beg my pardon, you can return to your old place and be as you were before."

A tremor ran through Joscelin's body. "Oh, no," he said. "It won't be the same."

"You can live down your disgrace."

"If you don't shut your mouth," Joscelin said quietly, reasonably, "I'll shut it for you. Go away and let me sleep."

"Joscelin—"

"Joscelin," he echoed bitterly. "Joscelin! Be a good lad, Joscelin. Smile nicely, Joscelin. Bow to the handsome Brother, Joscelin. And never mind the King, Joscelin. He's found a new darling and he doesn't need you any more." He laughed, a harsh strangled sound. "There now. I've let it out. I'm jealous, by God's left kneecap! My lord's got a new boy, a beautiful boy, and when he deigns to notice the old one, all he has is a smile and a pat on the head, and a penny for sweet charity."

Alf reached for him without thinking, as he would have reached for Jehan, to comfort him.

Violently Joscelin struck his hands away. "Get your filthy claws off me!"

For an instant they faced each other, deadly pale, Alf with horror and pity, Joscelin with hatred.

"Joscelin," he said gently, "I'm not the King's boy."

Again, that terrible, mirthless laughter. "Don't tell lies, pretty Brother. We're all good Sodomites here."

Alf shook his head. "Believe me. I'm not."

"Lies, lies, lies. Go away and take them with you."

"I will pardon you for all you have said and done to me, if you will only ask."

"*That* for your pardon!" Joscelin spat in his face.

Slowly, carefully, Alf wiped the spittle from his cheek. Equally carefully he said, "If you reconsider, send for me."

Joscelin laughed. His laughter followed Alf for a long while after.

18

When Aylmer could not sleep, he often found peace in the lofty quiet of the cathedral, winter-cold though it was, dim-lit by the vigil lamp above each altar. That night he had lain awake, listening as the great bell tolled each hour, until at last he rose and drew on the brown habit of his old Order, stepped over the novice-page who slept across his door, and went quietly out.

The cathedral was deserted in that dark time between Compline and the Night Office. He bowed low before the central altar, murmuring a greeting and a prayer, and turned toward the Lady Chapel.

In the dimness, he did not see the figure which lay prostrate upon the stones in front of the altar until he stumbled over it. A gasp escaped it; it rolled over swiftly, half-rising.

He knew who it was even before he saw the face; that feline grace was unmistakable. He held out a hand; Alf hesitated, then let the Bishop draw him to his feet. He looked very pale, shadow-eyed.

Aylmer heaved a mental sigh. This had kept him awake, and it seemed determined not to let him go. "Come into the sacristy," he said. "It's warmer there."

For a moment he thought Alf would refuse. But when Aylmer turned, the other followed.

As the Bishop lit a lamp in the sacristy, Alf stood among the holy things, his cloak drawn about him. At that moment, in that light, he did not look entirely human: a creature of the wild hills, trapped in a net of iron and of sanctity.

Aylmer sat on a low stool. "Well, Brother," he said. "You've been living hard, from the look of you."

Alf shivered, though not with cold. "Not living hard, my lord. Just—just living."

"Hard enough, from all I've heard. Were you fighting with the King tonight?"

Alf's lips tightened. "How did you know?"

"He sent me a message."

"I'm not to serve him again?"

"The message was: 'Brother Alfred is to ride with the King tomorrow morning at terce. And tell him to leave his damned skirts at home!'"

For all his troubles, Alf could not help but smile. It was a thin smile, almost a grimace of pain. "He forgives as swiftly as he condemns. And I gave him much to forgive."

Aylmer leaned against a richly carven chest. "First the King's squires, then the King himself. You're trying hard to make enemies."

"They make themselves."

"It takes two to start a war, Brother."

"True, my lord. It needs an attacker. And a victim."

"Do you see yourself as the victim?"

"Better that and dead, than living and a murderer."

"You have an urge to kill someone?"

For the first time Alf looked at him directly. His eyes had a strange gleam. "I could, my lord. I could commit every act that could possibly damn a man."

Aylmer rose and opened the chest. Amid its contents he found a violet stole. As he lifted it, Alf's hand stopped him. It felt thin and cold and not quite steady. "No, my lord. Don't put the seal of the confessional on this."

"Whether I wear the stole or not," Aylmer said, "the seal is there. Though I can't promise absolution."

"I ask no absolution. And no silence."

"Let me decide that for myself."

The Bishop returned to his seat with the stole in his hand. After a moment, Alf knelt facing him.

"I think," said Aylmer, "that I can spare you the agony of telling me a truth or two. St. Paul's monks have a reason to be after you. Don't they?"

Alf nodded tightly.

"A good reason, by their lights. You aren't exactly circumspect about yourself."

"You know," Alf whispered. "You know—"

"Enough," the Bishop finished for him. "If you'd wanted to protect your secret, you'd never have let yourself be sent on an errand for the King of Rhiyana. Especially to me. I've waited on Gwydion in Caer Gwent. I've seen his court. I know what the Fair Folk look like. And," he added, "a little of what they can do."

"Then," Alf said, "you think I'm one of them."

"I know you are."

Alf drew a shuddering breath. "How—how long?"

"Since I first saw you."

"But you never—" Alf stopped. He was seldom at a loss; yet Aylmer had never betrayed that he knew. Not even in his mind.

Carefully Alf mastered himself. "I meant to confess to you," he said. "I was gathering courage for it; but you came before I expected."

"What made you decide to tell me?"

The Bishop's face was stern, his gaze forbidding. And completely unafraid, though he knew what powers Alf had. Knew very well indeed. In their own country, Gwydion's people had few secrets.

Alf faced him with all disguises gone; he met the pale unhuman stare without flinching.

"My lord," Alf said, "I'm tired. I could lie and hide and pretend to be human, but I'm weary of it."

"Weary unto death?"

Alf caught his breath as if at a blow. Yet he answered with the truth. "Yes. Unto death."

"You're young to be so sure of that."

"No," Alf said. "Young, I am not."

Aylmer paused. A breath only, but long enough for a swift train of thought, a flare of recognition. He was not surprised, Alf realized. "Alfred of St. Ruan's," he said slowly. "Alfred of St. Ruan's. I was so proud that I knew what you were, and too blind to see . . . But if the *Gloria Dei* is yours . . . "

"It is mine." Alf's fists had clenched at his sides. "I wish to God that I had never put pen to parchment."

He looked up. To his amazement, Aylmer was laughing silently, a convulsion of pure delight.

The Bishop wiped his streaming eyes, struggling to regain his composure. "Your pardon, Brother. But if I were the Lord God, and I wanted to show the whole herd of theologians and canon lawyers what utter asses they are, I would have done exactly what He has done. Given them you."

"It was sheer hubris for me to dare to write what I did. But I never meant it to be a mockery."

"Nor did I. But the hair-splitters wax haughty in their conviction that man is the measure of all things, the center of the universe, the Macrocosm in microcosm. You show them that there's more in creation than they've ever dreamed of." Aylmer shook his head and coughed. "Brother, Master, you've restored my faith."

For a long moment Alf could only stare. "My lord, I don't understand you."

The Bishop's eyes gleamed upon him. "What! You can make clear the mysteries of Paradise, and you can't impose some sense on a lump of clay?"

"On strictly canonical grounds, you should be blasting the accursed witch-spawn to perdition."

Aylmer shook his head. "No, Brother. I'm a Bishop; I'm God's man; but thanks be to Him and all His angels, I'm no canon lawyer. I judge by what I see and hear, and not by what some mummified authority says I ought to."

"I have practiced witchery."

"Dark rites? Invocations of demons? Curses and black spells?"

"Dear God, no!"

"Not even a stray love philtre?"

Alf wanted to laugh; he wanted to weep. "My lord, I'm a poorer judge of men than I am of mummified authorities. But I know how you should be regarding me; and how others will regard me if the truth is known."

"Not if," Aylmer said. "When. Brother, I'm minded to send you away. Back to St. Ruan's if you want it, though you're not likely to be safe there. Or to Rhiyana, where God's Hounds can't go."

"I won't go, my lord. And if you know my kind, you know that nothing will hold me when I don't want to be held."

The Bishop's brows knit. "I do know it. I know that there's no arguing with a master of logic, either. What if I command you?"

"I'm afraid," Alf said gently, "that I will have to disobey you."

"Why? Why are you doing this?"

"I told you. I'm tired. And a trial and a burning, if burning there must be, will hold the King here until it's too late for him to destroy himself on the Marches."

"Do you really want to die?"

"I want to break this deadlock. With the King, with the Hounds, with myself. If I have to die to do it, yes. Yes, I want to."

"And if not?"

Alf was silent for a long moment. "If not . . . so be it."

"I understand you," Aylmer said. "I think you're a fool, but I understand you. I'll also do everything in my power to keep you from getting yourself killed."

"No, my lord. You'll do everything you can to assure that the King stays here and that he makes no effort to protect me. You will even support my enemies if necessary, for the King's sake. He must not go to war with Gwynedd."

"And you must not go to the stake."

"I don't matter. All Anglia hangs upon Richard's life and death."

"Have you ever considered what he might do to the men who condemn you? And what they might do to him?"

"There's no death for him in that, and no doom for his kingdom."

"You look like an adolescent angel. But you're as crafty as a Byzantine courtier. And somewhat colder-blooded." The Bishop rose with the violet stole still in his hands. "I've heard your confession. I grant you no absolution."

"You know I want none."

Aylmer kissed the stole and laid it away, and remained with his back to Alf. "Go to bed," he said.

Alf hesitated. Aylmer did not move. After a moment, he rose and bowed, and withdrew.

19

Alf burrowed in the box he shared with Jehan, searching amid their common belongings for the books he had brought from St. Ruan's. They lay on the bottom, lovingly wrapped in leather: the five treasures he had kept out of all that he had gathered. He uncovered them carefully and separated one from the rest.

"Brother Alfred."

He glanced over his shoulder. Reynaud stood in the doorway, smiling as he always smiled, without warmth; on the surface, all friendliness, and beneath, the eagerness of the hunting hound.

Alf took his time in setting the contents of the chest in order and in lowering the lid. When he turned, book in hand, Reynaud had come within arm's reach.

The Pauline monk nodded at Alf's habit. "Not hunting with the King today, Brother?"

"No," Alf said. "I'm to wait on him when he comes back. Meanwhile"—he tucked the book under his arm—"I have leave to amuse myself."

"Blessed freedom," sighed Reynaud. "And you'll do no more than read?"

Alf's smile was a wintry likeness of Reynaud's. "I'd rather read than hunt; I always find myself siding with the quarry."

"Even the wild boar?"

"Why not? In the end he lies on the table with an apple in his jaws, no more or less dead than the stag or the coney."

"But he gives a good account of himself before he dies."

"You expect him to turn Christian and bare his breast to the spear?"

Reynaud spread his hands in surrender. "I can't compete in words with a philosopher. My talents, such as they are, lie elsewhere."

"And where," Alf asked, "is that?"

He shrugged expressively. "In areas far from philosophy, or from serving kings. I preach God's word in my poor way; I serve His servants; I go where He bids me."

"So do we all." Alf glanced significantly at the door. "Do you have duties, Brother?"

"Nothing pressing. The weather is splendid for once. Come and walk with me."

Alf inhaled sharply. Danger always walked with Reynaud— surrounded him, wrapped him about. But that quiet request struck Alf like a blow to the vitals. For an instant he had seen through the veiled eyes; had caught a flare of raw emotion. Hate and hope and burning excitement. The mind of the beast before it springs for the throat.

It had come. So soon. The trap was laid; the quarry had only to walk into it.

Alf relaxed with an effort. "My thanks, Brother, but I promised myself a quiet morning."

Reynaud shook his head in reproof. "You'd mew yourself up in a cold library? For shame! Come out and let the sun warm you. Then you can go to your book with a clearer head."

But Reynaud's mind saw a barred cell and chains, and the stark shadow of the stake. Alf shrank from the horror of it.

Five days hence, Richard would depart for Gwynedd with a

hundred knights at his back, and the Marches would burst into a fire of war.

Alf battled to still his trembling. His decision was long since made. Was he to retreat now, when it came to the crux?

He sighed and shrugged. "Very well," he said. "A short walk."

Reynaud smiled. "A very short one. Yes. Come, Brother."

Jehan peered around a corner. The courtyard was empty, its much-trodden snow melting into puddles under the firful sun. He kilted up his habit and sprinted along the wall into the shadow of a doorway. Still no pursuit. After a moment he eased open a door, slipped down a passage, paused in the stable yard. The hound chained there wagged its mangy tail; he greeted it and offered it a bit of cheese. As it devoured the bribe, he walked boldly into the stable.

A day or two before, he had discovered that, if one settled into a corner of the hayloft near the dovecote, one could pass unnoticed by any who entered; there was light enough to read by, and warmth enough for comfort if one burrowed deep into the hay. And no one would ever think to look there for a truant.

He settled into his hiding place with a sigh of content, armed with Father Michael's precious copy of the Almagest and a pocketful of dried figs. With luck, he could read until it was time for arms-practice, and talk his way out of the punishment for evading kitchen duty.

"You'd better be able to, or what's an education for?"

Jehan choked on a fig. Thea sat astride a beam, dressed like a farm girl, laughing at his startlement. As he remembered how to breathe again, she dropped down beside him and pilfered a fig. "Ah! these are good. Where'd you find them?"

"Stole them at breakfast." He frowned at her. "You're hardly ever about. Where've you been?"

She shrugged. "Here and there. Keeping people guessing. Whose dog am I, whose wench am I, and what am I up to?"

"Everyone was sure you belonged to me till I said you didn't.

I made up a story about how you'd followed us from the lake; maybe you belonged to one of the rebels."

"I am a rebel."

"I never would have guessed."

She laughed again and shook her hair out of its rough knot. "I like playing country maid. It's market day today; I sold a basket of eggs and got a penny, and gave it to the beggar under Westgate. He told me all that's happened hereabouts. Amazing how much the kerns know. The King should ignore his lords and messengers and listen to people in the town."

Jehan watched her, and sighed a little. She was almost unbearably beautiful, yet her speech was as solid and earthbound as her ragged smock. She had no trouble accepting what she was. She simply *was*.

"I wish Brother Alf were like you," he said.

She paused, head tilted, half-smiling. "He is. But he's spent all his life trying to be something else."

"Why aren't you as confused as he is?"

"I wasn't brought up in an abbey, for one thing. My mother was a Greek, a doctor. My father was a Levantine merchant. The whole world used to pass through our house."

"And you left it?"

"One day we guested a prince from Lombardy. He was the ugliest man I'd ever seen and he stank like one of his own goats, but he was wise and he was clever, and I was tired of living in one place. I ran off with him."

"Did he marry you?"

"Of course not. He had a wife already. And three mistresses and a round dozen of children. After a while we parted on the best of terms, and I wandered about, taking whatever shape pleased me; and I came to Rhiyana, and to the King."

"Gwydion?"

"For us," she said, only half in mockery, "there is only one King."

Jehan lay on his stomach, chin in hands. "Brother Alf should go to him. I wager he'd know what to do with a monk who's also an elf-man."

"He might," she said. She ran her fingers through the splendor of her hair, that was as fine as Chin silk, rippling to her waist. "If the little Brother has his way, there'll be an end of all his troubles in fire and anathema."

"I'll stop him," Jehan muttered fiercely. "I'll make him stop."

She tilted her brows at him. "Will you now? Then you'd better hurry. The Hounds took him this morning."

Jehan sprang to his feet. The doves fled in a flurry of wings. "*What!*"

Thea caught a drifting feather. "He went voluntarily," she said.

"They'll kill him!"

"It's likely," she agreed.

He dragged her up as if she had been a wisp of hay, and shook her. "Where is he? *Where is he?*"

"You're not going to his rescue."

"God's feet!"

"God," she pointed out, "as First Cause, has no material shape. Therefore—"

"Shut up, damn you!"

She was silent. So, for a long moment, was Jehan. With great care he unclamped his fingers from her shoulders. "Where is he?" he asked at last, quietly.

"You will not go to find him. You will go and tell Bishop Aylmer what has happened, and do as he tells you."

"Bishop Aylmer can't—" Jehan stopped. Slowly he said, "I'll go. Where is Brother Alf?"

"In St. Benedict's Abbey," Thea answered him.

He bent and picked up the book which had fallen from his lap. It was open; he closed it gently, running his fingers over the worn cover. "Come with me," he said.

When he left the stable, the white hound trotted behind him.

"This is the man?"

"If man you may call him."

Fingers touched Alf's chin, turning his head this way and that. They were gentle, without malice, like the soft voice. "Certainly he has the look of the elf-brood. And yet . . ."

"Brother?" the other asked with a hint of tension.

"And yet. He let you take him on the first attempt."

"*Let*, Brother? He fought like a very demon!"

"He let you take him," the other repeated.

"Not until Brother Raymond struck him with an iron-shod cudgel. Then we managed to get a grip on him."

Alf lay very still, hardly breathing. His head felt as if he had caught it between a hammer and an anvil; his body ached. He could remember, in snatches—a deserted street, men in dark clothing; a battle, swift and fierce, and a swooping darkness.

And voices. One he knew, nasal, obsequious. In a moment, when it hurt less, he would remember a name.

The soft voice spoke again. "Guard him with all your skill. But be gentle with him."

"Gentle!"

"Yes. Gentle. Send me word when he wakes."

Only when the voices were long gone did Alf open his eyes. He lay on a pallet in a small cold room, no dungeon for it had a slit of window to let in the light, but bars blocked the opening, new-forged iron, newly set into the stone. The door too was new, heavy, bound with iron bands; as iron bound him, wrists and ankles, incised with crosses.

With great care he sat up. He still had his habit and his silver cross; beside him lay a jar and the familiar shape of his book.

The jar held water, touched with sanctity, which did not speak well of his captors' intelligence. Surely, if a demon could wear a cross next to his skin and handle the holy vessels of the Mass, then no sacred precautions could hold him.

He drank a little to quench his raging thirst, and splashed a drop or two upon his face. Gingerly he explored his aching skull. A great knot throbbed at the base of it, the worst of his hurts, though all his body bore the marks of battle.

He rose slowly, dizzily. Chained though he was, he could

move as he pleased about the cell, even to the door. Through its iron grille he saw a stretch of stone passageway and the back of a man's head, turning as if startled to reveal a stranger's face. A blast of fear and hostility struck Alf's reeling brain; he cried out and stumbled backward, half-falling against the wall.

The fear receded. He huddled upon the pallet, trembling violently, battling nausea.

Iron grated upon iron. The door opened.

Alf raised his head. Reynaud smiled at him. "Awake at last, Brother? How do you feel?"

"Betrayed," Alf said.

He winced. The blow upon his head had shattered his inner defenses; he could not shield against the other's anger.

Reynaud smiled through clenched teeth. "Do you think I betrayed you?"

"Is the price still thirty pieces of silver?"

"That," said Reynaud, "could be construed as blasphemy."

Alf swallowed bile. "I take a walk with you out of courtesy, and face an ambush. And when I wake I'm in chains. Is this how you demonstrate your friendship?"

It was some comfort to see Reynaud look uneasy. Yet righteousness flooded over the seeds of his guilt and drowned them. "I did as I was commanded."

"By whom? The Sanhedrin?"

Reynaud's hand flashed out. Alf darted away, but the blow caught him sidewise. His ears rang; his stomach heaved.

Reynaud's anger turned to disgust, and then to dismay. A firm yet gentle presence ministered to Alf, while a quiet voice said, "Go to my cell, Reynaud. I will come to you later."

The Pauline monk was gone. The other held Alf until he had recovered somewhat, cleaned him and dressed him in a fresh habit, a black one. "Your pardon, Brother," the man said, "but we have only Benedictine robes here."

Yet he wore Pauline white and gray: a tall thin man with the face of a Byzantine saint. His face was smooth, his skin as fresh as a boy's, but his hair was white; Alf sensed a great weight of years upon him.

He followed Alf's glance to his habit, and smiled. "And Pauline," he amended. "But I thought you would not want those."

"Nor would you," Alf said.

His smile faded. "Say rather, it would not be proper."

"No. The captive should not assume the garb of his captors."

"You speak wisely and well, young Brother. Though somewhat bitterly."

"You think I should not be bitter?"

The monk shrugged slightly. "I can understand, though not condone it."

"If our positions should ever be reversed, I'd like to hear you repeat that."

The monk's smile returned. "Perhaps I may not. I am human, after all." He paused; seemed to remember a thing he had forgotten; said, "My name is Brother Adam."

"You know mine."

"Do I?"

Alf sighed. "Ah. So the game begins. I'm called Alfred."

"Or Alf?"

"That, too," he admitted. "Reynaud has kept you well-informed. He's not going to welcome the need to treat me gently."

"You heard?"

Alf began to nod, decided against it. "Yes," he said. "I heard."

Brother Adam smiled again, wryly. "I see that I shall have to watch you more carefully."

"Reynaud was not happy. But he did try to obey you, until I provoked him. Don't be too harsh with him."

"And why did you provoke him?" Brother Adam asked, interested.

"I was angry. Inexcusably, but understandably. No one welcomes betrayal."

"Ah," said Brother Adam, "but if he had told you what he meant to do, then you would not have come."

"Maybe I would have," Alf said.

"Even into chains?"

Alf shook one. "They aren't pleasant," he said. "If I promised to behave, would you let me out of them?"

Adam's eyes were sad. "No, Brother. I would not. Certain sufferings are necessary, you see; those I cannot spare you."

"At whose orders? Why am I a prisoner?"

"Two questions," said Brother Adam. "Perhaps you know the answers to both."

Alf sat up. His head throbbed, but he would not lie still. "You have me, and this habit is Benedictine. Is this Bishop Foulques's doing? Is he holding me for ransom?"

"Brother," Adam said, gently chiding, "your innocence rings false. The Bishop knows and sanctions our actions here, but what those actions are, surely you know."

Alf regarded him with wide, gray, human eyes. Not all of the fear there was feigned. "I'm no heretic!"

"That, we will test."

"Sweet Jesu!" Alf knelt at his feet, a proud boy wakened suddenly to full knowledge of his peril. "Please, Brother, Domne. I'm a monk, a priest. I've loved God and served Him with all the faith that is in me. Would you make me suffer because two Bishops are at odds, and an Earl and a King have no love for one another?"

"We do not play the games of the world," Adam told him as gently as ever. "Lie down, Brother. You are not well enough yet to walk about."

Alf let himself be put to bed again, but he clutched the other's hand, his own frail and trembling. "I'm not a heretic, Brother. By all the saints I swear it."

"That may well be," Adam said. "But heresy is not the major charge." He disengaged his hand from Alf's. "Rest now. Later I shall return."

"Brother!" Alf cried. "For God's sake—what else can I be guilty of?"

The dark eyes were quiet. "Sorcery," answered Brother Adam. Even as he spoke, the door closed upon him.

Alf lay on his back, then, after a time, on his face. He no longer felt ill, only aching, and tired.

He rested his cheek upon his arm above the manacle. The fabric of the black habit was finely woven, soft. It lay lightly upon his bruised skin.

Brother. Light too that touch upon his bruised mind. He saw Alun sitting in an angle of sunlight in the cloister of St. Ruan's, hale to look on save for the bound hand and arm. His leg Alf could not see beneath the borrowed brown habit, but two knees bent for his sitting; he touched the right one. *This came out of its bonds yesterday*, he said. *Sooner than you predicted, Brother.*

Alf smiled in spite of his troubles. *Are you running races yet? Not quite yet.* The lightness left Alun's thoughts. *Are you well? Well enough*, Alf responded.

Weak as his barriers were, Alun slid past them with ease. His inner voice was almost harsh. *What is this? What has happened?*

Something I brought on myself, answered Alf. *Have you sent word to Kilhwch?*

Yes. Alun stood, balancing upon the strong leg and the weaker one, gray eyes stern. *So this is how you would delay the war until our messenger can reach Richard. Who has you? The King himself?*

The Hounds of God.

Alf reeled. Alun's serenity had shattered, baring for an instant the furnace-fires beneath. *God in heaven! Are you trying to destroy yourself?*

After a long moment, Alf found that he could think again. *My lord*, he said, *I'm doing what I have to do. Richard will be here when your messenger arrives.*

If Morwin discovers what he has sent you to, said Alun, *the knowledge will kill him. He meant for you to be healed, not to be slain.*

Maybe they're both the same. Alf knotted his fists. *My lord*, *promise me. Don't tell him what's happened. If I live, it won't matter. If I die . . . it's not his fault. It's not anyone's. Not even God's, though He made me what I am.*

Alun reached out through the otherworld. *Alf. Come to me. Now.*

His command was potent. Yet Alf resisted. *No. Be well, my lord. Recover quickly. And give my love to the Abbot.* He gathered the tatters of his shield and firmed them as best he might. Fear rose strong in him that the Rhiyanan would break them down and compel him to forsake his intent.

But Alun did not attack. When Alf ventured a brief probe, he was gone. No trace of his presence remained.

20

The narrow slit of window let in just enough light for a man to read by, more than enough for Alf's eyes. He sat under it, book in hand, reading as quietly as if he had been in the library in St.Ruan's.

Brother Adam watched him for a long while through the grille. He did not seem to notice that he had an observer, although when the monk entered he revealed no surprise. He did not even look up.

"Good morning, Brother," Adam said. "Did you sleep well?"

Alf raised his eyes. They were shining, remote. "Good morning," he said.

Adam's glance found a bowl of food by the pallet, its contents untouched. "You did not break your fast."

"I'm not hungry." Alf bent to his book again.

The other stood over him. "What are you reading?"

With a sigh, Alf shifted his mind fully from his book to his jailer. "Boethius," he answered.

"The prisoner and the Lady Philosophy. Very apt."

"Yes," Alf said. "It is apt. Too apt, perhaps. The prisoner was executed."

"But Philosophy consoled him most completely before he died."

"Did she? In the end . . . I wonder."

"If you are innocent," Adam said, "you will not die."

"I'm not sure I believe you."

"Do you deny that you have practiced sorcery?"

Alf stared at the page, not seeing the words written there, seeing his choices, truth or falsehood, death or life, and Kilhwch's messenger riding hard through the hills of Gwynedd. "What do you mean by sorcery?" he asked.

"You do not know?"

With his thumb Alf traced the cross graven upon one of his shackles. "People say I've bewitched the King. I haven't. He likes to look at me; he likes to listen to me. There's no sorcery in that."

"Except the old one of Venus."

"Jove had his Ganymede," Alf said, "and Achilles his Patroclus, but Richard has never had his Alfred. By witchery, or by any other way."

"Yet you could have cast a spell upon him if you had wished it."

"How, Brother? Have you found a grimoire under my pillow?"

Brother Adam sat on the pallet. "There are two types of sorcerers," he said. "Sorcerers proper, men of human blood and breeding, whose spells are the work of art and of skill, aided by the grimoires you speak of and by sundry devices of human or demonic construction: astrologers, alchemists, soothsayers and herb-healers. These are common and easily found out, and often converted to the path of righteousness. Yet there is a second, rarer brood, whom we call witches, elf-wights, people of the hills. Power does not come to these by study and by art; they need no books of magic, no powders or philtres or chanting of spells. No; the power is born in them, and fills them from the moment of their conception."

Alf laughed a little, incredulously. "You think I'm—what? Hob o' the Hill? Are you mad?"

From a pocket of his robe Adam brought out a disk of silver

no larger than his palm. When he held it up, Alf saw his own face reflected there. "Look," Adam said. "What do you see?"

"Myself."

"Have you ever seen such a face before?"

Alf blushed. "I—I'm not ugly. But I can't help that."

"Is your beauty a common, human beauty?"

Alf turned away from the mirror. "Must I be condemned because I look like this?"

"Not for that reason, but for what it indicates. God has marked the elven-folk that they may not be lost among the race of men— has made them surpassingly fair, as fair without as their hearts are black within."

"I am a priest," Alf said tightly. "A man of God."

"Truly?"

"The water of baptism did not sear the flesh from my bones; nor did the chrism of my ordination send me howling into the dark. I have raised the Host in the Mass, aye, more times than I can count; and never once have I been stricken down."

"For that, I have only your word."

Alf rose, trembling. "Test me. Give me the consecrated bread; make me drink of the wine. Say the Mass before me—say the very rite of exorcism over me. I am neither witch nor demon; I am simply Alfred of St. Ruan's."

Adam nodded slowly as if to himself. "So you say. You were a foundling, I am told."

"My mother died; I don't know who my father was. I was given to the abbey as a hundred other children have been, before and since."

"By three white owls?"

Suddenly Alf was very still. "Owls? Who told you that?"

"We have heard tales, round about."

"Owls." Alf shook his head. "That's absurd."

"You came to this city in the company of a hound. A wondrous hound, white yet with red ears, such as the old people say runs at the heels of the Lord of the Otherworld or on the trail of the Wild Hunt."

"Because," Alf said with taut-strung patience, "such beasts are bred all over Anglia. Of course Arawn or Herne the Hunter would have a pack of them."

"Then whence came yours?"

"She's not mine. She followed us; she might have belonged to one of the rebels the King's men slew. She comes and she goes, depending on whether one of us is disposed to feed or pet her."

"Indeed," Brother Adam said. "Do you deny that you have practiced sorcery?"

Alf lifted his chin. "Yes," he answered. "I do deny that I have practiced the black arts."

Adam stood, unruffled. "So. I am sorry that I interrupted your study of Master Boethius."

The other stared at him. "You won't let me go?"

"I cannot." Brother Adam sketched a blessing in the air. "*Dominus vobiscum.*"

"*Et cum spiritu tuo,*" Alf responded, signing himself with more defiance than reverence.

Adam smiled and took his leave.

The axe swung skyward; poised for a moment against the sun; flashed down. Its victim fell, cloven neatly in two.

"*That* for the cursed Hounds," Jehan muttered.

He set another log upon the block and sent it the way of its fellow. There was an odd, crooked comfort in that labor. At least it was action, if not the action he wanted.

He scowled at the block, seeing upon it Reynaud's thin sharp face, and smote with all his strength.

"Well smitten!"

He gritted his teeth. Company, he neither needed nor wanted. He reached for a log, hitched his habit a little higher, and raised the axe.

"Again," said his observer, "well smitten."

He turned, glaring, and stopped short. The King stood there in the mud of the kitchen garden, alone and unattended, and laughing at his expression.

He dropped the axe and knelt, bowing his head. "Sire," he said. "Majesty. I didn't know—"

The King cut him off. "Get up. You're not at court here." Although his words were sharp, amusement danced still in his eyes.

Jehan rose. Only one thing could have brought the King alone to this place; that knowledge turned his startlement to something very much like fear. With care under the other's eye, he rolled down his sleeves and let his habit fall properly to his feet. But there was no concealing his face. He arranged it as best he might and said, "You gave me a start, Sire. I thought you were one of the Brothers."

"I don't look much like a priest, do I?" Richard inspected the heap of new-cut wood and took up the axe, testing its balance. "So this is how Aylmer trains his knights. Practical. I should try it with my own men."

"Only if you want axemen, Sire," Jehan said.

"True enough. It's no good trying to hew wood with a sword. Though if I could set the swordsmen to harvesting grain and the mace-men to slaughtering sheep . . ."

Jehan laughed. "And the lancers could practice on cows, and what would Bishop Aylmer do for penances?"

"You're being punished, are you?"

"Yes, Sire." Jehan looked down, shamefaced. "I was reading in the hayloft instead of working in the kitchen. So I hew wood and draw water until my lord sees fit to let me go."

To his credit, Richard neither frowned nor smiled. "And when will that be?"

The novice shrugged. "When he pleases, Sire. But that's fair enough as penances go. I could have got a caning. Would have if I'd been in my old abbey."

"You sound singularly unrepentant."

Jehan raised his eyes. "Why, Sire! I'm most repentant—that

I have to spend my days here instead of in the tilting-yard."

The King grinned and placed a log upright upon the block. He measured it with his eye and raised the axe. It was not an ill stroke, Jehan thought, both amused and shocked that a King should want to try his hand at a villein's work.

"Sire," he said. "You really shouldn't—"

"I really shouldn't be here." Richard essayed a second blow. "In fact, I'm not here at all. I'm closeted with Bishop Aylmer."

Jehan was silent. The King set down the axe and dusted his hands on his riding-leathers. "This is easier work than hewing heads. A log can't hit back."

"The worse for the log," Jehan said. He did not move to resume his task. "Did Bishop Aylmer send you here, my lord?"

"Bishop Aylmer is cooling his heels in my workroom." The good humor had vanished from Richard's face; his eyes were fierce. "And what's His Majesty of Anglia doing running his own errands? Is that what you're thinking?"

After a moment Jehan nodded.

The King nodded also, sharply. "Some things even a King can't pass on to underlings. Or he passes them on and they disappear, and he never sees them again. That, boy, is called 'humoring the King.'"

"It's also called 'burying the evidence.'"

Richard laughed shortly. "So. You're smarter than you look. Are you too clever to tell the truth?"

"That depends on what you want to know, Sire."

"Nothing theological. Not even anything personal. Just a simple thing. It's so simple that I've spent a full three days trying to find it out, which has done my war no good at all. I've been sent by proxy from pillar to post, till I've had to set my own hand to it or never know at all." The King leaned close, so close that Jehan could see nothing but the glitter of his eyes. "Where is Brother Alfred?"

Jehan blinked. "Brother Alfred, Sire?"

"Brother Alfred," Richard repeated as to a witless child. "The tall one, with no color in him. Do you remember him?"

"Sire," Jehan said, "you came here just for him? But why to me?"

The King stepped back, scowling. "Just for him. Yes. And to you, you young fox with an ox's face, because he called you his friend. Which is more than he would do for me. Where is he?"

"You haven't seen him, Sire?"

"Boy," Richard said very softly, "I have not seen Alfred since he promised to attend me after I hunted, three days ago, and he never came. I thought it was one of his moods. But he didn't come the next day when I called for him, and the page I sent was told that he couldn't see the Brother, even at the King's command. And so the next messenger I sent, and the next. This morning I heard a whisper that Brother Alfred couldn't come because he wasn't there. More: he went out walking three days past, and never came back." The King spoke more softly still, a near-whisper. "Where has he gone?"

Jehan ran his tongue over his lips. "Sire. He is gone. But I can't tell you where."

"Can't? Or won't?"

"Can't, my lord. He went out, as you've heard. No one's seen him since. We—we think—someone took him."

"And why couldn't he simply have run away?"

"Sire," Jehan said hotly, "if you know him, you know that's not his way. He gets moods and he does strange things, but he'd never run off without telling anybody. Especially not on foot, with nothing on but his habit and a book in his hand."

Richard's eyes narrowed. "You saw him go?"

"No, Sire. Would to God I had! But I was playing truant, and when I came back, he—he was gone." Jehan struggled to keep his voice steady. "I know someone took him. I know it."

"Taken," Richard muttered. And, louder: "He's sent you no word?"

"No, Sire." Jehan's calmness shattered altogether. "Sire, don't you think I've tried everything I can? I even went to Bishop Aylmer and tried to get him to send out searchers. When he told me to wait, I yelled at him. That's why my penance isn't limited to a day or two. He—he told me to be patient and to let him do what he could, and—and not to talk to anyone about it."

"Did he?"

The King's tone made Jehan cry out, "He's no traitor! I'm sure of it. But he said, if Brother Alf's been taken, his takers must be your enemies. They haven't asked for a ransom; they must want you to go after him and fall into a trap, and maybe get killed. That's why my lord hasn't let you know the truth. He wants to find Brother Alf himself and spare you the danger."

"Fool," Richard said. "He'll find a corpse or nothing at all, and likely get his death by it."

"Sire!"

Richard hardly heard him. "I'll find him. As God is my witness, I'll find him, alive and whole and telling me I was mad to have tried it."

"Your Majesty," Jehan said, shaking but determined, "you can't do that. Your court—your war with Gwynedd—"

"Damn the court! Damn the war! Damn the world! I'll have that boy back, or I'll cast my crown in a dungheap."

"He's only one man."

"He's only my friend."

Long after he was gone, Jehan stood, trembling uncontrollably.

When at last he could command his body, he sat on the block and breathed deep. Now the King would ride out, searching for a traitor. Bishop Aylmer had wanted that; had all but challenged Richard to try it. But he would not search in St. Benedict's. That, the Bishop would make sure of. With the King abroad upon a fruitless chase and the war in Gwynedd forgotten, the Church would look after its own.

And the least of its novices would wait and pray, and try not to think of what the Hounds might be doing to Brother Alf. Jehan rose and took up the axe, and returned grimly to his penance.

* * * * *

Brother Adam sighed wearily. "Will you not confess?"

"No," Alf said with equal weariness. "I am not the Devil's minion. I know nothing of the black arts."

"But more of dialectic than any man ought, let alone one of the Night's brood." Adam shook his head. "Brother, I have done all that I can. There are those who urge me to resort to force. Is this what you would have?"

This too Alf had heard before. Without a tremor he said, "The answer would be the same."

Adam looked down at him where he sat upon his pallet, a dim figure by candlelight. He stared back without expression. He had eaten nothing since he was taken; he felt light, hollow, almost heedless. It has become a game, this constant resistance, four days and four nights of fruitless questioning. The other was haggard, unshaven, shadow-eyed; when he touched his own face, he could feel the jut of bones beneath the skin.

"Brother," he said, "I won't confess to a crime I haven't committed. Not even to spare you pain."

"Not even to spare yourself?"

Alf shook his head.

"I will not be your questioner in that extremity," Adam warned him. "Brother Reynaud will have the honor. He is well known for his skill."

"I'm not surprised," Alf murmured.

"That was not charitable."

"Neither is he." Alf lay back.

There was a pause. As it stretched to breaking, the other laid an icy hand upon his brow. "You are very warm. But you do not look fevered." He held the candle close. Alf turned his face away from it.

"Strange," Adam said. "In this room, in this season, you should be blue with cold. Yet I have never seen you shiver."

Alf shivered then; but Adam shook his head. "Too late, Brother. Your Master has shielded you well against the banes of your kind, cold iron and sacred things. Why, I wonder, has he omitted to take away the fire of Hell which warms you?"

"If it were Hell's fire," Alf said through clenched teeth, "it would sear your hand."

"Could it, Brother?"

"It is not Hell's fire."

"Then, pray, what may it be?"

"My own body's warmth. That is all."

"So simple a thing, to be so inexplicable."

"Inexplicable?" Alf asked. "Hardly. My fiery humors are in full blaze. I'm being held against my will; I'm charged with black sorcery; now you threaten me with torture. Can you wonder that my anger keeps me warm?"

"If all men were so made, we would have no need of clothing. Wrath alone would suffice."

"Though not for modesty," Alf said.

Adam was silent, his eyelids lowered, but he continued to watch Alf from beneath them.

"St. Ruan's Abbey," he said at last. "You were raised there, you say. Have you considered that if you persist in your obstinacy and are punished for it, your Brothers will suffer? For since it is what it is, where it is—surely its monks knew what dwelt among them: a creature of that elder race which ruled there before Christ's Gospel was borne into Anglia."

"My Brothers are guilty of no fault. They have seen nothing, recognized nothing, for I am no more and no less than any one of them."

Adam shook his head slowly, half in denial, half in sorrowful rebuke.

Alf sat up. "They are not guilty. There are no Elder Folk."

"There, Brother, you lie outright. For I have seen them. With my own eyes I have looked on them."

"But not in Ynys Witrin, Brother Adam. That I know. They do not haunt St. Ruan's cloister. Christ is ruler there; his cross rises above the Tor." Alf smote his hands together. "Accuse me if you must. But in the name of the God who made us both, let my Brothers be!"

Again Adam paused, pondering. "If you will confess, I may

be able to keep St. Ruan's out of the tribunal's consideration."

"I do not bargain with lies," Alf said. "Nor would you be wise to threaten more than my mere self. Remember that your Order is a new one, not yet as powerful as it would wish to be, and St. Ruan's is very large, very wealthy, and very, very old. Would you dare to set yourself against so great a power?"

"Would you dare to call upon it?"

The chill left Alf's voice to lodge in his bones. "I am the least of its children. I will not beset it with this shame."

"No shame to it if you are innocent."

"So am I condemned. I protest my innocence—I am commanded to confess. I speak of shame—it must be guilt, and not a foul and envious lie. Wherever I turn, whatever I say, I cannot be exonerated. My very face is held as evidence against me."

"So it is," Adam said. "So it must be until all the truth is known."

"The truth as you would have it."

"The truth of God." Adam signed himself and his prisoner. "May He keep you, and loose your tongue at last."

For that, he gained only silence and the turning of Alf's back.

Alf lay in the dark, luxuriating in his solitude, in quiet unbroken by that gentle deadly questioning. It would resume all too soon, to wear him down, to search out his weaknesses.

In the end he would confess. But not easily and not soon.
You may not be able to choose.

Thea's voice. He closed his mind against her.

There was a long stillness. Outside, his guard snored softly.

The bolt slid back. The snoring did not pause. Alf turned, for that was not Adam's slow sandaled tread. This was silent save for the faint rustling of cloth. He could see no more than a dark shape, clad and cowled in black.

"Thea!" he whispered fiercely. "Will you never learn—"

Her hand covered his mouth. "Hush, little Brother. You wouldn't talk to me the safest way, and I won't be put off."

"If anyone comes and sees you—"

"I'll be invisible, inaudible, and intangible." She knelt beside him. There was light enough from the guard's cresset outside for their eyes to see, but her fingers explored his face. "You're down to bare bone. But"—she examined the rest of his body, despite his resistance—"they haven't harmed you yet. I suppose you regret that."

Her hands had ended on his shoulders. He wanted to shake them off, but he did not. *Better there*, he thought, *than elsewhere.*

She laughed very softly. "Why, little Brother! Prison's been good for you. It's chipped off a layer or two of prudery."

"Is that all you came to see?"

"No." She released him and sat on her heels. "I've been eavesdropping. You haven't used power much, have you?"

"Only with my questioner, and only a little."

"That's what I was afraid of. I don't suppose you know what's been happening."

"The King is looking far afield for me. Bishop Aylmer is waiting for the Hounds to betray themselves. Kilhwch's messenger is coming."

"You're better-informed than I thought," Thea said. "Did you know that you're to be tried on St. Nicholas' Eve?"

Alf drew his breath in sharply. "Two days—but they were waiting for my confession!"

"The Hounds were. Earl Hugo and his imbecile of a Bishop have been getting nervous. They want you safely tried and burned before the King gets back. Aylmer they'll tell of the trial—far too late for him to gather any resistance. Then when Richard appears they can say that it was an ecclesiastical matter; that Aylmer was notified; and that the sentence was carried out promptly to prevent a public outcry against the terrible sorcerer. All in due and proper form. And you'll be a heap of ashes, and he'll have lost what he loves most."

"No," Alf said. "He doesn't love me. He loves my face. He lusts after my body."

"He loves you," said Thea. "God knows why."

Alf clenched his fists. "You are doing your best to talk me

out of this. You won't succeed. I know what I'm doing; I've considered all the consequences; I won't be shaken."

"You," she said in a thin cold voice, "are the most selfish being I've ever known."

"Why? Because I won't walk out with you now and forget both my duties and my troubles, and let you seduce me as you've tried to do since first we met?"

"Seduce you? *You*, you pallid, spineless, canting priest?"

"You sound exactly like the King," he said. "Do you fancy that you love me?"

When he could see again, she was gone. He lay where she had felled him, his brain reeling. Women, he thought foggily, were frail vindictive creatures, given more to tears than to blows. But this one had a heavier hand then Coeur-de-Lion.

Almost he called her back. He had meant to wound her; and yet, he had not.

Better for both of them that they not meet again.

He lay on his side, hand to his throbbing cheek, and tried to make his mind a void.

21

The Chapter House of St. Benedict's was a wonder of the north: a ring of pale gold stone, its vault held up with many pillars, and on each pillar a carven angel. Between St. Gabriel and St. Michael, beneath a gilded arch, sat Bishop Foulques. Robed and mitered, with an acolyte warding his jeweled crozier, he seemed no living man but an image set upon a tomb. His long pale face had no more life or color than one molded in wax.

On his right, beneath arches smaller and unadorned, sat figures cowled in black or gray, monks of St. Benedict and of St. Paul. On his left, somewhat apart, was Bishop Aylmer, dressed as he had come from Mass in the brown habit of a monk of St. Jerome. Set against the splendor of his brother-Bishop's garb, his simplicity was a rebuke.

Jehan, beside him, felt even larger and more ungainly than usual, crowded into a narrow niche with no more than a finger's breadth to spare on either side. He battled the urge to make himself as small as he might and sat erect and still, shoulders back, hands upon his knees. Opposite him, the monks stared and whispered. They had not expected Bishop Aylmer to appear on an hour's notice. Nor, Jehan suspected, had they thought to see himself.

Reynaud was not among them. After that first swift glance, Jehan ignored them.

A man in Pauline garb entered and knelt before Bishop Foulques, murmuring in his ear. The Bishop nodded once, imperially.

There was a pause, then a stir at the door, echoed round the hall. Jehan went rigid.

Four monks of St. Paul paced into the hall, burly men with hard grim faces. In their midst walked their solitary charge.

Jehan drew a shuddering breath. Brother Alf moved with the same light grace as always despite the chains which bound his hands; he bore no mark of violence. Yet he was alarmingly thin, his eyes black-shadowed, his skin so pale that it seemed translucent.

His guards brought him to stand apart on the Bishop's left, facing outward. If he saw Jehan, he did not show it. His gaze was strange, blurred, exalted, as if he walked in a trance.

Bishop Foulques rose slowly. The acolyte placed the crozier in his hand; he settled it firmly and straightened his cope. "My brothers," he intoned, "we are met in Christ's name by the authority of Holy Church. The Lord be with you."

"And with your spirit," the monks responded.

"*Oremus*," the Bishop bade them. "Let us pray."

Jehan barely heard the long ritual, prayer and psalm and prayer again, blessing and invocation and calling of Heaven to the labor of justice. His eyes and his mind fixed upon the tall slight figure of the prisoner.

The prayers ended; a monk came forward, he who had spoken to Bishop Foulques, with a parchment in his hand. He began to read from it in a voice both soft and clear.

"We gather here, my most noble and august Lord Bishop, to seek your judgment. Before you stands one anointed with the sacred oil of the priesthood, consecrated upon the altar of

God most high, yet accused of crimes most terrible and most unholy, forbidden by all the laws of God and man. By the testimony of many witnesses and by that of the prisoner himself, we have found due and proper cause to call him to this trial. Therefore, with God as our witness, we contend that this prisoner, known in this world as Alfred, once of St. Ruan's upon Ynys Witrin and now of the following of His Majesty's Lord Chancellor, is in fact a thing unholy and unclean, a changeling, a sorcerer, and a servant of the Lord of Hell; that he has knowingly and blasphemously profaned his sacred vows; and that he has cast a glamour upon His Majesty the King and upon His Majesty's Chancellor, blinding them to his demonic origins and shaping them to his infernal ends."

Jehan ground his teeth. Aylmer's hand had clamped about his wrist, else he would have risen. Perforce, he sat motionless and helpless, while the gentle voice wove its net of lies and half-truths.

As the monk went on, Jehan's wrath turned cold. In that grim clarity he became aware of a strangeness, a faint, maddening reverberation at the end of each pause. At first he did not trust his ears; yet with each brief silence he heard the echo more clearly. When at last the speaker ceased, there was no echo but a faint, distinct "*Amen!*"

Brother Alf had heard the charges without expression. But his eyes had focused slowly; had flickered about as if he searched for something. Others too cast uneasy glances round the room; one of the monks crossed himself.

Bishop Foulques seemed oblivious to the ghost-voice. "We have heard the charges," he said. "We will now hear the witnesses."

Was that a ripple of eldritch laughter?

The Pauline monk laid aside his parchment, genuflected to the Bishop, nodded to the man who guarded the door. He opened it to admit a young man at once arrogant and afraid. His eyes flicked at once to Alf and flinched away. He bowed low before Bishop Foulques, hesitated, bowed likewise to Aylmer.

As he straightened, the monk smiled at him. "Ah, sieur, you come in good time." He gestured; an acolyte brought a stool and set it in front of the Bishop. As the young man sat upon it, the monk said, "You would be Sir Olivier de Romilly, would you not?" The knight nodded; again he smiled. "And I am Brother Adam of Ely. My lord Bishop you know; it is to him that you should speak, although it is I who will question you."

Sir Olivier smoothed a wrinkle in his scarlet hose. "And the rest?" he asked.

"They will only listen," said Brother Adam. "I will speak and my lord will judge."

The other nodded.

Adam paused. After a moment he said, "Some days ago you told me a tale. Perhaps it would be best for my lord if you told it to him now, just as you told me."

Olivier obeyed. He would not look at Alf or at the silent Bishop; he spoke to the likeness of St. Michael with his flaming sword, in a high rapid voice as if reciting a lesson.

"A fortnight and more ago, I was riding with the King against Earl Rahere and his rebels. We fought in the hills by Windermere; a hard fight as they all are, though we had the victory. I was one of those who paid for it. I met a man with an axe—a Viking he must have been, as they tell of in old tales, a great blond giant of a man. I broke my sword on his axe; he dragged me from my horse and hewed me down.

"I was badly hurt. Very badly hurt, Brother, my lord. My yeomen carried me to the tent where the doctors were. There were strangers there. They were helping the doctors."

Olivier stopped. The listeners leaned forward, intent. Bishop Foulques frowned.

"They were helping the doctors," Olivier repeated. "I didn't think much of it. One doesn't when one's had an axe in the shoulder.

"One of them came to me. He gave me water. I was very glad of that. Then he . . . he touched me."

"Yes?" murmured Adam as the pause stretched beyond endurance.

"He touched me. I remember, he was looking at me—not at my face, but at my shoulder. I thought he must have been a clerk, but he was dressed like a squire. Then I thought it was strange that I could think at all. And then . . . then I knew." Olivier shivered. "I didn't feel any pain. None. Only a sort of warmth, like a patch of sun."

"And your wound?"

Olivier touched his shoulder and flexed it. "I was all over blood. But there was nothing there."

"No scar?"

"Brother, you know full well—" He stopped, composed himself. "There was a scar. My lord. But no wound. That, I've sworn to, on holy relics."

"May my lord see?"

Jehan had felt the blood drain from his face as the young knight told his tale. When he bared his shoulder and the deep livid scar there, the novice swallowed bile. He had not known of that healing; Brother Alf had never spoken of it. Which was most damnably like him. Had he been trying even then to get himself killed?

He seemed unmoved, although the eyes which turned to him held now a kind of horror.

"Prisoner," Bishop Foulques said, no name, no title. "Have you aught to say?"

Alf drew a breath to speak. In the silence, a thin eerie voice chanted: "*Kyrie eleison!*"

His lips tightened. "No," he said. "No, my lord. I have nothing to say."

Adam turned to him. "No, Brother? Is it true then as Messire has said? Did you work your sorceries upon him?"

"'And He healed them,'" sang that voice without breath or body: "'and the multitude wondered, when they saw the dumb to speak, the maimed to be whole, the lame to walk, and the blind to see: and they glorified the God of Israel.' "

Alf threw up his head like a startled deer.

Laughter rippled through the hall. Bishop Foulques half-rose; Olivier drew his dagger and spun about, hunting wildly for the enemy.

Brother Adam alone seemed unperturbed. "The air is full of sorcery," he said. He sketched a blessing over Olivier's head. "Go, and have no fear. No evil can touch you."

Olivier withdrew, white and shaking, his dagger still in his hand. One by one the monks settled back into their seats. The Bishop sat once more; his acolyte straightened his cope and crowned him again with the miter which had fallen from his head.

Brother Adam considered them all, so quietly certain of his victory that Jehan wanted to strike him down. "You have heard, Brothers," he said, "true and certain proof that we contend here with the work of the Enemy. For it is the way with demons that they make mock of what is holy. I would have you hear now of a night not long ago, when our prisoner revealed his nature for all to see."

The new witness was a stranger to Jehan, a man in the garb of a Benedictine novice. He had a handsome languid face and the air of a nobleman, but some ruthless barber had cropped his hair to stubble.

By that Jehan knew him. He took in the stranger's lazy grace, his expression of worldly ennui, and detested him, instantly, utterly.

He performed an obeisance which was proper to the point of parody and sat where he was bidden, enduring Brother Adam's introduction with every evidence of boredom. When he spoke, it was to Alf. "So, Brother. You look well in chains."

"And you," Alf said, "look ill in that habit."

Joscelin smiled. "Maybe it's your ham-handed barbering."

"Brother," Adam said, with the first small hint of sharpness Jehan had heard from him, "you are here to tell your tale."

"So I am," Joscelin agreed, unruffled. "Well now. How shall I begin?"

"At the beginning," Adam suggested.

Joscelin settled more comfortably. "So. The beginning. A good enough place, isn't it, pretty Brother?" He caught Adam's eye and grimaced. "Very well. I'll begin. I was the King's esquire then, and proud of it too. A little more than a sennight past, I walked out with friends for an evening's pleasure. On the way we met with yonder beauty."

Jehan clenched his fists. Olivier had told the truth as much as he might, but this was truth twisted out of all recognition. As Joscelin told it, he and his fellow-squires had taken Alf with them out of sheer goodwill, with a touch of censure for his most unclerical fondness for ale.

"And for the serving-wench," said Joscelin with a wry look, half the admiring young squire, half the new-hatched cleric.

Alf had gone upstairs with them, though reluctantly, Joscelin conceded; but then, he had been with the King not long before. No one mistook the implication. Alf stared at his feet, fists clenched about his chains.

"He was even more reluctant when he saw the woman," Joscelin said. "We did wrong, I'd be the first to admit it, my lords, but we were drunk, and so was he. We got him out of his habit." He paused, shook his head and sighed. "Brothers, before God, it was perilous to look at him. Nakedness of course is a sin, and when you couple it with such a body . . . *pardieu!* He looks a pretty fool, like a girl with her hair cut off, but the rest of him—"

"You stripped him," Adam broke in. "And then?"

One or two of the listeners sat back in ill-concealed disappointment. Joscelin sighed and resumed his tale. A sword had appeared in Alf's hand; Joscelin had tried to dissuade him; he had threatened, and the squire had lured him down to the common room, where the public eye might shock the monk back to his senses.

It did not. He covered himself in a robe of darkness and worked his magic with the sword, and before half a hundred startled men, he vanished.

Adam nodded as he finished. "We have found and questioned a number of the witnesses," he said, taking from his wallet a folded parchment and placing it in the Bishop's hand. "This, my lord, is their assembled testimony. All have sworn, separately and similarly, that he clothed his body with nothing more substantial than shadows and that he disappeared from the midst of them all. We have his habit and his cloak, taken from the room in the inn, certain proof of his presence there."

"And from thence he was taken up to heaven, alleluia."

Not a few of those there had expected it; but that uncanny voice roused them to superstitious terror. Brother Adam raised his arms. "In the name of Father, Son, and Holy Spirit, be thou still!"

For a long moment no one breathed. The voice was silent. Slowly each man relaxed, although he looked about uneasily, signed himself, and muttered a prayer.

Adam let his arms fall.

Eldritch laughter mocked all their folly.

A flush stained Adam's pale face. "Brothers," he said, "my lord Bishops, surely it is clear to you all that the Evil One lurks among us. One of his servants stands before you. The other you have heard; and of that one I have somewhat to say. For I have learned from witnesses that the accused is not alone in his sorcery. A familiar serves him, a creature of darkness which takes most often the shape of hound. It is a clever being, more clever if I may say it than its master, for we have been unable to capture it. Yet there are many who have seen it, and one man has observed it in its sorceries." He nodded to Joscelin, who retired to a seat among the monks, and raised his voice. "Brother! You may come in."

It was Reynaud who took his place before the judge, that hated face, that hated smile. Olivier had borne witness for fear, Joscelin for malice, but this man testified for the love of it. He had found

Alf, he had begun the pursuit; now he bent to rend the throat of his quarry.

He spoke calmly, distinctly, with none of the false friendliness Jehan had known. From the first day of Alf's arrival in the camp, he had watched and recorded and judged, and he had missed very little. His tale took in Olivier's and Joscelin's and the accounts of many witnesses, and shaped from them a larger whole, the portrait of a sorcerer.

And of his familiar. "A white hound," he said, "with red ears like the beasts of the pagan superstitions, and in its eyes the intelligence of a child of Hell. But when it chooses, it walks erect in human form."

"In what likeness?" Adam asked him.

"A shadow-shape, cowled like a monk but speaking with the voice of a beautiful woman."

And he told of the night in the stable, word for word. Eyes turned to Jehan as he spoke; the novice glared back. "Yes!" he wanted to shout. "I was there. I knew it all. Burn me, too!"

He could not speak. His tongue felt enormous, leaden; when he tried to form words, his mind blurred. He sat in silence, raging.

Reynaud ended at last. The monks stirred and murmured. "The *Gloria Dei*," someone said in a stunned voice. "He wrote the *Gloria Dei*?"

"Demonic mockery," Reynaud answered firmly, "intended to lead the young novice astray."

Jehan leaped to his feet.

The door burst open. A battle raged through it. Pauline white and gray, Benedictine black, and in the midst of it a whirlwind.

The struggle parted. Its center hurled itself forward, full upon Reynaud. Together they toppled.

Jehan plunged into the fray. A wild blur of faces—Bishop Foulques's beyond, crumbling into terror—a white shape, a tangle of bronze-gold hair. Jehan stared into Thea's wide feral eyes.

Adam's voice rose above the tumult. "What is this?"

The battle resolved into individual shapes. Reynaud sagged

in his fellows' arms, groaning, his face bleeding from a dozen deep scratches. No one else had come to harm.

Jehan let Thea go and backed away. She stood breathing hard, her hair falling about her face. Her gown was rent and torn; white flesh gleamed beneath.

She tossed back her hair. Some shrank from her; others started forward. She froze them all with her glare, her great eyes like a cat's, golden, wild. Her beauty smote Jehan's heart.

Again Adam spoke. "What is this?"

It was she who responded. Her voice they all knew, though this was born of throat and tongue and lips, a living voice as that other had not been. "I am not *what*. I am *who*. Is it a work of your famous Christian charity to wound a harmless woman?"

One of the monks called out, "It's a demon! It appeared before us; it tried to lure us away; Brother Andreas pretended to yield, and I struck it with the flat of my knife." He held it up, a small blade, too blunt for aught but cutting bread.

She whirled upon him. He raised the knife; she recoiled. "Aye," she cried, "he struck me, damn him to his own Hell; he burned me horribly." Across the palm of her hand spread a long red weal. She cradled it against her breast. "I shall demand redress."

Adam regarded her with an uncanny mingling of triumph and horror. "What sort of creature is this, that the flat of a blade will burn it?"

"The blade was iron," she said, shuddering, holding her wounded hand close. "Cursed iron. I would have gone free if he had not struck me with it."

"You should never have come!"

All eyes turned to Alf. He had fought his own battle to escape from his guards; two gripped him still, although he no longer struggled. "You should never have come," he repeated.

"What! and miss such a splendid game?"

"It is no game for me, nor now for you. For God's sake, escape while you still can."

"I can't," she said. "I'm bound."

"You're no more bound than—"

"Little Brother," she said to him, half in scorn, half in tenderness, "there's honor even in the hollow hills."

"That doesn't mean you have to die with me!"

"No?" She turned away from him to Brother Adam. "Yon holy saint, sir, is as witless as he is beautiful. My grief, for I saw him as he rode in the wood, and he was as fair as the princes of my own people; I set my heart upon him. But a greater fool never left an abbey. Would he dance with me? Would he let me sing to him? Would he be my paramour? No, and no, and no: and Lord have mercy, and begone, foul fiend, and back to his prayers again. Prayers, forsooth! and he so fair that the Goddess herself couldn't ask for better."

Adam's thin nostrils flared. Here was a gift to lay at the feet of the Pope himself: no mere witch or heretic, but a true child of old Night. "Are you aware that this is a trial, and that Brother Alfred is accused of serious crimes against the Church?"

"Crimes? He doesn't even know how to sin!"

"He stands accused of sorcery, for which the penalty is death."

"He?" She laughed, that same wild laughter which had run bodiless to the vaulted roof. "That child could walk among us and pass for one of us, but he's altogether a son of Earth."

"The evidence—"

"Lies," she said. "Lies and twisted truth."

Bishop Foulques moved suddenly to strike his crozier upon the floor. "This is a mockery! Brother, rid us of this creature."

She regarded him in amazement. "What! The stones can speak?"

A flush suffused the Bishop's waxen cheeks. "Adam! Do as I say."

Aylmer rose. Through all of that turmoil, he had not moved or spoken, had shown no fear or surprise. When he stood, it was as if one of the carven angels had stepped down from its pillar. "My lord Bishop," he said, "it is my understanding that you wish to determine the guilt of a sorcerer. The Brothers have gathered their evidence scrupulously enough, although I find certain of their methods somewhat questionable and their motives disturbing. It concerns me particularly that no attempt has been made on the part of this court to defend the innocence of the accused. Yet it seems to me that this lady, however unorthodox her arrival and her origins may be, has undertaken to do precisely that. Will you prevent her from doing so?"

Foulques seemed close to an apoplectic fit. "She has invaded the precincts of the Church's justice, has—"

"Justice?" Aylmer asked. "Is it justice to refuse to consider evidence of a person's innocence? In the court of His Holiness in Rome, even the Devil has his Advocate."

As Aylmer spoke, Adam had approached Foulques and whispered urgently in his ear. He shook his head, glowering; Adam persisted; at length, with obvious reluctance, he nodded.

Adam faced Bishop Aylmer. "My lord will permit her to testify. Yet she should be aware that her testimony may lead to her own trial and possible conviction; for we are committed to the destruction of all of Satan's works and creatures."

"Then," said Thea, "you would do well to burn your King."

Aylmer considered her for a long moment. "Maybe it will come to that, my lady," he said. "When the King's friend is in danger, can the King himself be safe?"

"The King has been bewitched," Adam said sharply. "We seek to protect him from such evil and to destroy the source of it."

Aylmer nodded to himself. "Ah, yes. I'm bewitched, too. Well then, continue with your mummery." He beckoned. "Come here, Jehan. Sit and let them entertain us."

Adam chose to ignore him. He glanced about, saw that a man guarded the door with drawn sword, faced Thea. "You say that you are bound. How so?"

She gestured toward the monk with the knife. "He touched

me with iron, and it has a stronger magic than mine. I can't leave unless he bids me."

"Indeed." Adam indicated the stool. "Sit."

"I prefer to stand."

He did not press her. "Very well. First, your name."

"Oh, no," she said. "Iron binds me tightly enough. I won't give you that power besides."

Reynaud shook off the hands which had supported him. "Thea. They called you Thea."

Her lip curled. "Jackal. Vulture. I scented you upon our path. Would to Annwn I had done as my heart bade me and torn out your throat."

"Your name is Thea?" Adam asked her quietly.

Her eyes burned upon him. "Yes. But you gain no power by it. It's not my true-name."

"Thea, then. Not a name of this land."

"And not the truth."

"So." Adam looked her up and down. "You are of the Fair Folk?"

"Haven't I said so? I saw your Brother Alfred as he rode through Bowland; I followed him."

"In the likeness of a white hound?"

"A hound!" She tossed her head. "Should I so degrade myself? I followed him; now and then I let him see me. He would have nothing to do with me. Such a little saint, he is. Either he tried to exorcise me, or he tried to make a Christian of me. I tempted him with enchantments; he prayed them away."

"Enchantments?" asked Adam. "How so?"

"So," she shot back. "One night three young hellions trapped him in a tavern. I want him to be a man and not a mumbling priest—but the Gray Man can have us both before I let any mortal woman have him. I gave him a sword and the skill to use it; I clothed him in spells; and he escaped. Did he thank me for it? No, before all the gods! He cursed me and bade me begone."

"That's not so!" Alf cried.

She raised her hand. He gasped and swayed. "Love is a blind god," she said, "and an utter fool, else why do I endure this? See how he tries to save me, who never had a kind word for me when I begged him to love me."

"You contend that he has practiced no sorcery?" Adam demanded of her.

"So does he," she pointed out.

"The sorceries ascribed to him are in fact yours."

"Sorceries," she said, "no. We don't traffic with the Dark. But the spells were mine. I was abasing myself to win that iron heart. I made his way easy for him. I warmed the water he washed in, I healed the man he tended, I set a hound to guard him. All useless. He's as cold as ever."

He stood mute as Jehan had stood, white with the strain of his resistance. She regarded him sadly. "Little Brother, I didn't know the humans would try to burn you for what I did."

"You say he is of mortal descent."

"Entirely."

"We have gathered certain evidence—"

"Nonsense," she said. "Look at him! No one of the true blood could wear a cross or bear such chains. All your so-called evidence is a travesty."

"So is your testimony!" Reynaud burst out. "I say that you are both witches and sorcerers; that you aided and abetted each other, and that you both should go to the fire."

She spat at him. "Cur! You would give your soul to gnaw our bones."

"Silence!" Adam commanded them. To Foulques he said, "My lord, I am inclined to support Brother Reynaud. I was not aware of this woman's existence or intervention, both of which alter the charges somewhat. That she may have worked her witchery as she has told us, I believe, yet I am not convinced of the other's innocence. Surely he yielded to her to some extent; he made use in the inn of the gifts she gave him, whatever he may have told her afterward."

"The stable," Reynaud said. "Their speech—"

"Devilish mockery, you said yourself," she broke in. "You can't have it both ways, jackal. If our little Brother, our beardless boy, is the greatest of your theologians, then surely he must be of our blood, for the book he wrote is twice as old as his face. But that can't be possible, can it? You didn't hear what you thought you heard, what you wanted to hear in your lust for his death."

"Witch!" he hissed.

"I madden you. You can't bear it that I should want him and not you. If I promised to take you, you would do everything in your power to have me set free. You'd even promise to free him — but that would be a lie."

Beneath the livid marks of her nails, his face was a mask of fury. "Demon! Tempter!"

"But not a liar," she said. "It's you who lie. You want him to die, for your own glory and for the King's grief. You haven't deigned to mention all the accomplices who must have known what our Brother was, raised him and trained him and made a monk of him — they're too many and too far away, and much too powerful. You haven't even called Master Jehan to account for his guilt, though in your tale he's as much at fault as the rest of us, for he doesn't matter to you and he has kin who could avenge him. The King's kin are his enemies and urge you on, and the little Brother has none."

Adam stepped between them. "We do not act at the bidding of any temporal power. Our part is to search out and destroy the enemies of the Church; here in this court we judge by that Law which commands, 'There shall not be found among you any one that maketh his son or his daughter to pass through the fire, or that useth divination, or is an observer of times, or an enchanter, or a witch, or a charmer, or a consulter of familiar spirits, or a wizard, or a necromancer. For all that do these things are an abomination unto the Lord.' And in speaking of punishment, the Law is most simple and most strict: 'Thou shalt not suffer a witch to live.'"

There was a silence. Thea seemed at last to have understood

what she had confessed. A tremor ran through her body; she
drew back a step, shying as her guard raised his knife. She
stopped and stood very still. "Brother Alfred is not a sorcerer.
If anyone is to die, it must be I, though life on this earth is very
sweet, and since they tell me I have no soul, Heaven is barred
to me."

"Hell will take you gladly," Reynaud muttered.

She hissed at him. "The Dark Lord is my bitter enemy, as
he is of all my people. We've thwarted him too often and too
thoroughly. But you he would welcome with open arms."

She turned to the Bishop. "This is not a trial. This is a
gathering of the King's enemies to destroy the one thing he cares
for. That one"—she indicated Adam with a toss of her head—
"believes in what he does, which is all the worse for him. But
the rest of you would kneel to a crucifix, and then spit on it."
Through gasps of horror and cries to seize her and cast her down,
she laughed without mirth. "Ah, you mortal men! The truth
sears you like cold iron. Shall I strike you again? You'll burn
the little Brother. The stake is ready; you have only to tie him
to it and light the fire. And then the King will come. What then,
Lord Bishop? While you kept to the abbey and plotted in secret,
he suffered you. But now you declare open enmity."

"He will not touch a man of God," Adam said. "He dares not."

Again she laughed, freely now, almost joyously. "Don't be
a fool. He'll tear down this abbey stone by stone and drive you
Hounds into the sea, and rend yon puppet of a Bishop limb
from limb and cast him to the dogs."

"Interdict—anathema—"

"You're babbling, pious Brother. Ask Bishop Aylmer if Anglia
or its King will suffer for vengeance taken upon traitors."

"*Silence!*" Bishop Foulques was on his feet, quivering with
passion. "The trial will resume. And I will hear no further
word from you, witch; or as God is my witness, I will cast you
out."

"My lord Bishop," Adam said soothingly, "she will not speak

again. We, for our part, have presented our case. We contend that the prisoner is guilty as charged, and we submit him to your judgment."

For a long while, Bishop Foulques did not respond. He had mastered himself; his face had returned from livid wrath to its former pallor. He seemed deep in thought, frowning, shooting swift glances at Alf, at Thea, at Aylmer: glances compounded of hatred and of cold terror. Slowly, repeatedly, his thumb traced the intricate carving of his crozier.

When at last he spoke, it was to no one and to everyone, in a firm voice. "I have heard both attack and defense. I have reached a conclusion."

He paused. Jehan found that he could not breathe. Alf was absolutely still, death-pale; Thea had turned toward him, holding him fast with her burning gaze.

The Bishop resumed. "No one has denied that witchcraft has been practiced in and about this city and the King. The doubt seems to lie in the identity of its practitioner. Either it is a woman of unknown origins and overweening arrogance, and a flagrant disregard of the dignity of the Church, its court, and its Scriptures; or it is a monk in the habit of the holy Order of St. Jerome, an ordained priest and an acknowledged favorite of His Majesty the King." Again he paused. Most of those there listened in puzzlement. But Adam's face had paled and Reynaud's gone livid. "The charges are grave. The penalty, as Brother Adam has informed us, is death."

Alf tore his gaze from Thea's and turned toward the Bishop.

Foulques raised his voice slightly. "It is my belief that both the accused and the woman are guilty of witchcraft, of sorcery, and of black enchantment. Yet in view of the evidence, it is also my belief that the guilt is not evenly apportioned. The prisoner has not confessed to his crimes, but has denied them; the woman . . ." He steadied himself with a visible effort. "The woman has admitted her guilt freely, insolently, and most unrepentantly. She also denies that the other shares that guilt;

of this I am not convinced. In my judgment, she was the instigator, he the accomplice; she the cause, he the sharer of their sorceries.

"Therefore," Foulques proclaimed, "I sentence them both. You," he said to Alf, avoiding the pale stare, "as a priest of God, have sinned most grievously. Yet you are young, of an age when the beauty of a woman may overcome the strength of your vows; the passion of your blood has tempted you to do what is most direly forbidden. You have not fallen wholly, as this woman has testified; yet for your transgressions you must pay the due and proper penalty. Here before the court of Holy Church, by her authority vested in me, I suspend you from your sacred vows. You shall not go up to the altar of God, nor perform the functions of a priest, nor admit yourself into the company of priests or of monks, until such time as you may have proven by the purity of your life and actions that you have atoned fully for your sin. Furthermore, to remind you that you are but dust and ashes in the face of the Lord, I command that you submit to the punishment of twenty lashes upon your bare back; and that with each stroke, you cry to Him for His mercy."

Alf stood rigid. His face was terrible, wholly inhuman.

The Bishop turned to Thea, his eyes glittering. "And you," he said. "You have cast your mockery in the face of Holy Church. You have given voice to lies born of the Devil your sire. And yet, in coming to this place, in crying your defiance, you have submitted yourself to our power. That power I invoke to its fullest extent. Woman of the hills, nameless one, corrupter of priests, you shall die by sacred and cleansing fire, and your bones shall be cast into a pit, and the curse of God's wrath shall lie upon them."

Alone of all those who listened, she seemed unmoved. Alf broke away from his guards. "No!" he shouted. "*No!* Let her live. I lied; I deceived you all. It is I who am the sorcerer. *I* worked the spells; I pretended innocence to confound you. *I* should go to the fire. Let me die in her place!"

"So completely has she corrupted him," the Bishop said, half in pity, half in satisfaction, "that he will defend her unto death. It grieves me to see such virtue turned to evil." He raised his hand. "I have spoken. So be it. *Fiat. Fiat. Fiat.*"

22

Early in the morning of the Feast of St. Nicholas, the towns-
folk of Carlisle began to gather near the east gate. In the space
before St. Benedict's Abbey, a new growth had appeared in the
night, a tall stake hung with chains. Heaps of brushwood stood
beside it.

By full day, a sizable crowd had taken shape. A newcomer,
ignorant of the cause, might have thought that they kept festival
under the rare cloudless sky and despite the winter chill. They
laughed and jested; among them moved peddlers and pick-
pockets, a traveling singer and a troupe of jugglers. On the fringes
a huddled circle, a chorus of shouts and jeers, proclaimed a
cockfight.

Only the space about the stake remained clear. Pauline monks
guarded it, interspersed with men-at-arms who wore the blazon
of the Bishop of Carlisle.

Beyond the throng in the lee of the abbey's wall, workmen
had erected a canopied platform. Figures began to take their
places there as the hour approached terce: Benedictines, Paulines, a layman or two. Earl Hugo appeared with his lady and
half a dozen attendants, settling on the right of the vacant high

seat. Not long after, Bishop Foulques swept in to take the chair of honor, escorted by the Abbot of St. Benedict's. Servants saw them settled and wrapped in warm robes against the cold.

The crowd boiled. Bishop Aylmer strode through it on foot and simply dressed, with a troop of monks at his back. Eyes widened and grew wise. Not one of the escort was armed or armored, and none wore spurs on his sandaled feet, but the smallest overtopped the burly Bishop by half a head.

Aylmer bowed curtly to the dignitaries on the dais, and paused a moment. The high ones exchanged glances; one or two half-rose as if to make room for him.

The King's Chancellor turned on his heel and took his place close to the stake, with his monks in a half-circle behind him.

At the stroke of terce, the great gate of the abbey swung open. A hush fell; eyes stared, necks craned, fathers swung children onto their shoulders.

It was a small procession for so great a matter. A tall thin Pauline monk carrying a book and a scroll; a pair of novices, thurifer and crucifer; monks chanting a psalm. And behind, guarded by mailed men with drawn swords, the prisoners. The first stood taller than his guards, a familiar pale face ravaged now with fasting and with sleeplessness, and beneath it a thin white tunic which afforded little protection from the biting wind. Chains bound his wrists, but he walked with his head up, seeing nothing and no one.

But the second made the crowd jostle and crane, straining to see. She was harder to catch a glimpse of, tall but not as tall as the other, her long tangled hair half-hiding her face. Her tunic was much like his, but her chains were far heavier, of black iron, weighing down her slender body.

A growl rumbled in a hundred throats, swelling swiftly to a roar. A stone arced over her head; others followed it. Men-at-arms surged forward, striking with fists and flattened blades.

Thea paid them no heed. Nor did she heed Alf, who continued his nightlong mental barrage. For each shield he had battered down, she had erected another; he could not reach her mind. *Thea!* he cried. *Thea, for the love of God, answer me!*

Her shield held fast. And he had nearly exhausted his mind's strength. A last desperate shaft struck not at her mind but at her chains.

It rebounded to pierce his own bruised brain. He staggered; a hard hand held him up.

Out of madness and frustration and sheer perversity, Alf let fall the illusion which shielded his eyes. The guard gasped and crossed himself.

With a small tight smile, Alf walked on. He had not restored the seeming. If enough people saw soon enough, he would go to the stake with Thea.

It loomed before him now, half again his own height, a great lopped tree-trunk. Beside it stood a hooded man, in his hand a long whip. He wore lay garb, but Reynaud's mind laughed within the hood. Adam had not let him touch the precious prisoners, but Bishop Foulques had been more amenable, had let him take the executioner's place. In that much, he would have his revenge on them all.

The procession arrayed itself round the empty circle. Adam performed obeisance to the high ones, and at Bishop Foulques's nod, mounted the dais. In a clear voice he began to read the charges.

Alf did not listen. The stake held his gaze and his mind. They were economical, these people. He would be flogged first at that stake, and afterward they would bind Thea to it, heaping high the fuel. And then—

They were dragging him forward. Adam had come down from the dais; he met the monk's eyes. The mind behind them mingled regret, compassion, a touch of genuine liking; and a fire of zeal for his calling, that leaped high as the truth struck his consciousness.

Denounce me, Alf willed him. *Make them burn me. Make them!*

Adam's deep eyes hooded. He stood aside as the men-at-arms chained Alf to the stake, back to the air, face to the rough bark.

It was sweet-scented, seasoned pine; it would burn well and swiftly.

Hands tore at his tunic, baring his back. Vulgar jests rang in his ears. He pressed his cheek to the wood, aware of Morwin's cross caught between breast and stake. Adam had let him keep it. Gentle, cruel Brother Adam.

There was no gentleness in Reynaud. The whip whistled as he whirled it about, teasing, taunting him with the anticipation of pain which never came.

Pain. A trail of fire across his shoulders. Remember the discipline. Remember. *Pie Jesu, miserere mei:* sunlight upon apple boughs, chanting in the choir, a child bathing in both up in he oldest tree, the Lady Tree, that had once been sacred. Remember sweet scent, sweet singing, sweet freedom-from-pain. Ride on scent, song, light, up and up to Light. *Lux. Fiat lux*, and light was made; and He looked upon it and saw that it was good.

Far below in the dark place, a small soft thing clung to a stake. Red weals marred its back. A black ant labored, striking and striking and striking again. Voices cried out to him: to stop, to slow, to go on, to beat, to strike, to kill. He laughed.

Men ran forward, small robed shapes, to seize the hand as it swung upward yet again, to wrest the whip from it, to hurl the madman laughing and struggling to the ground.

Alf plummeted. Agony—agony—

He gasped and gagged. Blood lay heavy upon his tongue. He had bitten it through.

They loosed his hands. His knees held him. Control, yes. It took control. He turned. The faces nearest him held horror. "Fifty lashes," someone said. "I counted fifty."

"Sixty," another insisted.

"More. It was more."

He dared not breathe, nor move hastily. He shook off the hands which reached to aid him, walked slowly forward. Reynaud was gone, his laughter silenced.

He stopped where his guards bade him stop. Dimly he was aware that they did not wear mail or the Bishop's blazon, but dark robes; they were tall, as tall as he or more. One face he knew, but he could put no name to it. A strong bony face, a great Norman arch of a nose, a tousle of straw-colored hair.

It blurred. Beyond it men heaped faggots about the stake, taking their time, letting the crowd work itself to a frenzy. The words and rituals of the Church sank into that uproar and vanished.

Thea stood in the center of it, very pale, very still. Tall though she was, as tall as most men, she seemed terribly frail. She tossed back her hair and turned her face to the sky; upon it, a look almost of ecstasy. When Adam made the sign of the Cross over her, she smiled. Her lips moved. "Lord of Light," she said, "*Christos Apollo, chaire, Kyrie . . .*"

It seemed an incantation. But Alf understood. She prayed in her own Greek tongue, entrusting her soul to the Light.

Her soul.

She believed that. He tried to spring forward.

She bound him with power, bonds he did not know how to break.

They chained her to the stake—face outward, she, so that all could watch her die. She was smiling still; and she changed her speech to Latin. In sudden silence, her voice rang silver-pure. "*Deum de Deo, lumen de lumine*—God from God, light from light . . ."

Alf's hand sought the silver cross. With a swift movement, he broke its chain and hurled it flashing and glittering across the wide space.

Bound though she was, she caught it. Kissed it for all to see—all those who thought her the Devil's kin. One of her guards thrust a torch deep into the fuel at her feet. Drenched with oil, it blazed up.

The flames coiled about her, caressing her with a terrible tenderness. She stretched out her hands to them. Her face was rapt, serene, untouched by pain or fear.

A howl welled from the center of Alf's being. He tensed to break free of the hands that gripped him.

And cried aloud; but not with the beast-roar that had been born in him. For the fire had enfolded her; she had melted like mist in the sun.

Out of the pyre rose a white bird with a cross in its bill. It soared up and up into the vault of the sky, winging for heaven.

The fire licked hungrily at an empty stake.

23

Alf lay on his face. His body rested in blessed comfort, but his back was a fiery agony. He had a dim memory of fire and shouting, swift-moving shadows, the call of a trumpet, a thunder of hoofs. And Jehan's face, drained of all color, with eyes that held death. *No*, he had tried to tell him. *No vengeance, Jehan. For your soul's sake, no vengeance!* But his voice would not obey him; darkness closed in.

For yet a while longer he rested. There was someone with him, and someone fretting at some little distance; he did not extend his inner senses more than that. It was too pleasant simply to lie still and know that he was well, and more, far more, that Thea lived.

He opened his eyes. The King stared back, surprise turning to relief so sharp it was like pain. "Alfred?" he asked, trying to soften his voice. "Brother?"

Alf smiled. "Good—day? Sire."

"It's night."

"Is it?" Alf raised himself on his hands. He was clean, naked but for trews of fine linen, his back salved and bandaged. As he sat up, the King reached for him in protest but shrank from touching his hurts.

He drew a breath carefully. Movement had awakened new pain, the price of his folly. He set his teeth against it and looked about. "Sire! This is your own bed. How did I come here?"

"I brought you," Richard answered. "You shouldn't be moving about."

"I'm healthy enough. What's a stripe or two to a born eremite?"

The King's eyes glittered. "It was a lot more than two. And a lot more than twenty."

"Sire," Alf said, "don't harm anyone for my sake."

"They were eager enough to harm you for mine."

"I started it, Sire. I sought it out."

Richard fixed him with a steady amber stare. "I know you did. I should hang you up by the thumbs. Do you have any conception of what it did to me to be chasing wild geese all over Cumbria, and to find out too late that you were right under my nose? If you weren't half-flayed already, I'd have your hide for that."

Alf's head drooped; his eyes lowered, shamed. "I'm sorry, Sire. Most sorry."

"You ought to be. While I was out hunting will-o'-the-wisps like the scatterbrained fool I am, half my knights decided they'd rather spend Yule at home by the fire than fight in the snow on the Marches. It's paltry satisfaction that I smoked out a nest of rebels and got an excuse to hamstring those cursed Hounds."

"Sire!" Alf cried. "What did you do to them?"

"Little. Yet. They and their traitor Bishop are locked up safe and sound in the abbey. Tomorrow Aylmer and I will give them a somewhat fairer trial than they gave you."

Alf staggered to his feet, heedless of pain and of gathering darkness. "My lord. I beg you. Don't punish them."

The King swept him up with ease. Yet even when he had been set in bed again, he would not be quenched. "You must not!"

"Boy," Richard said, half in affection, half in exasperation, "I seem to spend a great deal of precious time fighting off your Christian charity. But this time you won't extort a surrender. His two-faced Excellency is going to discover that he didn't divert me by burning the wrong prisoner; and the Hounds have had this coming to them for a long, long while. It was their mistake to let Foulques talk them into going after you."

"It wasn't Foulques. They would have pursued me no matter who I was."

"Would they?"

"Yes," Alf said. "I told them the truth, Sire. I'm no demon nor any demon's servant. But that was only half of the truth they looked for. The woman they tried to burn . . . was no less human than I."

Richard's face did not change. "The holy angel? So she was like you. I thought so. Clever of her to make such a spectacular exit."

Alf was speechless.

Richard laughed. "Thought I was just another mortal fool, didn't you? I grant you, for a long time I was. But while I was combing the Fells for you it all came together. Even the most dutifully Christian monk doesn't take a foreign king's command to heart unless he has good reason. Such as that that King is his kinsman."

"My ancestry—"

"Probably it's as low as you want to think it is. But you're one of Gwydion's kind. They hang together, those Fair Folk in Rhiyana. Did he send the woman to help you?"

"She came of her own accord."

"Ah," said Richard. "Was she as beautiful as you?"

"More so."

"Impossible." The King stretched. "Rather interfered with your attempt at martyrdom, didn't she?"

Alf's cheeks burned. "I was acting like a fool, my lord. She knew it. And so, at last, do I."

"Someday I'll find a way to thank her for that. When I realized what you were, I knew where you had to be. Nigh killed a good horse getting back here—just too late. If you'd had your way, by then you'd have been a pile of ashes."

Alf shivered. Richard struck his brow with his fist. "What am I doing, wearing you out with things you'd rather not hear? Waiter! Food and drink, and water the wine!"

It was not the King's servant who brought the meal, but Jehan. Richard scowled at him but said nothing. He set the cups and bowls upon the table by the bed with such admirable self-control that Alf smiled. He did not even look at the invalid, although he bowed to the King, every inch the royal page.

"Jehan," Alf said, "are you angry with me?"

The novice spun about. His face had the stiff haughty expression it always wore when he was fighting back tears. "Angry, Brother Alf? *Angry?*"

"I've made you suffer terribly."

"Not as much as you've made yourself."

"Ah, but I wanted it."

"I know. Idiot." Jehan looked him over with a critical eye, only a little blurred with tears. "You look ghastly. When's the last time you ate?"

Alf could not meet his gaze. "I don't remember."

"*That* long? *Deus meus!*" Jehan sat on the side of the bed and reached for a bowl. "Broth then and nothing else, till we've got your stomach used to working again."

"But I'm not—"

"You're never hungry. That's most of the trouble with you. Will you eat this yourself or shall I feed you?"

Beyond Jehan's head, Alf could see Richard's broad grin. With a sigh he took the bowl and raised it to his lips.

"He rode into Carlisle like the wrath of God," Jehan said when Richard had gone to contend with his court, "galloped through the crowd, scattering them right and left, and stopped dead in front of Bishop Foulques.

"Odd," the novice went on. "I expected him to blister our ears with curses. But he just sat there on his heaving horse with his men straggling up behind him, and stared. The Bishop turned the color of a week-old corpse and started to babble. The King put up his hand; old Foulques lost his voice altogether.

"The Hounds were howling like mad things about witches and sorcerers and spells; the kerns were yelling about saints and martyrs and miracles. Some people were fighting, the guards who were Hounds against a bravo or six from the town.

"The King had his man blow his trumpet. That quieted people down a little. 'Aylmer,' he said and pointed to the people on the platform, 'take these men into custody.' Bishop Aylmer did, except for Earl Hugo and his lady, who'd scampered for cover as soon as they heard the King's trumpet.

"The King didn't stop to watch. He took you up on his saddle—had to fight me for you, too, till I saw the sense in it—and carried you to the keep. Nobody got in his way." Jehan shivered. "I hope I never see anyone look like that again. He was almost as white as you, and he looked as if he wanted to cry but couldn't, and the not being able to made him want to tear the world apart."

Alf rested his forehead upon his arm. His voice was soft, muffled. "Did he curse me?"

Jehan hesitated. Then: "Only after his doctor said you'd be all right. He has an impressive vocabulary." After a moment, when Alf made no response, he added, "He stayed with you all day. He wouldn't go out at all, for anything."

There was a long silence. Jehan thought Alf had fallen asleep, until he said, "Thea is gone."

"As soon as it's safe, she'll be back."

"No. She's gone. She's kept me from getting myself killed; she's had enough of me. She's gone back to her own people."

"I suppose you're relieved," Jehan said. "You never liked her much, did you?"

Alf did not answer.

* * * * *

The King did not submit Bishop Foulques and his allies to the disgrace of a public trial. His revenge was more subtle. He spoke privately with the Bishop, with the Earl, and with the Paulines; and each emerged in somewhat worse state than when he had entered.

"It's what we intriguers call a 'settlement,'" Aylmer explained to Alf afterward. "Foulques has changed his allegiances rather than find himself Bishop of Ultima Thule. Hugo has become the most loyal of the King's men, with his eldest son for a surety. And our Brothers of St. Paul have found sudden and urgent reasons to leave the kingdom."

Jehan laughed. "*Urgent* is the word. None of them dares to show his face out of doors. The kerns are in a rage, that the priests of holy Church have tried to burn one of God's own angels; they'd gladly put a Hound or two in the fire."

"I'd gladly oblige them," the King said, "but I know I'd never have any peace if I tried."

Alf smiled. He had managed to bathe with Jehan's help and dress in a cotte of Richard's, and sit propped carefully with pillows. With the King and the Bishop and the novice about him and a page waiting to serve him, and half a dozen servants hovering within call, he knew how a prince must feel.

"You're the people's darling now," Jehan told him. "Everyone who said you were a sorcerer is swearing up and down that you're a saint, and that God sent His angel to save you from the fire. Sir Olivier's been going about declaring that you healed him with Divine power, and promising every farthing he has to charity because he testified against you."

Alf's smile turned to a look of dismay. "I'm anything but a saint. I'm not—even—" His voice died.

"You are," said Bishop Aylmer. "I've revoked your suspension."

They waited for him to wake to joy. But he shook his head. "My lord, I'm most deeply grateful. And yet . . . No. I haven't functioned as a priest for a long while. Not since I became fully aware of what I am. But I couldn't bear to give up the duties and offices of a simple monk, mockery though they were, performed by one who was not a man." All three moved to speak; he silenced them with a glance. "I know; you think I'm wrong. Like Abbot Morwin, you think a child of the Fair Folk can be as good a priest as any mortal man. Maybe one can; maybe I can. But I know what the Church says—know it as well as the Paulines knew. Until I'm certain of the truth, I can't call myself a man of God."

"You are," Jehan said. "You *are!*"

Alf touched the other's knotted fist, lightly. It tightened; then it sprang open to grip his hand with painful force.

"Brother Alf," Jehan said, though he shook his head at the title. "You'll always be that to me. But . . . if this will help you, or heal you . . . then do it. Only, don't tear your soul apart for a few empty words."

"Sometimes one has to be torn apart in order to grow." Alf smiled his familiar wry smile, that Jehan had not seen in a long while. "See: I'm even getting wise in this my old age. There may be hope for me yet."

Alf promised to sleep if he were left alone. That won suspicious glances, but at length even Jehan withdrew.

He did sleep a little despite a rebirth of pain. In his dreams he endured again the stroke of the lash; and suddenly he held the whip, and the prisoner chained to the stake had a woman's white body and a fall of bronze-gold hair. He dropped the whip in horror; she turned in her chains. Her eyes held the old familiar mockery. "What, little Brother! Can't you even flog me properly?"

"I'm not a priest anymore," he said.

She laughed and stretched, sinuous as a cat. The chains fell away. "Not a priest? You? I don't believe it."

"I decided I needed to grow up. They were right in St. Ruan's, you know. The sacrament cast a spell on me; I stayed a boy, mind as well as body. But I've broken the spell. I'll be a man now."

"Truly?" She approached him. He stood his ground, although he trembled violently. Her hands tangled themselves in his hair, that had grown thick and long, shoulder-long; she drew his head down. He felt his body kindle. Only with her, he thought. Only, ever, with her.

"Such a handsome boy," she said. "Will you be a man?"

"Yes," he whispered. "Yes."

He started awake. No warm woman's body stirred beneath him; no wild pale mane brushed his shoulders. He staggered up and groped for the watered wine Jehan had left for him.

A deep draught steadied him somewhat. He sat on the bed, head in hands. "Poverty," he said. "Chastity. Obedience. Poverty, chastity, and obedience. Three vows, little Brother. Only three. And she is gone away and will never come back."

He drained the cup. Again he stood, swaying. Among the King's belongings he found a voluminous dark cloak. He settled it about his shoulders, flinching as the weight of fabric roused his back to pain.

No one saw him leave the King's chamber. He went slowly, concealing his face from those he passed; thronged to bursting as the castle was, he passed unnoticed.

It was raining without, a gray cold rain. He bent his head beneath it and made his way through the town.

Brother Adam paced the length of St. Benedict's cloister, heedless of the wind which swirled round the carved and painted columns to fling rain in his face. No one else had braved the weather, save one latecomer who paused in an archway, wrapped from crown to ankle in a dark cloak. Yet, swathed though he was, the stranger wore neither shoes nor sandals; his feet were bare, spattered with mud as if he had walked a distance in the wet.

He let his hood fall back. Adam regarded him without surprise. "Brother Alfred," he said.

"'Brother' no longer," said Alf.

"No?"

"You of all people will admit that it is fitting."

"Perhaps."

Alf drew nearer to him, undisguised. He shivered slightly but stood his ground. His mind was a wondrous thing, elegantly ordered, shaped for the glory of God. Yet its foundations had begun to crumble.

Adam's voice was very quiet. "Get out of my mind."

"You know what I am," Alf said.

Still quietly, without malice, Adam responded, "You walk as a man, you pass as a man. But a man you can never be."

"You didn't denounce me."

"Perhaps I should be damned for it."

"For mercy?"

"For suffering a witch to live."

"It's a strange thing," Alf said. "We deny the power of the Old Law; we revile those who follow it still. But when it suits us, we follow it to the letter."

"A witch," said Adam, "has set the keystone upon our theology. Alfred of St. Ruan's, you are such a creature as would drive Rome mad."

"Rome, and you, and myself. I'm learning, slowly, that sanity lies in acceptance. The world the Church has made is a world of men, but does it encompass all of the world that God has made?"

"You tread upon the edges of heresy."

"Don't we all? When you defined yourself to me, you implied that evil had created me, that God had no part in it. And that, Brother, is the error of the Manichees."

"It is a dilemma," Adam said. "You are a dilemma. It is a sin and it is a child's folly, but I would that you had never been born."

"Or that I had truly been evil?"

Adam's face was drawn as if with pain. "Yes. Yes, God help me. There are priests who live lives far less pure than yours, witch-born though you are, and no one censures them. And I knew this, and I kept silence in despite of the Law."

"You are a compassionate man."

"I am a fool!" He controlled himself with a visible effort. "I shall do penance. I am leaving my Order; I shall set sail over sea to Hibernia and dwell there in solitude, far from any man. Perhaps I shall learn to forget you."

Quietly Alf said, "I can make you forget."

Adam threw up his hands as if to avert a blow. "No!"

Alf bowed his head.

The Pauline monk drew a breath, struggling to steady himself. At length he managed a faint, bitter smile. "You were a far better prisoner than am I. Does it amuse you to see how low I have fallen?"

"No."

Adam shook his head in disbelief. "Come now. Surely you came to taste your revenge. You have overthrown a great Order in Anglia and driven Reynaud mad beyond all healing, and cost the King's enemies two of their strongest supporters. Are you not human enough to be glad of it?"

"No," Alf repeated. "You called me. I came as soon as I could."

"I never—" Adam fell silent. He looked his full age, sixty years and more. Hard years, all of them, and this the hardest of all.

Alf laid light hands upon his shoulders. He shuddered and closed his eyes, but did not draw away. "Brother. Alone of all my enemies, you did what you had to do, for the love of God and of the Church, and never for yourself."

"That I should hear such words from one of your kind . . ." Again Adam shuddered. "Yet you mean them. Soulless, deathless, inhuman—you mean them."

"Perhaps I have no soul, but I am as much God's creature as any other being upon this earth."

" 'Let all the earth proclaim the Lord . . .' Ah God! You torment me."

Alf let his hands fall. "I meant to heal you."

"I think I may be beyond any healing but God's."

"Then I pray that He will make you whole again."

"Perhaps," Adam said, "He will hear you."

The other drew up his hood and gathered his cloak about

him. "If I were a man, I would want to be your friend. Since I am not, may we at least part without enmity?"

Slowly Adam nodded. "That . . . I can give you. I too regret that we are what we are."

Alf bowed to him as if he had been a great lord. "The Lord be with you," he murmured.

For a long while Adam stood where Alf had left him. At last he raised a trembling hand and sketched a blessing in the air. Very softly he whispered, "And with your spirit."

24

"The Devil's Crown." Richard held it up to the light: the great Crown of Anglia, set with rubies like drops of blood. "That's what my father used to call it." He set it on the bed beside Alf, rubbing his brows where the weight had plowed deep furrows in the flesh. "He used to call us the Devil's brood, and say that his grandmother would be delighted to see what we'd turned into."

"There's no taint of evil in you," Alf said, venturing to touch a point of the crown with his fingertip. "Nor in this," he added, although he sensed power in it, the power almost of a sacred thing.

"I'm the great-grandson of a devil," Richard said.

"The Demon Countess? Maybe she was one of us."

"Hardly. She'd sit through Mass just up to the Credo, no more. The day her lord made her stay longer, she held on until the Consecration; then she grabbed up the two closest of her offspring and flew shrieking out of the window. No one ever saw her or the boys again. Likely enough, when Father went to his well-deserved place in Hell, he found his uncles there already, stoking the fires."

"I think you're proud of it."

The King grinned at him. "Why not? It's a noble ancestry, though it's come down a bit in the world."

"My lord!"

Richard laughed aloud. "You look like a virgin in a guardroom."

"I *am* a—" Alf bit his tongue. "Sire, I'm learning to live as a worldling, but couldn't I do it slowly?"

"All at once, or not at all," Richard decreed. He tilted a jar, found it still half full of spiced wine, poured a cupful for each of them. "Consider it a punishment. Because of you, I'll be riding to war with half the men I need and with winter breathing down my neck."

Alf held the cup but did not drink. "You persist in this madness?"

"In spite of all your tricks," Richard answered, "yes."

"When?"

"Tomorrow."

Alf took the crown and laid it on his knee. It was very heavy, too heavy, surely, for a mortal head to bear. "Take me with you," he said.

The King paused. Alf did not look at him. "What would you do on a winter campaign?"

"Ride," Alf answered. "Tend the wounded."

"And browbeat me into surrender. No. You'll stay here and mend. When the court goes to Winchester for Yule, you'll go with it."

"I would rather go with you, Sire."

"You'd rather I didn't go at all." Richard drained his cup and retrieved the crown from Alf's lap. "When I get back I'll have another of these for you to play with."

"You'll have a wound that will drain your life away, and two kingdoms in revolt, and the Flame-bearer ravaging your coasts."

Alf's eyes were blurred, unfocused, his voice too soft to be so clear. The King shivered with a sudden chill. Yet he spoke lightly. "So. You're a prophet, too."

"No. I see the patterns, that is all."

"My pattern has two crowns in it and Jerusalem at the end of it."

"Two hundred years ago," said Alf, "there was a very learned man who rose to the Papacy. He had been promised that he would not die until he had seen Jerusalem. Being a clever man, he decided to live forever, for he would never leave Rome. But one day he fell dead upon the steps of a church within sight of his palace. The name of the church was Jerusalem."

"I should put you in a bottle like the old Sibyl, and never uncork you."

Alf smiled faintly, set his untouched cup aside, and rose.

"You're not supposed to get up until tomorrow," the King said.

"Really?" Alf asked. "I walked to St. Benedict's this morning to see Brother Adam, who was my questioner. I've shaken his faith very badly; I wanted to give him what comfort I could." He sighed and took up his tunic. "I didn't give him much."

"Was there ever anyone like you?" the King demanded of him.

Carefully Alf drew on the tunic, and then the cotte. As he fastened the belt he said, "If you're leaving tomorrow, I'd best get all your letters done today. There must be a week's worth to do."

"You'll do nothing of the sort. Get back into bed and stay there."

"Not to mention your mother's letter, which you've put off answering. And the matter of the estate in Poitou—"

"Alfred."

"Yes, Sire?"

"Go to bed."

"Saving your grace, Sire," Alf said, "no. I suppose my writing case is still in the solar?"

Richard snarled in exasperation and let him go.

Alf set down his pen. He had finished his third letter, and he was more weary than he cared to admit.

He looked about the solar. The King conversed quietly with one or two of his knights, considering matters of the war. The usual complement of servitors moved about or stood at attention. No one glanced at the clerk in his corner, although there had been stares enough when first he came. He had disappointed them by seeming the same as ever but for his hollowed cheeks and his secular dress, and by settling quietly into his old task of writing letters for the King. They had expected more of one charged with witchcraft and proven a saint.

He reached for a new sheet of parchment. His back twinged; his half-smile turned to a grimace. He moved more carefully to sharpen his worn quill.

A disturbance drew his eyes to the door. The guard within conferred with the guard without and turned. "Sire!" he called out. "Owein of Llanfair, courier of the King of Gwynedd, asks grace to converse with Your Majesty."

Alf crossed himself. "*Deo gratias*," he murmured, no more than a sigh.

The man entered with dignity, although he was wet to the skin and plastered with mud. He wore no livery nor any sign of rank, but the brooch which clasped his cloak bore the dragon of Gwynedd and the eyes which scanned the room were proud, almost haughty. They fixed without hesitation upon Richard; the messenger limped forward to sink to one knee before the King.

"Your Majesty," he said in a clear trained voice, "your royal brother of Gwynedd sends his greetings and his respect."

Richard's amber glare had passed him by to burn upon Alf. *Your doing*, it accused him. *Damn you!*

Alf smiled. A vein pulsed in the King's temple; it took all of his control to say, "Anglia responds with similar sentiments."

The envoy bowed his head and raised it again, and took from his wallet a sealed letter. "My royal lord bids you accept this epistle, and with it his goodwill."

Richard took the letter but did not break the seal. "What is his message?"

"'To our dear brother of Anglia,'" responded the messenger, "'we have held our throne now for two years and two seasons, since the lamented death of our father, whom God cherishes now among His angels; in our poor fashion we have endeavored to govern his kingdom as he desired it to be governed. In particular, we have attempted to maintain relations with our neighbor and dear friend in Anglia, for whom–'"

Richard cut him off. "Never mind the bombast! I can read it easily enough myself. What does Kilhwch want?"

Owein's face did not change, although his eyes flickered. Amusement, Alf realized, and reluctant admiration. "Your Majesty, the words he spoke to me were blunt and without embellishment. But he bade me couch them in the terms of courtesy."

"Courtesy be damned. What did he say?"

Alf had come quietly to stand behind the King. The messenger's eyes widened a little; he closed his mouth upon his protest and bowed slightly, yet with more respect than he had shown the King himself. "His Majesty of Gwynedd said to me, 'Pretty it up, Owein. But make sure you let him know that his barons are raising hell on my borders, and that my barons are like to raise hell in return; and that's no good to either of us. I'll see him and talk to him in any place he chooses; maybe we can put out this fire that's threatening to burn us both out of our kingdoms.'"

Richard's brows had drawn together until they met; his eyes had begun to glitter. "Kilhwch won't fight?"

Owein maintained his serenity. "My liege desires a conference. The place is to be of your choosing; he asks that you come as he will, with no more than twenty knights in attendance and in certainty of his friendship."

"He wants peace? Bran Dhu's son wants peace?"

"The King of Gwynedd desires what is best for his kingdom."

Richard broke the seal and skimmed the letter, muttering to himself. "'Kilhwch of Gwynedd to Richard of Anglia, greeting . . . Conference . . . alliance . . . friendship . . . Given in Caer-y-n'Arfon, four days before the Calends of December.'" He looked up sharply. "It took you this long to ride to me?"

The messenger nodded briefly. "Yes, Sire. My horse was shot from under me as I passed the border; I walked until I found another; there were other difficulties."

"Pursuit," Alf said softly. "Battles. A wound. And cold and famine and this deadly rain."

Again Owein bowed, with respect which came close to reverence.

Richard looked from him to Alf, tugging at his beard. At length he said, "I'll consider my reply. Giraut, take this man and see that he's well cared for. I'll call for him later."

For a long while after the messenger had gone, escorted by the King's page, no one moved or spoke. Save the King, who paced like a caged beast.

He came to a halt in front of Alf. His glare swept the solar. "All of you. Out."

They obeyed swiftly. One or two shot pitying glances at Alf. The King's wrath looked fair to break upon his head.

When the last small page had passed the door, Richard smiled sweetly. "Now, my fair young friend," he said. "Suppose you tell me exactly how you managed to concoct this plot with the King of Gwynedd."

"To concoct what plot, Sire?"

Richard shook his head. The rubies flashed and flared upon his crown. "No, Alfred. Don't play the innocent here. Just tell me the truth."

"Very well, Sire," Alf said calmly. "The truth is that Kilhwch of Gwynedd is a wise man, and he sees no profit in a war between your kingdoms. And you, Sire, are furious, and ready to force a conflict for pride and for folly."

The King's breath hissed between his teeth.

Alf nodded as if he had spoken. "Yes. I dare much. Overmuch, perhaps. But only because I wish you well."

"You wish me hamstrung and unmanned."

"I wish you strong upon a strong throne." Alf sat at the King's worktable with grace which concealed his growing weakness.

"Sire, if you agree to this meeting you suffer no disgrace. Your friends will be glad that you don't try to sap the kingdoms' strength with a useless war; your enemies will be mortified. They're relying on your falling into the trap."

"Weaselling words. Maybe you're my enemy."

Alf held out his hands, the wrists bearing still the marks of chains. "I won't contend with blind anger that knows full well that I speak the truth. For Anglia's sake, Sire. For your own. Agree to meet with Kilhwch."

"You take a lot on yourself, for an unfrocked priest."

"Yes," Alf agreed. "I do."

"Damn you!"

Richard raged about the room, fists clenching and unclenching, jaw working. Alf watched him and tried to forget the pain which darkened the edges of his vision. He could not faint now—must not. He gathered all of his waning strength and held it tightly, waiting for the King's temper to cool.

It calmed long before Richard wished it to, nor would it rouse again. Cold reason dulled the fire; calculation slew it altogether. The King stopped and glared at Alf, who seemed intent upon a letter. He looked pale, haggard; a dark stain was spreading over the back of his cotte. The hand which held the letter trembled just perceptibly.

Richard snarled and cursed him. He did not look up. But Richard had seen enough men on the edge of endurance to recognize another.

And he had done it all with quiet, monkish obstinacy, to get what he wanted.

"Damn you," Richard said again, little more than a whisper. "You're worse than a woman. Or is that what you are?"

Alf smiled and shook his head. "In the words of your former squire, I have a face like a girl's. But the rest of me . . ."

"The rest of you ought to be roasted over a slow fire."

Alf had gone back to his reading.

Richard snatched the letter from his hand and dragged him to his feet. "All right, damn you. I'll go to meet this wonder-child, this wise old sage of seventeen."

"Nineteen, Sire. Nearly twenty."

"What! So ancient?"

"So ancient," Alf said. "I'm glad you've come to your senses."

"I think I've lost them altogether."

Alf smiled again, but his lips were white. "Sire, if you don't mind . . . may I sit down?"

"You're going back to bed."

And Richard carried him there, past staring faces and in spite of his protests. When he lay in the royal bed with the King's surgeon tut-tutting over his reopened wounds, Richard said, "You've won. It's cost you your vocation and half your hide, but you've won."

Alf winced as the surgeon probed too deeply, and blinked away tears of pain. But he spoke as clearly as if he had been lying at his ease. "Sire. If you really want to do this, I know where you can meet with Kilhwch."

"Of course you do. You plotted this months ago."

"Days, Sire. There's a place not two days' ride from Gwynedd across Severn's mouth, with room enough to house two kings and their escorts; the Abbot there—"

"Abbot, sir?"

Alf nodded. "I'm speaking of St. Ruan's, Sire."

"I suppose the Abbot's in the plot, too?"

"If plot you choose to call it. The man whose errand I took on myself is still there, a lord of Rhiyana who can speak for the Elvenking. Think of it, my lord! Three kings and three kingdoms united in amity, with the Church as witness. Your enemies will gnash their teeth in rage."

"You can play me like a lute," Richard said. "God knows why I stand for it."

Alf smiled. "Because, Sire, you need my meddling. Your reputation forbids you to be sensible, but if you can blame it on my plotting, you can do whatever is wisest, and confound your enemies without awakening them to the truth."

"Flatterer. Go to sleep and leave me in peace."

Obligingly Alf closed his eyes. Richard stood for a while, watching the surgeon's deft gnarled hands, flinching from the sight of the outraged flesh. "Goddamned martyr," he muttered.

The pale face did not change. Richard's hand crept out to touch it; stopped short; withdrew. He turned on his heel and strode out.

25

Kilhwch's messenger left at dawn, well-fed and newly clothed, with the King's horse under him and the King's letter in his satchel, and gifts of gold and food and safe-conduct to ease his way to Gwynedd.

Richard rode out well after sunrise with twenty knights at his back, and among them, Aylmer and a grim-faced novice. And, falling in behind as they left the keep, a rider in blue on a gray mare. His hood was drawn up against the cold, the rest of him well-muffled.

The King's men exchanged glances. One or two dropped back; two more fell in on either side of him, concealing him from the crowd which had gathered to see the King go.

It was the wind which betrayed him. As they neared the south gate—as the King passed beneath its arch—a gust blew back his hood, baring his head. A flash of sunlight caught it and broke into rays about it.

A shout went up. A single voice at first above the cheering for the King: "The saint! The saint!" Two joined it, three, a dozen, a hundred; the crowd surged forward. Voices, faces, minds beat upon all his senses. "Let me touch you—don't go away—my baby's sick—my eyes, my sore eyes—my leg—my arm—my hand—it hurts—oh, God, I hurt—"

The gate arched above him. The voices thundered in the hollow space, beating him down.

And suddenly he was free. The mare moved into a canter, keeping pace with the beasts about her. The shouting faded behind them.

Alf did not look back. His protectors moved away; the mare lengthened her stride. She ran as lightly as a deer among the heavy destriers.

Just behind the King, she slowed. Richard rode between Aylmer and Jehan; only the novice acknowledged Alf's presence. He reined back his mount to keep pace with the mare, and regarded Alf with a wild mingling of joy and anxiety. "Brother Alf! You weren't supposed to come."

"Should I have stayed behind in *that?*"

Jehan glanced back. Carlisle huddled within its red walls, crowned with its red keep; about its gate seethed the crowd which had sought to overrun Alf. He looked at his friend, who rode with eyes fixed forward, face white and strained. "I am not a saint," Alf said. "I am—*not*—a saint."

"You're ill," Jehan said.

Alf shook his head sharply. "I'm somewhat battered, and I'm a little weaker than I should be. That's all."

"A *little* weaker!"

"Would you be able to keep from shaking if you'd just been canonized?" Alf stared at his hands. In spite of his words they were almost steady. "She said it would happen. They would canonize me, or they would burn me. They tried both."

"Brother Alf—"

He straightened in the saddle. "Don't call me that."

"Brother Alf," Jehan said stubbornly, "you're trying to uncan-onize yourself by proving just how nasty, disobedient, and downright human you can be. Don't you know by now that you don't have to prove anything to me?"

"Maybe," murmured Alf, "I need to prove it to myself."

Richard looked back, a fierce amber glare. "Take my word for it. You are nasty, disobedient, and downright human. And damnably clever. I should send you back to Carlisle and make you find your own way out of the mess you made there."

"Sire! I—"

"Look at that," Richard said to Aylmer. "Injured Innocence, done to perfection. Should I send him back? Or should I let him find out for himself that he's not half strong enough to keep the pace I'll set?"

Aylmer met Alf's glance with a dark steady stare. To the King he said, "He was determined enough to come over your express command. Let him stay. He can pay whatever penalty he has to pay."

Alf nodded. "Just because I've been a priest, Sire, doesn't mean you have to treat me as if I were a woman or a child. I can do whatever I have to do."

"Do you mean that?" Richard demanded.

"Yes, Sire."

"Well then. You've cost me an esquire. Take his place. That means you'll be treated exactly like any other squire—the good and the bad. You'll be bowed to, but you'll have to work; if you slack up you get a beating. And you'll be exercising at arms whenever you get the chance. Do you still want to ride with me?"

"Yes, Sire," Alf replied without flinching.

"That's a commitment, boy. From the moment you take my hand and swear on it, you're mine until I see fit to let you go." Richard held out his mailed hand. "Will you take it? Or will you go back?"

Alf hesitated only briefly. He clasped the King's hand and met the King's eyes. "I shall try not to disgrace you."

"You'll do more than try. I'll give you till evening to learn what you've got yourself into." Richard turned his back on him and clapped spurs to the red stallion's sides. "*Allez-y!*"

Jehan dropped back with Alf to the rear of the column. "I think he planned that," the novice called over the thunder of hoofs.

"I know he did. Look—not a single royal squire in all this riding."

"And you *let* him?"

"I came, didn't I?"

Jehan shook his head. "It's a long leap from saint to squire, and you started as a monk. You've got a lot to learn."

"Then you'd best teach it to me. I've only got till evening."

"Thank all the saints you're clever, then."

To Jehan's amazement, Alf laughed. "Too clever, maybe. Come now, Master, your pupil's ready. Will you keep him waiting?"

By nightfall the travelers had found lodgings in a baron's drafty barn of a castle, driving that provincial notable to distraction with the honor and the terror of playing host to the King. In such confusion, any number of errors could have gone unnoticed. But Alf labored to do exactly as Jehan had taught him. He won no reward for his effort, not even a glance from Richard, but he had expected none.

The lord and his lady boasted the luxury of a chamber to themselves, an airless cell behind the hall, nearly filled with a vast featherbed. This Richard was given as his due, nor in courtesy could he refuse it. He sought it soon enough, if none too soon for his newest squire, who had served as cupbearer through an interminable feast. Alf had locked his knees with an effort of will, else he would have collapsed in the hall with every eye fixed upon him.

But Richard, it seemed, had not yet forgiven his disobedience. Even as the King rose from the high seat, he crooked a finger. "Alfred. You'll wait on me."

Alf bowed as deeply as he could. He knew he looked stiff, arrogant; he was past caring. His sight had begun to narrow. Grimly he focused it on the King and on the path he must take. Across the dais, up a steep railless stair, through a heavy curtain. Somehow he had acquired a lamp, a bowl filled with tallow, its wick a twisted rag. As if his eyes needed—

They fixed before him. Not far. Not far at all. Slowly. They
would take it for stateliness, the proper gait of a servant before
his King. The lamp's smoke was rank; oddly, the stench revived
him a little. He set his foot upon the stair.

Richard inspected the bed and pulled a face. "Fleas in the
mattress for sure," he muttered, "and lice, and worse things yet,
I wager. And this sheet hasn't been washed since King Harold's
day."

Alf set the lamp in a sooty niche. However cramped this
chamber was between two tall men and a bed as broad as a
tilting-yard, it lacked at least the press of bodies below. He could
see again; he could speak, though not strongly. "There are no
vermin here now, Sire."

The King's eye flashed upon him. "Don't like you, do they?"

"Like you, I prefer to live without them."

"And you, unlike me, have the means to assure it. Would you
happen to have a similar predilection for clean sheets?"

Alf granted him half a nod, the bowing of the head but not
the raising. Gently, completely, his knees gave way beneath
him. At least, he thought, it was a clean bed he fell to.

Would have fallen to. Richard had caught him, eased him
down, pulled off his surcoat. "You're bleeding again. Idiot."

Alf tried to shrug free, but for once Richard's hands were too
strong. "I'm strong enough still; I can serve you. Later—Jehan
can—"

"You're weak as a baby. Where'd those fools put—ah. There."
Richard had Alf's own baggage, opening it, searching swiftly
through it. In a moment he brought out the rolled bandages
and the salve the doctor had made, that Alf had made stronger
with his own healer's skill.

"Sire," Alf said, "how came these to be—"

"A squire stays with his lord. Particularly if he doesn't want
the world to know that he's out on his feet." Richard began to
ease the shirt from Alf's shoulders. Here and there it had clung

where blood had dried, fusing linen to bandages and bandages to torn skin.

"Majesty. You can't wait on me like this. I won't allow it."

"A squire allows anything his King commands. Hand me the basin. Ah, good. Clean water at least. Hold on, boy. This will sting."

Like fire. But it was a clean fire, and Richard was surprisingly skillful. With a small sigh Alf accepted the inevitable. He let his body rest, sitting upright, eyes closed. Richard's voice was a soothing rumble in his ear. "Well now. I haven't lost much of my skill. I used to be a good hand at field-surgery—from necessity at first, then I rather liked it. It's a good thing to know when you're on the field and your men are falling everywhere, and you need every hand you can muster."

If the water had stung, the salve was agony. Alf's jaw clenched against it. With infinite slowness it passed, bound beneath the clean bandages.

Carefully but firmly Richard completed the last binding. Alf mustered the will to move, at least to turn his head. The King had fallen silent, sitting very close, his gaze very steady.

Alf's throat dried. Between exhaustion and pain, he had closed his mind against invasion—and against perception. He had only done as he was bidden, gone where he was sent, endured until he might rest. Bringing himself to this.

The King would not ask. Not openly. Nor would he compel. Yet, at ease though he seemed, every muscle had drawn taut.

Richard laid his hand on Alf's brow as if to test for fever. "You're burning," he said. But his palm was hotter still.

Alf swallowed painfully. He was not afraid, but he could have wept. Should have, perhaps. Richard hated tears; they put him in mind of women.

Alf forced himself to speak in his wonted voice, light, cool, oblivious. "It's not a fever I have, Sire. I'm always so. My power causes it." He managed the shadow of a smile, moving as if to seek comfort for his back, sliding as by chance from beneath

the King's hand. "It's a very great advantage in a monk. All those
cold vigils . . . I make a wonderfully effortless ascetic."

That shook laughter from Richard, though it held less mirth
than pain. "There's no need for a vigil tonight. I'll look after
myself. Lie down and sleep—the bed's big enough for my whole
army."

"Sire—"

"Lie down."

There was a growl in Richard's voice, the hint of a warning.
Mutely Alf obeyed him. It could not matter now what people
thought or said, and the bed was celestially soft.

Richard stripped with dispatch and without modesty, took
his generous half of the bed, and fell asleep at once. There was
a royal secret, to lose no sleep over what could not be mended.

Alf had no such fortune. Now that he was almost in comfort,
laid in the bed he had longed for since midmorning, his strength
had begun to repair itself; it grew and spread, filling him, driving
back the mists from body and brain.

For a long while he lay awake, now on his side, now on his
face. The lamp sputtered and died. Richard snored gently. In
the hall, a hound snarled; a man cursed; the hound yelped and
was abruptly still.

At last Alf rose, moving softly lest he wake the King. He drew
on his shirt, gathered his cloak about him.

The stair from the hall continued upward to emerge upon
the barbican. The wind smote Alf's face, clear and cold; the
stars blazed in a sky from which all clouds had fled. He turned
his eyes to them and breathed deep. His exhaustion had vanished, and with it his heart's trouble. He felt as light and hollow
as he had in the trial, stripped of his vows and of his sanctity,
made anew, squire-at-arms of the King of Anglia.

His hand went to his head. His hair was growing with speed
as unhuman as his face; in a month or a little more, no one would
know that he had ever been a priest. Even here, even now,
his host had regarded him with interest but no curiosity, taking

him for a young nobleman whose family had recalled him from the priesthood. Such men were common enough.

And could he play that part as he had played the other? Fifty years a priest and a scholar, fifty years a squire, a knight, a lord of the world. And then—what then? Priest again, or something else?

The stars returned no answer. They were older than he and wiser, and content to be what they were. They did not need a flogging to shake them into their senses.

Carefully, gingerly, he flexed his shoulders. With time and patience he would heal; the pain was his penance. The pain and the scars. His vanity had suffered nearly as much as his flesh itself.

Someone mounted the steps. He moved away, pricked irrationally to annoyance. The newcomer paused as if to get his bearings, then turned toward him. He leaned upon the parapet and pretended to be absorbed in his thoughts.

"Little Brother," said a voice he knew very well indeed, "are you so sorry to see me?"

Thea regarded him with eyes that caught the starlight, turning it to green fire. He had forgotten how very fair she was.

"Thea," he said through the thundering in his blood. "Althea. I thought you weren't coming back."

"I? I'm not so easily disposed of. Besides," she added, "I had this." She held out her hand. Silver gleamed in it. "I knew you'd want it back."

He did not move to take the cross. "Keep it."

"It's yours."

He shook his head. "I gave it to you. You can sell it if you don't want it."

"Of course I want it!" she snapped. "But it belongs to you. Will you take it or do I have to throw it at you?"

He kept his hands behind his back. "I'm not a priest now. I'm the King's squire. I want you to keep the cross."

"That is supposed to be a logical progression?"

The blood rose to his cheeks. "Will you please keep it?"

Thea's fingers closed over the cross. "All right. I will. Though I know what your Abbot will say."

"Morwin will say that I had a noble impulse, and leave it at that."

"Will he?"

Alf turned outward, letting the wind cool his face.

"I've met him," she said. "I like him. He's wise and he's sensible, and he's not at all afraid of the female race."

"All that I lack, he has." Alf glanced at her. "Alun let you find St. Ruan's."

"Finally," she said. Her voice changed, hardened. "And no wonder it took him so long. Prince Aidan is going to raise Heaven and Hell when he sees what's been done to his brother."

"Not if Alun can help it."

"Alun is going to have his hands full. And since he's only got one he can use, he's likely to lose the fight."

"He didn't lose it to you."

"I'm not Prince Aidan."

"So I noticed."

She laughed. "Why, Brother! You've grown eyes."

"My name is Alf. I'd thank you to call me by it."

"Pride, too," she said to herself. "The monk's becoming a man."

"I was always proud, though maybe I was never much of a man."

"Don't say that as if you believed it." She stood very close to him, almost touching; the wind blew a strand of her hair across his face. "What did you think of my miracle?"

He could hardly think at all. Yet words came; he spoke them. "We're part of local hagiography now. The saint, and the angel who saved him from the fire. The Paulines are furious."

"I meant them to be. But what did *you* think?"

"I thought you were blasphemous, sacrilegious, devious, and splendid."

"Not hateful?"

"Maybe a little," he admitted.

"Swiftly and virtuously suppressed. Alfred of St. Ruan's, I don't know why I endure you."

"I'm afraid I do."

"Afraid, little Brother?"

"Afraid, little sister."

"Now I know how to break you of your bad habits. Peel you out of your habit, clap you in chains, and whip you soundly."

"And threaten to burn the woman I—a woman of my own kind."

"The woman you what?"

He would not answer.

She made a small exasperated noise. "It's the tender maid who's supposed to blush and simper and pretend to be modest. Why don't you come out and say it?"

"Why don't you?"

For the first time since he had known her, he saw her blush. Brazen, shameless Thea, who had cast defiance in the face of holy Church and set out coolly to seduce a priest—Thea blushed scarlet, and could not say a word.

Her confusion gave him more courage than he had ever thought he had. "It was easy enough when I was only a pretty innocent to tease me into tears. Then you realized that I mattered. I, not the diffident little Brother, not the fool who tried to fall on his sword because he discovered that he could use one and to be put to death because he couldn't face himself. When you flew out of the fire, you mocked all my pretensions; you made me see them for what they were."

"I'd have done that for anyone," she said sharply.

With breathtaking boldness he touched her cheek. It was very soft. "Would you have come back for anyone?"

"The cross—"

"Morwin could have kept it for me. It was his, first."

"You are the worst possible combination of divine wisdom and absolute idiocy."

"And you are as prickly as a thorn tree and as tender as its blossom." He laughed a little, breathlessly. "Thea, you make my head whirl; and I'm still in Orders though I've suspended myself from my title and my duties. What are we going to do?"

"You can go and pray and mortify your flesh. I—" She tossed her head proudly. "I'll find myself another Lombard prince and run away again."

"Maybe that would be best."

She whirled upon him. "Don't you even care?"

"I care that I can't be your lover, and that we would only torment one another."

"You're not a gelding."

"No. I'm worse. I'm a priest who believes in his vows. And you care now for me, or you'd have seduced me long since. Your thorns are thick and cruel, Thea, but your heart is surpassingly gentle."

"It's black and rotten, and it damns you."

"I think not."

"You bastard!"

"Probably."

She struck him, a solid, man's blow that sent him careening to the stones. As he struck them, he cried out.

Her own cry echoed his. He rolled onto his face; she dropped beside him, reaching for him. Without warning the pain was gone. She knelt frozen, her face a mask of agony.

He dragged himself to his knees and shook her. "Thea," he gasped. "Thea, for the love of God, *don't!*"

The pain flooded back, almost welcome in its intensity. Thea sagged in his hands. "I tried to heal it," she said faintly. "I don't have the gift. I can't even—Oh, how can you bear it?"

"Not easily. But I provoked you."

"I didn't have to hit you. Now it's all opened again, worse than before, and you—how you hurt! Let me take some of it. Just a little. Just what I added to it."

"You didn't add much." He drew a breath carefully. "It's passing. You took the worst of it."

"I had to. I always hurt what I care for. Always. Always."

"Thea, child—"

"I'm not a child!"

"Nor am I so very little a Brother; and I'm much older than you."

"Not where it matters."

"Maybe not. But, Thea, you see what I can do to you."

"And I to you." Her composure had returned, ragged but serviceable. She shook her head. "Little Brother, after you a Lombard prince is going to be very dull."

"Peaceful."

"No. Dull. What will people say if your white hound comes back?"

"That my familiar has found me again."

"That won't do," she said. "I'll think of something else."

"You could wait with Alun in St. Ruan's."

"I could." She stretched as high as she might and kissed his brow, lightly. "Good night, little Brother."

He bowed so calmly that he might have seemed cold, but his heart was hammering. "Good night, little sister," he said.

26

They rode hard from castle to castle, round Bowland and its shadows to the dark hills of the Marches and the flood of Severn, swollen with rain; and at last, the dim and misty country about the Isle of Glass. Only a month ago, Alf had left it, yet he looked on it with the eyes almost of a stranger. Literally indeed when his mind touched Thea's, flying with her on falcon-wings, soaring high above him. *I was a monk when I left*, he thought, *driven into exile. Now I'm—what?*

An eagle learning to fly, she answered him.

I feel like a roast swan. Plucked, gutted, and done to a turn.

Her laughter was both an annoyance and a comfort.

The last day began in a driving rain, but toward noon the downpour eased, freeing the sun. Jehan pushed back his hood, shook his sodden hair, and laughed. "There!" he cried. "St. Ruan's!"

The King wrung water from his cloak and sneezed. "The first thing I'll ask for is a draught of their famous mead."

"Roast apples," Jehan said. "Warm beds. Baths."

"No more water for me!" cried the knight behind him. "I've had enough to last me a good fortnight."

Richard grinned. "Come on. First one to the gate gets a gold bezant!"

The gray mare was swifter by far than any of the heavy chargers, but she ran far behind. Jehan held in his own mount in spite of his eagerness, looking back with troubled eyes. Now if ever Alf's brittle new mood would shatter.

He seemed calm enough, although he kept Fara to a canter. He even smiled and called out, "Won't you race for the bezant?"

"Won't *you?*" Jehan called back.

He shook his head.

Jehan hauled his destrier to a heavy trot and waited for the mare to come level with him. "Are you going to be all right?"

Alf's smile turned wry. "Poor Jehan. You're always asking me that. What will I do when I don't have you to look after me?"

"Fall apart, probably. Are you sure you're up to this?"

Alf looked ahead to that race which was like a charge of cavalry, and to the abbey waiting beyond. It floated before them on its Isle of mist and light, but solid itself like the bones of the earth. Its gate was open; he could see figures within, brown robes, faces blurred with distance. "It's odd, Jehan," he said. "I thought I'd hardly be able to stand it—that I'm here, and I don't belong anymore. But it all seems very far away, like something I knew when I was a child."

"I know what you mean." Jehan's gelding snorted and fought his strong hand on the bit. "I'll race you for a bath. Loser gives the winner one."

"Done," Alf said, and gave the mare her head.

They passed the slowest of the knights running neck and neck. Jehan grinned; Alf grinned back and leaned over Fara's neck. She sprang forward, running lightly still, taunting the big gelding with her ease and grace. Jehan had a brief and splendid view of her flying heels.

She thundered through the gate half a length ahead of the

King and wheeled within, tossing her head. The monks had
scattered before the charge, slowed though it was, the more
prudent arriving at a trot. Richard laughed and tossed Alf a coin;
he caught it, face flushed, eyes shining.

The monks stared openmouthed as he slid from the saddle
with the bezant still in his hand.

"Well, Brothers," the King said in high good humor, "I've
brought back your prodigal."

"In grand style," Morwin observed, stepping from behind a
pair of tall monks. "Welcome to St. Ruan's, Your Majesty."

The King knelt to kiss his ring, as was proper even for royalty
in the Church's lands, and turned to present his followers.
Novices took their horses; others led them, once presented,
to the guesthouse.

Alf stood apart with Jehan hovering behind him. None of the
Brothers approached them, although Brother Osric half-moved
toward them and stopped. The King's presence, and their own
air of the world and its splendors, made them strange.

Morwin completed his courtesies. It was odd to watch him
as if he had been a stranger, a small elderly man in an Abbot's
robe, very clean but somewhat frayed.

At last he looked at Alf, a quick encompassing glance,
measuring this falcon he had cast from his hand. Suddenly he
scowled. "This is a fine way to greet an old friend. What are
you hanging back for?"

Alf came to his embrace. He was as thin and fragile as a man
made of sticks, but he was still wiry-strong. He grinned at Alf,
blinking rapidly. "The good Brothers will never get over it.
Gentle Brother Alf who used to have to be dragged bodily out
of the library to see what the sun looked like, roaring in at the
head of a troop of cavalry. The next thing we know, Brother
Edgar will be reading Aristotle."

The other laughed with a catch in it, for Morwin's tight
embrace had kindled sparks of pain.

The Abbot held him at arm's length. "You look as if you've
got a lot to tell me. As soon as I've settled things here, come

and talk." He glanced beyond him, at Jehan. "You make a pair of bashful maids, to be sure. Or are you so used to rubbing elbows with kings and bishops that you can't spare a good-day for a mere abbot?"

"Good day, Dom Morwin," Jehan said obediently, with a glint in his eye.

"That's better." Morwin flung his arms wide. "Welcome back, you two. Welcome back!"

The Brothers crowded round them then, reticence forgotten. In that babble of greeting and of gladness, none but Jehan noticed Alf's pallor. With each hearty embrace it increased; although he smiled and spoke cheerfully enough, his face was drawn with pain.

"You should rest," Jehan said in his ear.

Alf shook his head almost invisibly. "Yes," he said to Brother Osric, "I had a look at some new Aristotle. And a copy of Albumazar in Arabic, from the Crusade. . . ."

"So," said Morwin. "You're the King's squire."

Alf stood by the window of the Abbot's study, gazing at the orchard, bleak now and gray, fading into the early darkness. "Nothing's changed," he murmured. "Nothing at all."

"But you have."

Alf did not answer. Morwin prodded the fire, rousing the embers to sudden flame. He fed it with applewood; the sweet scent crept through the room.

"It's so quiet here," Alf said. "Nothing happens from year's end to year's end, except what's always happened. The trees bloom; the apples ripen; they fall, and the winter comes. The world races past, but no one heeds it, except to spare it a prayer."

"Do you think I shouldn't have sent you out into it?"

Alf sighed. "I've been like a man from the old tales, taken away to the Land of Youth for a night, but that night was a lifetime long."

"It's all too easy to stay a child here, even if your body can grow old."

"I know. Oh, I know!" Alf faced him. "I've been seventeen years old for half a century. And suddenly I feel as if I could advance to eighteen if I tried hard enough."

"So," the Abbot said with a wicked glint, "you've finally caught on."

"God knows, it took me long enough."

"Sit down and tell me about it," Morwin commanded him. "How did you get from monk to royal squire in a little over a month – and half of it spent traveling?"

Morwin listened to Alf's tale, standing by the fire, neither moving nor speaking. When Alf spoke of the trial and of his punishment, the Abbot's face grayed; his eyes glittered. "Show me," he said.

Alf did not move to obey. "There's no need. I'm mending; I'm content."

"Let me see."

"No."

"Alfred," Morwin said, "I want to know what you paid for your foolishness."

"Less than Alun paid for his, and more than you would like." Alf shifted in his seat, and shook his head as the Abbot began to speak. "Let it be, Morwin. It's part of my growing up; you can't protect me from it."

"You don't deserve to be protected."

"Everyone seems to agree with you, myself included."

The Abbot glared at him. He smiled back. Little by little Morwin softened. "Well. You haven't done so badly since. The King seems fond of you."

"I'm fond of him. He reminds me of Jehan. Hot-headed, impetuous, and exceedingly wise when he has to be."

"And fond of letting people underestimate him," Morwin said. "Are you going to stay with him?"

"I'm sworn to it."

"But do you want to?"

Alf stared into the fire. Slowly he answered, "I don't know

what I want. I'm a little afraid to take up a career of arms—it's so alien to all I've ever been or taught. And yet I have a gift for it. Weapons fit my hands."

"You aren't carrying one," Morwin said.

His hand went to his belt where a sword should have hung. "Not yet. But I will. If I continue."

"You doubt it?"

He closed his eyes and shook his head. "I don't know what I'm saying. Of course I'll go on. The King has bound me; I've made up my mind to it."

"It's going to be odd to see you riding about in mail with some lady's sleeve on your helm."

Alf rounded upon him.

Morwin laughed. "That's part of the world, too, Alf. Don't tell me you're that innocent!"

"I'm no more innocent than you."

"Nonsense!" Morwin snorted. "Remember the year in Paris? Every girl we met sighed after you, and you didn't even know what it meant."

"Of course I knew. I was the one who explained it to you. Horrified, you were. *People* did that? But that was for animals!"

"You blushed furiously all the while you told me, too, and swore you'd never stoop so low." Morwin's eyes danced upon him. "You're blushing now. What will you do when you get to court?"

"Nothing," Alf snapped. "I wouldn't want to do anything. I've discovered something horrible, Morwin. I can't bear the thought of . . . making love . . . to human women. They revolt me."

"Whores and sluts would revolt me, even if I weren't under vows—and I'm as human as they are."

Alf shook his head sharply. "It's all women. All human women. And men too, if it comes to that. I can love my fellow man, but not—not carnally."

"And what led you to that sweeping conclusion?"

He would not answer.

Morwin shrugged. "Talk to me again when you're a made knight, and we'll see if you say the same."

"I will."

"We'll see," Morwin said. Even as he spoke, he glanced over his shoulder; his eyes lighted. "My lord! Come in."

Alf had been aware of the listener for some time; he turned, rising, bowing with new-learned grace.

Alun left the doorway, walking unaided although he limped noticeably. His eyes smiled upon Alf; his mind touched the other's, the familiar gentle touch. Alf clasped his good hand and would have kissed it, had not his glance forbidden. "Brother," he said. "Well met."

"Well indeed," Alf responded, looking him up and down. Even lame and with his hand still bound in a sling, even in the brown habit Alf had left him, he looked strong and proud, a knight and a prince.

The smile found its way to the corner of his mouth. "I make a very poor monk, my brother, though I've done my utmost short of actually taking vows."

"He has," Morwin agreed. "Brother Cecil is almost resigned to the loss of his best tenor from the choir since he's gained a splendid bass-baritone in exchange. When you go, God only knows what I'll do to pacify him."

Alf smiled. "And have they put you to work elsewhere?" he asked of Alun.

"No, but not for my lack of trying. Apparently I'm still an invalid."

"Almost," Alf said, "though if you asked, I might let you ride."

"I wasn't going to ask. I was going to do it."

"Fara will be glad to have you back again."

The Rhiyanan shook his head. "I gave her to you, and she has come to love you. Keep her, my brother; in your new station, you need her."

"But—" Alf began.

"It's her wish as much as mine. Take her, Alf."

"My lord, I can't."

Alun sighed. "You can't, but you shall." He sat by the fire, warming his good hand. "Now. Tell me what your King will do."

"Won't you see him yourself?" asked Morwin.

"Not until tomorrow, when Kilhwch comes." Alun's gaze crossed Alf's, held for a moment, flicked away. "Then we'll meet, all three of us."

"Gwynedd and Anglia and Rhiyana," Alf said. "That will be an alliance to reckon with."

"It will indeed," said Alun.

27

The King of Gwynedd rode into St. Ruan's in the late morning, his dragon banner leaping and straining in a strong wind, the sunlight flaming upon his scarlet cloak. Richard waited in the courtyard with his knights about him, vivid figures among the brown-robed monks.

Kilhwch reined his mettlesome stallion to a halt and sprang down. At first glance he seemed ordinary enough, a short stocky young man with a heavy, almost sullen face. But the eyes under the black brows were striking, steel-gray, piercing; flashing over the assembly, taking in each face. They paused several times, at Richard, at the Abbot, at Aylmer. And, for a long moment, at Alf.

He stepped forward, stripping off his gloves and thrusting them into his belt. "Well, my lord of Anglia, you're here before me." His voice was harsh, clipped, his manner abrupt.

Richard's eyes were glinting. "I left as soon as I saw your messenger off. He arrived safely?"

"Safely and in good time, with plenty of good to say about you." Kilhwch's eyes flicked to Morwin. "My lord Abbot, you're generous to lend us your hospitality. If your Brothers would see to my men, we could get to our business."

The Kings ate at the Abbot's table with Bishop Aylmer and one or two of the knights, attended by their squires. In spite of his impatience, Kilhwch seemed content to debate the merits of Frankish and Alemannish chargers and to tell long tales of the hunt and of the joust. He did not move to speak of either war or peace.

He watched Alf steadily, with a look almost of puzzlement. He glanced from the strange face to the royal leopards ramping on the tabard, from the hands which poured his King's wine to the head which bent to catch a comment from the hulking lad in the Bishop's livery. With each glance his frown deepened.

At last he leaned toward Richard. "Your esquire. Who is he?"

Richard bit off half a leg of capon and chewed it deliberately. "Why? Have you seen him before?"

Kilhwch shook his head impatiently. "How long has he been with you?"

"Not long at all. Less than a month."

Kilhwch sat back. His bafflement was turning to anger. "He's been tonsured. Did you snatch him out of a monastery?"

"Yes. This one, in fact." Richard grinned at Morwin. "The Abbot's generosity is legendary."

The young King turned toward Alf, who stood with the other squires by the wall. "You, sir! Come here."

Alf came quietly, with that calm of his which could have passed for haughtiness. "My lord?" he asked.

"What is your name?" Kilhwch demanded.

"Alfred, Sire."

"Alfred? Is that all?"

"Of St. Ruan's, Sire." Alf smiled a very little. "I have no lineage to speak of. If it's that you're looking for, you should talk to my lord Bishop's esquire. He has pedigree enough for both of us."

"Your pedigree doesn't concern me," snapped Kilhwch. "I had

a message from one of the Folk, who gave me to think that
he was with my lord of Anglia. But you're not he. Where is he?"

"Here."

Kilhwch leaped up. Aylmer too had risen, his face as unread-
able as ever.

The young King all but vaulted over the table, and dropped
to one knee. "My lord!" he cried. "What have you done to your
sword hand?"

"Little," Alun answered him, raising him and embracing him
as a kinsman.

He pulled away, eyes blazing. "You went to Rhydderch. After
all my warnings, you went to Rhydderch. And he well-nigh killed
you, from the look of you. I'll have his hide for a carpet!"

"You will do no such thing." Alun's soft voice had a startling
effect. The King of Gwynedd subsided abruptly, like a child
rebuked by his father.

Richard watched them with great interest. "So," he said,
"you're the one who ran afoul of my baron."

Alun nodded, bowing slightly. "My lord of Anglia. I am glad
that at last we meet."

"I've you to thank for my new esquire—and for the fact that
I'm here and not waging war against Gwynedd. You're a shameless meddler, Sir Rhiyanan."

Kilhwch whipped about. "Keep a civil tongue in your head, sir!"

Richard's teeth bared. "I may be rough-spoken, but I don't
run like a dog at some hedge-knight's heel."

"Damn your insolence! Would you speak so of a king?"

"King?" Richard laughed. "King of what? Rags and patches?"

Aylmer stirred. "No," he said. "Rhiyana."

While his King stood speechless, he approached the man in
the brown robe and knelt as Kilhwch had knelt. "Your Majesty,
I thought perhaps it was you."

"And why did you think that?" asked Alun, who was Gwydion.
The hand with which he raised the Bishop flamed with the blue
fire of his signet.

Aylmer shrugged. "It was like you to do something of the sort."

"Nonsense!" Richard burst out. "Gwydion of Rhiyana is unspeakably ancient. This is a boy with his first beard. How old are you, lad? Twenty? Twenty-two?"

"Eighty-one," said the Elvenking, limping forward. Jehan, closest of the squires, leaped to offer him a chair at the end of the high table.

Richard shook his head stubbornly. The gray eyes rested upon him, quiet, amused, and uncannily wise in the smooth youth's face.

"Sire," Alf said. "He is who he says he is."

Richard glared at him. "You knew?"

"From the beginning."

"And you never said—"

"I did not wish it." Gwydion accepted a cup of mead from Alf's hand and sipped it. "It's one thing for the King of Rhiyana to ride abroad alone and under a false name, and another altogether for him to suffer violence at the hands of a foreign king's vassal."

"That," growled Kilhwch, returned now to his place, "it surely is. Before God, that swine shall pay for it."

Richard tugged at his beard, scowling fiercely. "Did he know who you were?"

"Only that I was Rhiyana's ambassador," Gwydion answered.

"And in Rhiyana, do they know?"

"No." Gwydion set down his cup. "My brother's face is the image of mine. I left him holding the crown and the throne; those of our people who saw me go thought I was Aidan, fleeing the peace of Caer Gwent. They think so still."

"Not for long," Kilhwch muttered. "Wait until Aidan finds out that you've been stirring up scorpions' nests on the Marches of Anglia. Half the exploits he's known for are yours—but this one was harebrained even for him."

Gwydion's face grew stern, although his eyes glinted. "Hush, lad! You're giving away state secrets. As far as anyone knows, I sit serenely and pacifically on my throne, and Aidan rides far and wide upon his errantries. Would you ruin the reputations we've labored so hard to build?"

"You've already done it. Spectacularly. And it will be even more spectacular when Aidan gets wind of it."

"Not if we turn failure to success," Gwydion said. "Here we sit all together, which is a thing Lord Rhydderch never looked for. Shall we thwart him further?"

"How?" demanded Richard.

"That's for us to decide. Shall we begin?" He glanced to Morwin. "By my lord Abbot's leave."

Morwin bowed his assent. "Alf—bring out the best wine, the Falernian. And see if Brother Wilfred has any cheese."

Jehan followed Alf on his errand. In the odorous dark of the wine cellar, he gave himself free rein. "Brother Alf! Is Alun really Gwydion?"

"Yes." Alf blew dust from an ancient jar and peered at the inscription upon its side. "Greek wine," he muttered.

"You really have known all the time?"

"Almost." The second jar was Greek also; he frowned.

"How did you know?"

"I was in his mind. He thinks like a King. High, haughty, and most wise." Alf sneezed. "Pest! where is it?"

Jehan held up a small cask. "Here."

Alf glared, and suddenly laughed. "Why didn't you tell me?"

"I wanted you to talk to me. What do you think the kings will do?"

"Kilhwch and Richard will squabble and drink and squabble some more. Gwydion will keep them from each other's throats."

"And then?"

"With luck they'll come to an agreement."

Jehan tucked the cask under his arm and followed Alf among the cobwebbed shelves, past the great tuns of ale. As he mounted the steps to the pantry he said, "They ought to bring Rhydderch here and make him answer for all he's done."

"That's not an ill thought."

Jehan almost dropped his burden. "Thea, for the love of God! Can't you ever come on gradually?"

She laughed and stepped back. Alf closed and locked the door, not looking at her, but Jehan could not tear his eyes away. She stood resplendent in the garb of a high lady, a gown of amber silk embroidered with gold and belted with gold and amber; a golden fillet bound her brows. Rather incongruously, she carried a great wheel of cheese wrapped in fine cloth.

"Where did you get the gown?" Jehan asked her.

"From the air," she answered. "Where else?" She set the cheese in Alf's unwilling hands and pirouetted in the narrow space of the pantry. "Do you like it?"

"You look beautiful," Jehan said sincerely.

Her eyes danced from him to Alf, who had said nothing at all. "You don't agree, little Brother?"

He met her gaze. "Lady, you are beautiful, and you know it."

"And you." Her mockery was brave but shaky. "You make an extraordinarily handsome young squire."

"And an extraordinarily dilatory one. Many thanks for fetching the cheese; will you let me by to take it to Their Majesties?"

"Better yet, I'll go with you."

He opened his mouth to protest, closed it again. "Come then."

The kings were deep in converse with the Abbot and the Bishop, but Thea's arrival silenced them abruptly. Kilhwch grinned a sudden, startling grin. "Thea Damaskena! What are you doing here?"

"Waiting on my liege-lord," she replied with a flash of her eyes, "since he won't let me give his game away to his noble brother."

"And performing an occasional miracle on the side," Richard put in, rising. "Demoiselle, you have my deepest gratitude for saving the life of a certain worthless cleric."

She sank down in a deep curtsey, but her eyes were bright and bold. "You are welcome, Majesty."

Alf had set the cheese on the sideboard and begun with great diligence to cut it. Richard looked from him to Thea, and smiled with a slight edge. "May I ask you something, Lady?"

She inclined her head.

"Why did you do it?"

"Why not?"

Richard laughed. "I can see you're a match for him."

"She's a match for any male alive," said Kilhwch.

"What woman isn't?" She settled between Gwydion and the young King. "Well, sirs. How goes the battle?"

Kilhwch sat back with folded arms, glowering at the table. "Nowhere," he muttered, "and to no purpose. I won't have Anglia's army on my lands, even to round up Rhydderch's troops."

"And I can't control him if I can't get at him," snapped Richard. "If he's not in his castle, I'll damned well have to go after him."

"Take his castle and hold his people hostage."

"That won't be enough. He'll raise the whole Marches around me."

"Then take the whole Marches! Or aren't you king enough for that?"

Richard rose, hand to dagger hilt.

Thea laughed like a clash of blades. "Don't be such witlings! There's a better way than that."

"And what may it be?" Gwydion asked.

"It's not my idea," she said. "Come here, Jehan. Tell them."

The novice started and nearly poured wine into Aylmer's lap. Deftly the Bishop relieved him of flask and cup and said, "Speak up, boy. What would you do if you were a king?"

He swallowed. For the merest instant, he hated Thea cordially. But they were all staring, even Brother Alf; and something in Thea's eyes made him forget fear.

"It's just a simple thing," he said. "You talk about armies and invading each other's lands and stopping uprisings. Why can't you send for Rhydderch and make him come here? He'll have to obey a royal command, especially if it comes from three kings at once."

Gwydion nodded, for all the world like Brother Alf when he had just asked a question and got the answer he wanted. "A point well taken. How could you be certain that he wouldn't destroy your messenger, and claim afterward that none had come?"

"I'd be very careful to send someone with rank enough that his loss would be noticed. And I'd give him a strong escort— half from Anglia maybe, and half from Gwynedd. With a binding on him that if he weren't heard from within a certain length of time, then both kings would fall on him with all the power they could muster."

There was a silence. Jehan's palms were damp; he wiped them surreptitiously on his hose. Both Richard and Kilhwch were frowning. Gwydion, who seldom wore any expression at all, was staring into his cup.

It was he who spoke. "Well, my lords? Would it please you to bring Rhydderch face to face with his crimes?"

"The one against you most of all," Kilhwch said fiercely. "Yes, by God. Yes!"

Richard arranged crumbs in careful order on his trencher, line by line. "One would almost think," he said idly, "that my lord of Rhiyana had had this in mind all the while."

"And if he had," asked Thea, "would it matter?"

He added another line to his army, and over it a banner of rosemary. "I suppose not. Who would go if we agreed to do this? One of us?"

Thea rested a light hand on Gwydion's bandaged one. "That would be tempting fate. It has to be someone whose life isn't vital to the survival of the kingdom. And," she added, for Alf had started forward, "who isn't one of our people. Rhydderch has learned to hate us; we want him to come as quietly as possible, not bound and raging. But since he's madder than a wild boar, his keeper had better be strong enough, and clever enough, to handle him."

Richard nodded slowly. "If I agree, will you give me the right to choose the messenger?"

"Whom would you choose?" Kilhwch asked sharply.

"The best man I know of: well-born, strong as a bull, and clever as a fox."

They were all staring at Jehan again. He stared back and tried not to shake.

Kilhwch's black brows met. "He looks more than strong enough; he seems clever. But he's only a boy."

Thea laughed. Kilhwch's scowl grew terrible. "My ancient lord," she said, "even children have their uses. You were one once. Remember?"

He flushed darkly. "I wouldn't have entrusted myself to Rhydderch's tender mercies."

"Wouldn't you? Who was it who went after a boar with his bare hands? Give in, Kilhwch. Just because you can't go doesn't mean you have to hold him back."

"If he wishes to go," Gwydion said.

Jehan drew a shuddering breath. "Of course I want to. Though I don't deserve the honor."

"Why not?" asked Richard. "You're a Sevigny; you're trained in arms and a scholar besides; and no one who looks at you could possibly think you have a brain in your head. If anyone can lure Rhydderch out of his lair, you can."

He bowed low, unable to speak.

Richard struck the table with the flat of his hand. "Well. That's settled. Alfred, wine for everybody, and double for our ambassador."

As Alf filled Jehan's cup, he met the wide blue stare. His own held fear for the other's safety, but pride also, and deep affection. The novice smiled crookedly and toasted him with a remarkably steady hand, and drank deep.

28

Night was falling with winter's swiftness, but what light clung still to the low sky cast into sharp relief the castle upon its rock.

Jehan muscled his red stallion to a halt; behind him his escort paused. A thin bitter wind tugged at their banners, Gwynedd's scarlet dragon, Anglia's golden leopards.

He stared up at Rhydderch's fortress, his face within the mail-coif grim and set. He liked the sight of the castle as little as Gwydion had. Less.

But Gwydion had not ridden up to it with a dozen knights behind him and two kings' banners over him. Jehan turned in his saddle, scanning the faces of his company. Strong faces, a little disgruntled perhaps to be under the command of a half-grown boy, but warming to his gaze. He grinned suddenly. "Well, sirs. Shall we see if the boar's in his den?"

The drawbridge was up, a chasm between it and the track. Jehan rode to the very edge of the pit, so close that the stallion's restless hoofs sent stones rolling and tumbling into space. No light shone above the gate, nor could he discern any figure upon the battlements.

He filled his lungs. "Hoi, there!" he bellowed.

No response.

Again he mustered all of his strength and loosed it in a shout. "Open up for the King's messenger!"

After an intolerably long pause, a torch flickered aloft. A voice called out: "Which King?"

"Anglia," he shouted back, "and Gwynedd."

Rhydderch's man raised his torch a little higher. Jehan could see a sharp cheekbone, an unshaven jowl. "Take your lies somewhere else and let us be."

One of the knights urged his mount to Jehan's side. Light flared, illumining a thin nondescript face, a straggle of brown beard. But the eyes were Thea's. She raised her brand high, casting its light upon the banners that strained in a sudden blast. Dragon and leopards seemed to leap from their fields toward the guard upon the battlements.

"Open up," Jehan commanded, "and take me to your lord."

"He isn't here," the man said harshly.

Jehan's mount snorted and half-reared. "Then by Saint George and Saint Dafydd, let me in to wait for him!"

The torch wavered. After a moment it dropped from sight.

With a groaning of chains, the drawbridge lowered; the iron portcullis rose. Light glimmered within. Jehan sent the red stallion thundering to meet it.

Jehan sat in the high seat in Rhydderch's hall, his mail laid aside for a princely robe, Kilhwch's gift as the stallion had been Richard's.

Gwydion's gift contemplated the array of dishes which the cook had hastened to prepare for them, and nibbled fastidiously on a bit of bread. "Barbarians," she said in her own voice, although her face remained that of the young knight from Gwynedd.

He nodded, holding his breath as a squire leaned close to refill his cup. The youth had not encountered soap or water in longer than he cared to think. He looked about, surveying

Rhydderch's domain. Caer Sidi was a fortress above all; upon the bare stone walls of its hall hung neither tapestries nor bright banners but ancient shields blackened with smoke. The men beneath them, the servants who moved among the tables, had a dark wild look, ever-wary, like hunted beasts.

"I've seen such faces elsewhere," Thea said in Jehan's ear. "In Sicily in the cave of a bandit chieftain. In Alamut among the Hashishayun."

He shivered and set down his new-filled cup.

She laughed softly. "All men who follow madmen have the same look. But this is only a petty madman and a fruitless madness. You're easily a match for both."

"I'm not so sure," he muttered under his breath.

As the hour grew late, Rhydderch's men waxed boisterous with wine. But Jehan's knights clustered together near the high table, drinking little and eating less, casting longing glances toward the weapons heaped just outside the door. The air about them was heavy with hostility, the servants' conduct hovering on the edge of insolence.

The knights endured it grimly, for they had been chosen with utmost care. But they had their pride. The youngest of them bore with fortitude the wine poured down his rich tunic, but when the offender grinned at him, he struck the man down. The servant leaped up with a long knife gleaming in his hand.

Jehan sprang to his feet. What he felt, he realized later, was not fear but cold fury. His voice cracked through the hall. "Put down that knife!"

Silence fell abruptly. Among Rhydderch's men, eyes rolled white. Half a dozen blades clattered to table or bench or floor, the servant's among them. Jehan caught the knight's blazing eye and willed him to return to his seat. Slowly he obeyed.

Jehan sat himself, trying not to shake. With reaction, or with laughter that was half hysteria. He pushed his cup aside and gathered himself to rise again, to put an end to this mockery of a feast.

And froze. Men had come and gone often, as always during a banquet, but those who strode in came armed and helmeted, their cloaks dabbled with mud.

A short broad man walked at their head, clad in mail with no surcoat. But once one had seen his eyes, one forgot all else — strange, almost as light as Brother Alf's, but red-rimmed and glaring like a wild boar's.

He halted in front of the high table, his men fanning out behind him. Eight, Jehan counted, no more than an escort. But there were five times that in the hall, watching him as the hound watches the huntsman, with hate and fear and blind adoration.

Jehan leaned back, running a cold eye over him. "Is it the custom to walk armed into hall?"

"In my hall," Rhydderch answered, "I make my own customs. Who are you, and what are you doing, lording it in my castle?"

"*Your* castle?" Jehan's eyes were wide, surprised. "Are you the Lord Rhydderch then?" He rose and bowed as equal to equal. "Jehan de Sevigny, body-squire to the Lord Chancellor of Anglia and ambassador from the Kings of Anglia and of Gwynedd, at your service, sir."

Rhydderch's nostrils flared; his knuckles whitened upon his sword hilt. "Anglia?" he demanded. "Gwynedd? Anglia *and* Gwynedd?"

"You heard me rightly," Jehan said. "Come, my lord. Share the feast. Your cook's outdone himself tonight by all accounts."

The baron did not move. "Gwynedd and Anglia together?" He seemed stunned. "What do they want with me? I'm but a poor Marcher lord."

"Let's say," said Jehan, "that you're not as insignificant as you'd like Their Majesties to think you are."

"But not so significant that I'm worth a made knight."

"Well," Jehan said. "There are twelve of them with me, and I'm bigger than any. And the alternative was war." Rhydderch's eyes gleamed; he smiled. "The two kings against you and your men. But they've been feeling compassionate lately. It must have hit you hard when Sir Alun escaped."

It was a long while before Rhydderch could master his voice. "Sir Alun?"

"Of Rhiyana. A remarkable man, that."

"A spy," grated Rhydderch.

"An ambassador," Jehan countered. "Like me, but not quite so well-attended. Nor so well-treated. Through sheer stubbornness he found his way to an abbey. The Abbot sent word to the King, and the King met with Kilhwch of Gwynedd."

"Peaceably?"

"Perfectly so. They're two of a kind, after all."

Rhydderch did not sneer. Not quite. "And why have they honored me with your august presence?"

"Out of longing for your own. You're bidden to attend them on Ynys Witrin as soon as you can ride there."

"I?" Rhydderch asked. "What can I do for Their Majesties?"

"You can go to them and ask."

"And if I don't?"

"If you don't," Jehan said, "they come and get you."

"Am I to be punished for arresting and dealing with a spy?"

"I don't know about punishment, but my lords would like to talk to you," answered Jehan. "You have a day or two to think about it."

"And then?"

Jehan's smile was affable. "If I'm not back in St. Ruan's by the third day from now, in your company, both kings will come to find us. On the other hand, if you ride with me, Richard might be disposed to be friendly. Even if he can't exactly condone his vassals' warmongering in his absence and without his consent, he can understand it."

Slowly Rhydderch shrank in upon himself. He had planned for every contingency but this one, that the kings would ally against him; his swift mind raced, seeking wildly for an opening.

He bowed his head as under a yoke, fierce, hating, yet

apparently conquered. "I'll do as my King commands. We ride out tomorrow at dawn."

Jehan nodded. "Excellent. You may take one man. Be sure he has a good horse."

As Rhydderch turned away, Thea left her seat beside Jehan and followed him. She paused only once, to retrieve her sword from its resting place near the door and to meet Jehan's eye. Her own was bright and fierce. With the slightest of bows, she strode after the baron, silent as his shadow and no less tenacious.

Jehan released his breath slowly and beckoned to the hall steward. "More wine," he commanded.

Somewhat to his surprise, the man obeyed him. He returned to Rhydderch's seat and sat there, lordly, unconcerned, and shaking deep within where no one could see.

29

Half a mile from St. Ruan's, where three days ago Richard's knights had begun their race for the gold bezant, a figure stood alone. From a distance he seemed a lifeless thing, a stone or a tree-trunk set upon the road, dusted with the snow which had begun to fall a little after noon. Now and then a gust of wind would snatch at his dark cloak, baring a glimpse of brightness, scarlet and blue and gold, or plucking the hood away from a white still face that turned toward the north and west.

The snow thickened. He paid no heed to it, nor tried after the first time or two to cover his head, although the flakes clung to his hair and lashes, half-blinding him.

He heard them long before he saw them, the pounding of hoofs, the jingle of metal, the harsh breathing of horses driven fast and hard over rough country. Through a gap in the swirling snow burst a company of knights.

Their leader well-nigh rode over him. The red stallion reared, its iron-shod hoofs seeming almost to brush his face. Its rider cried out, "Brother Alf! For the love of God!"

The stallion stood still, trembling and snorting. Alf laid a gentle hand upon its neck and regarded the company, and Rhydderch a shadow in their midst. He shivered slightly. "You're back," he said, looking from Jehan to Thea. "We've all been waiting for you."

"Obviously." Jehan held out his hand. "Come up behind me."

He shook his head. "Your poor beast has all the burdens he needs." Yet he clasped Jehan's hand, a brief, tight grip, fire-warm, and smiled. "I'm glad to see you safe." He turned away too quickly for Jehan to answer, and swung up behind Thea on the gray mare of Rhiyana.

The kings received the arrivals in the Abbot's hall, in royal state. Even Gwydion had put aside his brown robe for a cotte which seemed made of the sky at midnight, a deep luminous blue worked with moonlit silver in the image of the seabird crowned. Both Richard and Kilhwch, to his right and his left, blazed in scarlet and gold.

Through all the journey from his stronghold, Rhydderch had spoken no word. When royal guards relieved him of his weapons and monks bathed him and trimmed his hair and beard and clothed him as befit his rank, he offered no resistance. He seemed half-stunned by the failure of all he had plotted.

He came before the kings as docilely as an ox led to slaughter, following Jehan blindly, hardly aware of the guards about him.

Before the three thrones they drew away to leave him standing alone. The ambassador named each of the kings for him, and each bowed a high head: Kilhwch of Gwynedd, Richard of Anglia, Gwydion of Rhiyana.

The Elvenking regarded him with a level gray stare, and deep within it a flicker of green fire. Rhydderch started as if struck. For an instant the mute submission dropped away, revealing the black rage beneath.

"Well met, Lord Rhydderch," Gwydion said softly, "and welcome."

Rhydderch's eyes hooded; he bowed low. "I came as you commanded, Your Majesties. What will you have of me?"

"Your company," Richard said, toying with the heavy chain he wore about his neck. "I'm glad you came so quickly. It would have been uncomfortable for us to have to go after you."

"I've always labored to do as my King commands."

"I'm pleased to hear that." Richard gestured; Alf brought a chair. "Sit down and be comfortable. We're all friends here."

Rhydderch sat quietly enough. He had not looked at Gwydion since that first terrible glare. "It pleases me to see Your Majesties so friendly."

"Your doing," Kilhwch said. "Sir. We'll have to thank you properly when there's time."

"My doing, Sire?" Rhydderch asked, as if incredulous. "How can that be?"

"You don't know, my lord?" Kilhwch smiled. "Perhaps my lord of Rhiyana can enlighten you. He's tasted your famous hospitality, has he not?"

Rhydderch frowned slightly. "I can't recall, Sire, that I've ever had the honor of guesting a King."

"Not even the Dotard of Caer Gwent?"

Gwydion stirred. "Kilhwch," he said very low. The young King's mouth snapped shut. He himself leaned back, cradling his broken hand as if it pained him. "I'm not what you expected, am I, Lord Rhydderch?"

"You are precisely what the tales say you are."

"Then you'll admit that you knew who he was?" demanded Kilhwch.

The Elvenking raised his hand. "This is not a trial," he said. "Lord Rhydderch has ridden hard and far, and he has not slept well of late. He is hungry and weary, and much bemused, I am sure, by the suddenness of our summons. Let us eat and sleep; in the morning we may turn to deeper matters."

"I don't like this," Jehan said. "I don't like any of it. I wish I'd never brought that man back!"

It was very late. The kings had long since gone to their beds, but he sat with Alf and Morwin in the Abbot's study. Of all the praise he had had for a task well and swiftly done, theirs was the sweetest. But he had not earned it.

"He came too easily," he went on, "without even trying to fight. Either he's a complete fool—or we are, and he's about to prove it."

Morwin shook his head. "He's a clever man and a vicious one, but he knows better than to set himself against three kings. He planned to prick them into killing each other, without letting them know who was responsible. Unfortunately, one of his provocations turned out to be the very King he wanted to provoke."

"True enough," Jehan agreed, "but you're forgetting something. He looks sane and ordinary, but he's neither. He's had a terrible blow, and he knows he doesn't have much to hope for. The best he can expect is to get his lands back, with a ruinous tax on them and a knight's fee he'll have to struggle to meet. He'll die a pauper, who wanted to be a King. Who knows what he'll do if he breaks?"

"He's here and very well guarded, not in Caer Sidi hatching war. And tomorrow—"

"'And seven alone returned from Caer Sidi.'"

Alf's voice startled them both. He had been sitting quietly, apparently drowsing; his eyes were half-shut, blurred as if with sleep. He sighed deeply and shivered. "He calls his castle by the name of the Fortress of Annwn. Death walks in his shadow. How cold it is!"

Jehan opened his mouth to speak, but Morwin hushed him.

Again Alf shivered. His eyes cleared; he looked about as if bewildered. "I must have been dreaming. I thought someone had died, and Rhydderch had killed him."

Morwin laid a hand on his brow. It was burning hot, yet he shivered violently. "No one's dead, and no one's going to die, least of all at his lordship's hands. Look, Alf. Jehan is back safe and sound, and Rhydderch's surrounded by every guard the kings or the abbey can spare. There's nothing to be afraid of."

Jehan brought him a cup of mead. He drank a little; his

shivering stilled. He tried to smile. "I shouldn't stare into the fire; it makes me see horrors. And Rhydderch isn't a pleasant man to think of. Even Gwydion can't see very far into his mind. It's too dark and too twisted and too wild, like the black heart of Bowland."

"Don't talk about him," Morwin said sternly. "Don't even think about him. That's for the kings to do."

"Low station can be a refuge, can't it?" Alf drank the last of his mead and stood. "We all need our sleep. Come, Jehan."

Morwin had risen with him. "I'm not sleepy yet. I'll walk with you."

"There's no need for you to—"

"What's the matter, Alf? Do you expect me to be waylaid in a passageway?"

Jehan laughed. Alf paled and shuddered, but did not speak.

When Alf lay on his pallet near Richard's door, Morwin drew Jehan aside. "Watch out for him," he said. "When this mood is on him, he's apt to do anything." Jehan nodded, understanding; he smiled. "Good night then. God be with you."

"And with you, Domne," Jehan murmured.

The Abbot blessed him and turned away, walking as lightly as a boy.

30

Rhydderch lay motionless and sweating under thick blankets. Across his door, his own liege-man snored softly. Outside in the passage, two knights slept deep, clasping their swords to their breasts. One was of Anglia, one of Gwynedd.

Carefully he opened his eyes. The moon escaped from its wall of cloud and hurled a bright shaft across the room, transfixing the hilt of his sword. He was not a prisoner. No one had chained him or bolted his door; the guards were for his honor and protection.

His lip curled. They mocked him, those fools of kings. Richard, cheated of a war, turned weakling and woman-heart. Kilhwch, who thought himself so clever and so cruel, who set his man to watch the guest and to kill him—by accident—if he ventured to escape.

And Gwydion. Gwydion, with his bandaged hand which he kept always in sight, and his cold gray eyes, and his too-handsome face. Huw had had orders to break that eagle's beak of a nose; he would lose his own when Rhydderch won free of this gilded trap.

Rhydderch growled deep in his throat. Gwydion had brought

him to this. Gwydion, who refused to age as a man ought, who looked on his enemy with cool and royal scorn. He had not been so haughty when Dafydd plied the hot iron; his blood, royal and immortal though he was, had flowed as redly and as readily as any villein's.

With infinite caution Rhydderch rose. He had kept on his tunic and hose against the cold. Soundlessly he crossed the room.

His hand eclipsed the moonlight upon his sword hilt. He froze for an instant; his guards did not stir. Taking up the sheathed sword, wrapping himself in his cloak, he crept toward the door.

The Lady Chapel glimmered softly by the light of the vigil lamp. It was the fairest of the abbey's chapels, Morwin thought as he paused in its doorway, and the most wonderful, walled with a tracery of pale stone, its altar of white marble inlaid with lapis lazuli. When Morwin was young, some forgotten artisan had painted the curving ceiling the color of the sky at night and set it with golden stars.

He knelt in front of the altar and contemplated the face of the carven Virgin behind it. A gentle face, a little sad, as if it looked upon the ills of the world and mourned for them. But beneath the sadness lay a deep serenity.

He did not pray in words. Somehow the Lady of Comfort was beyond them.

Instead, he remembered. Good things, ill things. Apple blossoms in the spring; plague in the village. The Brothers chanting the *Te Deum*; soldiers chanting a war chant and men screaming. The day of his ordination, he and Alf taking their vows side by side, each serving the other at his first Mass; the day he realized that his hands were twisting and stiffening with age, and that the hairs which fell from the barber's shears were more gray than red; and that his friend, who had been a boy with him, had not changed and would never change.

He sighed. The hands on his knees were like the branches of an ancient apple tree, gnarled and almost sapless. "And I still

don't have a likely successor," he said to the Virgin. "Alf's wings
have spread too wide and he's flown too high. *Mea culpa*, Lady,
mea maxima culpa. I sent him out, knowing what would happen;
that the world would claim him – and heal him a little.

Has it? the calm eyes seemed to ask.

"I don't know. I think it's too early to tell. The scars are still
too deep."

For a while longer he remained there, head bowed. The lamp
flickered. It needed refilling, he thought inconsequentially, and
smiled at himself. That was age and power, to worry about lamp
oil when his mind ought to be on the Infinite.

The abbey was a labyrinth, vast and unlit and stone-cold, and
apparently deserted. Rhydderch's nose wrinkled at the holy stink
of it, rotting apples, long-dead incense. Once or twice a monk
prowled the empty passages; he hid until the shadow passed,
itching to test his blade on priestly flesh. But he had promised
it a better offering.

Light at once alarmed and attracted him. He inched toward it.

A heavy door stood ajar. The light shone beyond it, dim and
unsteady, hanging over an altar. He had found a chapel. From
his vantage point he could see a kneeling figure, a dark robe,
a bowed white head. An elderly monk at prayer, all alone.

Rhydderch drew his cloak over the hand which held the sword
and advanced boldly.

"Excuse me, Brother," he said, softening his voice as much as
he might. "I got up to go to the privy, and I seem to have
taken a wrong turning."

The monk turned. Rhydderch did not pay much heed to the
sharp-featured old face. They all looked alike, these shavepates;
he had another face before his mind's eye, quite another face
altogether.

"Lord Rhydderch," the monk said. He did not sound surprised. "Your room has its own garderobe. Don't tell me your
guard forgot to remind you."

Rhydderch ground his teeth. Thwarted, always thwarted. The

damned witch. He picked a man's mind clean and told the world what he had found.

The sword gleamed naked in Rhydderch's hand. The monk regarded it almost with amusement. "Isn't that a little excessive, my lord? A simple request will do. Shall I take you back to your room, or do you have somewhere else in mind?"

"You," Rhydderch growled. "I ought to know you."

The monk smiled. Small and sharp-nosed and deep-wrinkled as he was, he looked like a bogle from an old nursery tale. "We've been introduced, my lord, though the light's not good here. Just call me *Brother* and tell me where to take you."

Rhydderch raised his sword and rested the point very lightly against the withered throat. "Take me to the Witch-king."

It did not seem to trouble the monk in the least that death pricked his adam's apple. "Well, my lord," he said, "that's a hard thing to do. We're inundated with royalty here, I grant you, but there's none who answers to the name of—"

"Gwydion," snapped Rhydderch. "He calls himself Gwydion."

"And what do you want with His Majesty of Rhiyana at this hour of the night? I can tell you now, my lord, that he's long since gone to sleep and that he oughtn't to be disturbed. Unless, of course," the old babbler added, "it's deathly urgent."

"Urgent. Yes, it's urgent. Take me to him!" A red film had drawn itself over Rhydderch's eyes; his tongue felt thick, unwieldy; his fingers trembled on the sword hilt. The point wavered; the monk winced. A minute, glistening droplet swelled from his throat.

"Now, sir," he said reprovingly. "There's no need to hurt anybody. Why don't you put your sword down and say a bit of prayer with me? Then we can decide if your message is important enough to break into a King's sleep."

"If you don't do as I say," Rhydderch said very low, "I'll hack off your head, tongue and all."

"It's a mortal sin to shed blood in a sacred place, my lord. Not to mention the fact that you'll have to get past three kings and their men to escape. And then where will you go? Come, sir. Let me take you back to your bed, and we'll both forget we ever met each other."

He was smiling. Smiling, damn him, as if he were the one who held the sword, and as if he pitied the poor misguided victim. The witch had smiled so with those cat's-eyes of his, not hating, only pitying. Poor Rhydderch, with his ragged army and his hovel of a castle and his mad dreams of kingship.

The sword retreated. The monk's smile widened. "Ah, my lord, I knew you'd—"

The bright blade whirled in an arc and flashed down.

Jehan spread his pallet next to Alf's, undressed and settled on it. His friend seemed to have fallen into a restless, tossing sleep. He moved as close as he could without actually touching, and tried to think calmness into the other's mind.

After a while it seemed to work, or else Alf had relaxed of his own accord. Jehan dared to close his eyes.

He drifted lazily between sleep and waking, not quite ready to let go. A dream hovered just out of reach.

He started awake. Alf sat bolt upright, his face so terrible that for an instant Jehan did not even know it.

The novice reached for him. "Brother Alf," he whispered. "Brother Alf, it's all right."

The body under his hands was rigid, the eyes all red. "Rhydderch," Alf hissed. "Murder. Sword. Morwin." His lips drew back from his teeth. They were very white and very sharp, the canines longer and leaner than a human's. Jehan had never noticed that before. "Chapel—chapel—*Morwin!*" It was a cry of anguish.

Even before Jehan had scrambled to his feet, Alf was almost out of sight. The other bolted after him.

Rhydderch stood over the crumpled body, breathing hard, the sword dangling loosely from his hands.

A whirlwind swept him up. The blade flew wide; he fell sprawling. His head struck the floor with an audible crack.

Alf dropped beside Morwin. Blood fountained from the deep

wound in the Abbot's breast. Desperately he strove to stanch it, but it spurted through his fingers.

"It's no use, Alf."

In the gray and sunken face, Morwin's eyes were as bright as ever. He grinned a horrible, death's-head grin. "Well, old friend, Cassandra was right after all. I'm sorry I laughed at you."

Alf shook his head mutely. All his strength focused upon the gathering of his power. Slow, so slow, and Morwin's life was ebbing with the tide of his blood. Yet the power was there, as it had not been for Gwydion's healing. It was ready to gather, to grasp—

"*Alf!*"

Morwin's cry brought him to his feet. Rhydderch's sword clove the air where his head had been; madness seethed behind it, a black fire of hate. Kill the monk, kill the witch, kill—

Alf's eyes flamed red. Without a sound he sprang.

Rhydderch fought like a wild boar. But Alf was a cat, too swift to catch, too strong to hold. They swayed back and forth, twined like lovers, battling for the bloody sword.

It fell with an iron clang. Swifter than sight, Alf seized the hilt.

For an instant, the world stood still. So one held the sword. So one raised it, beyond it the hunched black shape, fury turning to fear, fear to blind terror.

In that timeless moment, Alf was completely sane and keenly aware of all about him. The chapel with its gentle Virgin and its golden stars; the Abbot drowning in his own blood; the huddle of stunned figures in the doorway, Jehan foremost, white as death. And Rhydderch.

Rhydderch, who had killed Morwin. Coolly, leisurely, with effortless skill, Alf hewed him down.

31

Very gently Alf cradled Morwin in his arms. The Abbot's body seemed light and empty as a dried husk, but a glimmer of life clung to it still.

He tried to speak. Alf laid a finger on his lips. Already they were cooling. "In your mind," he whispered, "the old way."

The old way, Morwin thought. *Not long now . . . Alf. Promise me something.*

"Anything," said Alf.

The Abbot smiled in his mind, for his grip on his body was loosening swiftly. *Say my funeral Mass.*

Alf flinched. Quietly, steadily, he said, "I murdered a man in cold blood in God's own sanctuary. I am in the deepest state of mortal sin. I can't say Mass for you. It would be blasphemy."

No! Morwin snapped with a ghost of his old vigor. *You said you'd do anything.* Anything, *Alf.*

"Morwin—before God—"

Before God, Alfred, ego te absolvo. . . .

"Morwin!"

Friend, brother, son, thy sins are forgiven. Say the Mass, Alf. For love of me, for love of God. And for your soul's sake, see to his rest the poor creature who killed me.

Morwin's eyes were fading; he blinked, peering through the shadows. *Such a fair face, to be the last thing I see. Are there tears on it? Poor lad. When you've laid this bag of bones in the ground and made your peace with Rhydderch, find your own peace in the City of Peace. What is it that the Jews say? "Next year, in Jerusalem."*

"You—you bid me make a pilgrimage?"

For peace, Alf. To Jerusalem. The darkness was almost complete. But on the very edge of sight glimmered a light. Morwin reached for it. So far, so fair . . . *Alf! Alf, look. It shines. It shines!*

Alf raised a tear-stained face. Jehan was standing over him. "He's gone," he said. His voice was soft, level. "I couldn't follow him. It was too bright." Suddenly, luminously, he smiled. "But he went on; I saw. I felt. There was joy, Jehan. *Joy!*"

The novice stared at him as he crouched there with the Abbot's lifeless body in his arms, his hands red with the blood of the man he had slain and the man he had defended—and on his face, pure joy.

Jehan swallowed hard. Others crowded behind him, an alarming number, the kings, Aylmer, Thea, a handful of knights, several monks, all in various states of undress. Their faces were white with shock; even the kings seemed frozen with the horror of it, a chapel turned to a charnel house, an Abbot foully murdered.

Jehan frowned. Three crowned kings—and not one had the wits to act. He singled out the solid dark figure of Aylmer. "My lord Bishop, you'd best take over the abbey and see that the Brothers know what's happened. Brother Osric, Brother Ulf, take Dom Morwin to the mortuary; you, sir knights, had better see to Rhydderch. Brother Owein, roust out a party of novices to clean up the chapel; it will have to be purified later. And if you please, my lord Gwydion, would you take care of Brother Alf?"

* * * * *

Jehan hesitated at the stair's foot. Gwydion had left Alf in his old cell, by Alf's own choice, for it was quiet and isolated, and it had a door which could be bolted against the world.

With sudden decision, Jehan strode forward. The door was shut; he knocked softly.

"Come in," Alf said.

He sounded like his old self. Jehan lifted the latch and stepped into the cell.

It was the same as it had always been, very plain and very bare. Alf sat cross-legged on the hard narrow bed in his shabby old habit, as if he had never left St. Ruan's at all.

Jehan found that he had nothing to say. Alf looked quiet, serene; he even smiled. "Have they finally let you go?"

"I let myself go." Jehan sat on the bed and looked hard at him. "Brother Alf, are you bottling yourself up?"

Alf shook his head. "I've been talking with Gwydion. That's all."

"But you're so *quiet*."

"Ah," said Alf. "I should be raving and trying to find a sword to fall on." He turned his hands palm up and flexed his long fingers. "Yes. I should be. I killed a man. He killed one who was dearer to me than a brother. And I have to say Morwin's funeral Mass, witch and murderer that I am, suspended from my vows."

"You're none of those things."

He sighed deeply. "Am I not? It's very strange, Jehan. I've tormented myself for so long for so little; now that I have a reason, I find that I can't. I am what I am; I've done what I've done; I can't change any of it."

"Is that acceptance or indifference?"

"I'm not sure yet. Gwydion says it's part of my healing. Thea says I'm finally coming to my senses. I think I'm numb. Either I'll come burning back to life again, or I'll mortify and fall away."

Jehan swallowed, but could not speak.

"'I am the Resurrection and the Life; he who believes in me will never die.'" Alf spoke softly, wonderingly. "To believe that, and to *know* it . . . When I looked into the middle of the Light, Jehan, for a moment I saw Morwin. He was a boy again; and he was laughing."

Jehan could not bear it. "Brother Alf! Don't you understand? It's my fault he's dead. It was my idea to bring Rhydderch here; I brought him; and he—he killed—"

So young, so strong; he had borne all that Alf had borne, and been a shield and a fortress, and never wavered or fallen. "Jehan," Alf said. "Jehan. It was none of your doing."

"It was!" he cried.

Alf shook him. "Jehan de Sevigny, Rhydderch's coming put an end to the war and to the quarrel between kings. When he died, when no one else could move or think, you did both, splendidly."

"I started the whole thing. The least I could do was put an end to it."

"Which you did, most well. You're fit to walk among kings, Jehan."

"I'm not fit to walk with a dog." Jehan dashed away tears, angrily. "I wish people would stop praising me and see what an idiot I am."

"You are yourself. That's enough."

Jehan's brows contracted. "Here you are, giving me my own advice. And you're barely in any condition to bear your own burdens, let alone mine."

"No," Alf said. "I think I'm stronger than I ever was." He settled his arm about the tense shoulders. At first they tightened, but little by little their tautness eased. Jehan drooped against him.

He smoothed the unruly hair, gently. "Just before Morwin went to the Light, he paused. He turned back to me with the joy already on his face, and said, 'Don't mourn for me, Alf. And don't mourn for yourself. I'm not leaving you alone; you have Jehan to be friend and brother and son. Love him, Alf. Love him well.'"

Jehan buried his face in Alf's robe and wept.

Alf held him until he had no more tears to shed, and for a while after as he lay spent, without speech or thought.

When he stiffened, Alf let him go. He sat up, scrubbing his face with the backs of his hands, sniffing hard. "A fine great booby I am," he said. "You must be mortally ashamed of me."

Alf smiled and shook his head. His own cheeks were wet. "We both needed that. Do you feel better?"

"Yes. Yes, I do." Jehan tried a smile. It wobbled, then steadied. "Thank you, Brother Alf."

The other looked down. Gratitude had always embarrassed him.

Jehan's smile warmed. "You've changed completely, and yet you haven't changed at all. If you're going to say Mass again, does that mean you're going back to being a priest?"

"I–" Alf's fingers knotted; he stared at them as if their pattern held an answer. "I don't know. Morwin left certain things for me to do. For atonement. The Mass was one. And I'm to go to Jerusalem as a pilgrim. Whether I'm also to go as a priest, he didn't say."

"But of course you should. Isn't that what you are?"

"That's the trouble. I'm not sure I am. I'm still Richard's squire. And Gwydion–Gwydion and Thea–talked to me for a long while. Gwydion will be going back to Rhiyana very soon now, before his brother comes raging into Anglia. He's asked me to go with him as a kinsman."

"Do you want to?" asked Jehan.

Alf raised his eyes. "When I'm with him or with Thea, I feel as if I've come home. I'm no longer a witch or a monster or even a peculiar variety of saint; I'm only Alf. They could set me free to be what I was truly meant to be. Maybe even, still, a priest. A priest of the Fair Folk." His lips twitched. "The theologian in me is going to have to do some very agile thinking."

"You'll do that then," Jehan said.

"Maybe." Alf unlocked his fingers, one by one. "Maybe not."

Jehan shrugged. "It doesn't matter to me. I don't care in the least where I go, as long as it's with you."

For a long moment Alf was silent. His face was very still, his eyes at once clear and impossible to read. "Jehan," he said at last, "I love you as a brother. As a son. When I had fallen as low as I could fall, you lifted me up again and showed me how to be strong. You've been living your life for me." Jehan opened his mouth; Alf raised a hand. "Jehan, you're young. You have a whole life to live, a life of your own. You'll be a warrior, a scholar, a prince of the Church. You'll walk with kings; you'll counsel Popes; you'll even win the respect of the Infidels, who deny the Christ but who know what a man is."

"You can do all that," Jehan said. "We can do it together."

"No, Jehan. Maybe our paths will cross. Maybe they'll even converge for a space as they have now. I pray they will. But whatever you do, you must do on your own, for yourself. If I go to Rhiyana or to Jerusalem or to Winchester with the King, you must not follow me, unless your own path takes you there."

"It will—because it's yours."

"Child," Alf said, though he bridled at the word. "Your way lies for now with Bishop Aylmer."

"He'll free me if I ask."

"Don't."

Jehan glared at his feet. Great ugly feet, like all the rest of him. And in the center of him, a terrible ache.

"Jehan." He refused to look up. Alf went on quietly. "I'll tell you the truth. If we have to part, it will not be easy for me to bear. But I want you to go your own way, wherever that is, without regard for me. Please, Jehan. For my sake as much as for yours."

Jehan's shoulders hunched; his head sank between them. His voice when he spoke was rough. "If you go one way and I go another, will I ever see you again?"

"Yes," Alf answered him. "I promise."

Muscle by muscle Jehan relaxed. He drew a deep breath. "All right then. I'll grow up, and stop dangling at your tail."

Alf smiled.

He scowled. But Alf's smile was insidious. It crept through

the cracks of his ill-humor, and swelled, and shattered it, for all that he could do. He found himself smiling ruefully; then more freely, until they were both laughing like idiots over nothing at all.

32

Rhydderch's body rested in the room in which he would have slept, guarded as he had been while yet he lived. Even now he seemed to scowl, hating those who had tended him and made him seemly, clothing him as a lord and according him due honor.

Alf stood over the bier, too still and too pale. He did not respond when Richard came to stand beside him; his eyes were fixed on the dark furious face.

"If ever a man looked like the Devil's own," Richard said, "this one does."

Alf shuddered.

The King clapped him on the shoulder; he winced, for his back was still tender. "There now. He was damned long before you put the seal on it, but he'll get the Christian burial you wanted for him. There's no need to shed tears over him."

"I'm not weeping for him," said Alf. "I'm praying for his soul."

"God knows he needs it."

"Who doesn't, Sire?"

Richard laughed. "Aylmer says you have the face of an angel, and the Devil's own wit."

"A fair face and a black heart. That, say the Paulines, is the essence of elf-kind."

"Your heart is as pure as a maid's and somewhat softer." He met Alf's bright strange gaze. "We've decided to be kind to this carrion. After you've buried your Abbot, it goes back where it came from, with a company of knights to keep off the birds and bandits and a good man to hold the lands and the folk until I find a proper lord for them. One who's loyal, and who'll wait for me before he starts any wars."

"Are you going to turn against Kilhwch after all?"

Swift anger flashed across Richard's face. "Kilhwch is a splendid fellow. So is His Majesty of Rhiyana. And I'm not such a scoundrel that I'll break up a pair of noble friendships. There'll be no fighting on either side of Anglia while those friendships hold." His anger faded. "Imagine, Alfred. A King who can ride wherever he likes and leave his brother with crown and throne, and who knows that he can come back and take both without having to shed even a drop of blood. And I'm going to have a chance to see this prodigy. There's to be a tournament in Caer-y-n'Arfon in the spring, and Gwydion says the Flame-bearer will come; I'll have a chance to see which one of us is stronger."

Alf smiled. He was no longer quite so pale.

"And you," Richard said. "Aylmer's trying to steal you back from me. Anyone can see, he says, that you belong in the priesthood. You and that great clever ox of a Sevigny—you'll be the right and left hands of the Church Militant, and half the body besides."

"I know," Alf murmured. "He came to talk to me this morning. He wants me to resume my vows in full and to take up knightly training, and to teach theology to one or two of his priests."

"Will you have time to eat or sleep?"

"Occasionally."

Richard stood squarely in front of him. "Tell me now," he said. "Tell me the truth. If you were free to do whatever you chose, would you go with him?"

"Once upon a time," said Alf, "two men disputed the ownership of a fine hound. One had raised it from a pup; the other had found it wandering in the wood, and taken it and fed it and trained it to hunt. They took their case to their liege lord. He heard each side of the story, and deliberated for a long while; at last he had his men draw a circle on the floor of his hall and place the hound in it. The owners stood on opposite sides and called to it."

He stopped. Richard frowned. "So? What happened?"

"The beast lay down," Alf replied, "and calmly went to sleep."

The King glared, then laughed. "The Devil's wit, indeed! Who's calling you?"

"Aylmer, for one. Gwydion wants me to go with him to Rhiyana. My Abbot, when he died, bade me make a pilgrimage to Jerusalem. And you, Sire." Alf smiled wryly. "I haven't forgotten the promise I made to you, though you've been most kind to let me see my Abbot to his rest as if I were still one of his monks. When his Mass is over, if you command me, I'll put on your livery again."

"And if I don't command you? If I leave you free to choose?"

Alf was silent. Richard could find no answer in his face, nor in his eyes that were the same color as the winter sun.

The King's voice roughened. "When you have a hawk, there comes a time when you have to set it free. If it comes back it's yours. If not . . ." He drew a breath. "I'm freeing you. You can go with your priests or to your Fair Folk. Or you can rule Anglia with me. In Winchester I'll make you a knight and give you lands and riches, and set you among my great lords. And in the spring after the tournament in Gwynedd, we'll start planning a new Crusade. You'll have your pilgrimage to Jerusalem, Alfred, and a kingdom there if you want one. And after that we can travel to Constantinople, just as we said we would when we were riding to Carlisle." His face was flushed, eager, lively as a boy's. "Tell me, Alfred. Tell me you'll do it. With you by me, there's no one in the world who can conquer me."

"Sire," Alf said. He moved away from Rhydderch's body, that weighed like a stone upon heart and mind. Richard followed him until they stood together by the cold hearth. "Sire, I've been offered so much. Aylmer promises to set the Church at my feet; Gwydion opens the realm of the Fair Folk to me. And you spread before me all the kingdoms of the world."

A shadow crossed Richard's face. "Is that all I am to you? A tempter?"

"My lord, you know that's not so."

"Do you realize that you've never called me by my name?"

"You're my King, Sire. I wouldn't presume—"

Richard struck the wall with his fist. "Damn you! You've presumed to rule me, heart and soul, since the day you met me."

"Richard," Alf said. "Richard, my lord. You see so much, can't you see that I look on you as my friend?"

"I see it," Richard answered harshly. "I wanted to hear it."

Alf, who spoke as much with touch as with words, had never touched Richard. He laid his hand very lightly upon the King's shoulder. "You never once tried to overstep the boundaries I set. For that I learned to love you."

Richard trembled under his hand.

He did not draw it away. "Richard. I have so many choices, who never had any, who needed to have no thoughts of my own but only to do as I was bidden. Each choice is one I would make gladly. But I can't have them all. Only one."

"And that's not mine."

"No!" Alf cried. "Don't you see? I don't know. I can't choose. Bishop Aylmer thinks I should go back to Winchester for Yule and do my thinking there; then I can go where I will."

"That makes sense."

"Do you think so?" Alf let his hand fall from Richard's shoulder. His eyes were troubled. "Sire, I have to think. I have to pray. But whatever I choose, remember. Remember that I'm still your friend. Your brother, even, if you will."

For a long moment the King stared at him, as if to commit to memory every line of his face. Suddenly, swiftly, Richard embraced him, and let him go, stepping back. "I'll remember," he said. He turned away, striding past Rhydderch's body, paying it no heed.

Alf drew a shuddering breath. "There," he whispered to the empty hearth, the dead shape, "truly, is a King."

* * * * *

> "*Sing praise to the Lord, you His faithful ones, and give thanks to His holy name.*
> *For His anger lasts but a moment; a lifetime, His good will.*
> *At nightfall, weeping comes in, but with the dawn, rejoicing.*"

Such a contrast, Alf thought, between Rhydderch and his victim. Morwin lay in state in the chapel, surrounded with candles and incense and the chanting of monks. He seemed strange, lying so still, who had been lively and restless even in sleep; the robes of a Lord Abbot had displaced his old brown habit. But his face bore a hint of his wicked smile.

Almost Alf could hear his dry humorous voice. "All this fuss for a silly old fool. I should sit up and grin, and give them all a proper fright."

Alf smiled and touched the cold hand. Something glittered beneath it upon his breast. Alf's fingers found the shape of a cross, the cool smoothness of silver, and a memory of Thea's presence.

> "*To you, O Lord, I cried out; with the Lord I pleaded:*
> '*What gain would there be from my life-blood, from my going down into the grave?*'"

The chanting rolled over them both, living and dead. From where Alf stood, he could see the shadow that was the doorway of the Lady Chapel, a faint glimmer as of painted stars. The lamp there was extinguished, the chapel forbidden until it should be cleansed of the stain of murder. Bishop Aylmer would do that tomorrow after the funeral Mass.

> *"You changed my mourning into dancing: You took off my sackcloth*
> *and clothed me with gladness,*
> *That my soul might sing praise to You without ceasing; O Lord,*
> *my God, forever will I give You thanks."*

Alf knelt beside the bier and bowed his head over his folded hands.

"Brother? Brother Alfred?"

The chapel had been silent for a long while. Alf straightened slowly, stiffly. Several monks stood near him, watching him: Brother Osric, Brother Owein, and old Brother Herbal.

Looking into their faces, he realized that they had always thought well of him. The younger ones had been his pupils; Brother Herbal had taken vows a year or two before he had. Familiar, all of them, and yes, beloved.

Brother Osric cleared his throat. A bright lad, he had been; aging now, his eyes, never good, peering myopically through the dimness. "Brother," he said again. "We've met in Chapter, all of us, to elect our new Abbot. Some of us wanted you to be there. But . . . well . . . you were sent out and you came back a layman, and there's the matter of—of—"

Osric had always lost all fluency when he was agitated. Alf finished the sentence for him. "Murder," he said. "I know, Brother. I understand. And I appreciate your coming here to tell me." He looked from face to face. "Whom shall I congratulate?"

They would not answer. Yet they had chosen someone; that much Alf could read, even without witchery. Someone important, and someone controversial, from the gleam in Brother Owein's eye and the set of Brother Osric's jaw.

Brother Herbal frowned. Like Morwin, he had never had much patience. "Well, Brothers? Isn't anybody going to tell him?"

Alf stood. His knees ached; his back was twinging. He had lost the knack of kneeling for long hours on hard stones. "What's the trouble? It can't be anyone I'd object to very strenuously; I'm not such a fool that I'd demand another Morwin."

"Good," said Brother Herbal. "Because Morwin, you're not."

"What do I have to do with—" Alf broke off. He knew. God help him, he knew.

He wanted to burst into wild laughter. Four times now. Would they never learn? And five choices, it made. Five. He would go mad.

"Now look here," Brother Owein said sternly, as if he had been a stubborn novice. "This is becoming a ritual. Elect Brother Alfred; argue with him; lose the argument; and go through the whole foolish process again to elect someone less able but more willing. I know Dom Morwin wanted you to be Abbot after him—and so did Dom Andreas, Dom Willibrord, and probably Dom Lanfranc, too. Haven't you got the message by now?"

Alf sank down upon the altar steps, so pale that Brother Herbal hastened to him. He waved the old man away. "I'm not going to faint. I'm not going to shout at you, or howl, or even weep. I'm not even going to remind you that I'm still recovering from trial for witchcraft, or that I killed a man on sacred ground."

He held out his hands to them. "Brothers, you honor me more than I can say. To gather, all of you, and to elect me your Abbot, even knowing what I am and what I've done . . . I think I shall weep, after all."

Brother Herbal grimaced. "Go ahead. But tell us first. Yes or no?"

Alf looked at each in turn. "You know that I have a charge from Morwin to seek absolution in Jerusalem."

"We know," Osric answered. "If you go now, you go as Abbot, and some of us will go with you. By your leave, of course."

He wanted to laugh again, for pain. "Oh, Brothers! Do you know what torment this is? I stand upon a peak in the desert with all of heaven and earth spread about me, and voices whispering in my ear, bidding me look and choose. A warrior-priest in the Bishop's train, a lord of Anglia, an elven-knight of Rhiyana —and now, Abbot of St. Ruan's. Dear God! What shall I do?"

Brother Owein stood over him, hands on hips. "All of a sudden your worth is catching up with you. I don't doubt you'd make a good knight or lord or priest; you'd certainly make a better Abbot than most." He glanced at his companions. "We had orders to make you accept, by force if necessary. But we didn't know how many others had been at you. The abbey can manage as it is for a day or two. Take the time. Meditate. Pray. Say the Mass and ask for guidance. Then tell us. Yes, or—God forbid—no."

They left him then, with many glances over their shoulders. The last, as they passed the door, found him upon his face before the altar. His shoulders shook. Weeping, they wondered, or laughter?

33

Reverently, lovingly, Alf lifted the vestments from the press where he had laid them away, so long ago. They bore a sweet red-brown scent, for the press was of cedar of Lebanon. Amice and alb, white linen of his own weaving; the cincture from his first habit, soft with age; maniple and stole; and the chasuble of black Chin silk, embroidered with silver thread, heavy with pearls.

He laid out each garment as an acolyte would have done, but the novices who would serve him, and the Bishop and the priests of St. Ruan's who would concelebrate the Mass, had busied themselves elsewhere in the sacristy, leaving him alone with his priesthood and his God. He found that his hands were shaking, nor could he stop them; his heart pounded. To say the Mass, and this Mass of all others, with such burdens as weighted his mind and his heart, and perhaps also his soul, if soul he had . . .

He leaned against the wall, breathing deep again and again. *Dear God*, he thought. *Morwin, make me strong. It's been so long, so long; and I am not worthy. I am — not —*

Jehan's concern pierced through his barriers. He forced himself to straighten, to take up the amice. His hands, his mind, remembered. He touched the garment to his head and laid it about his shoulders, murmuring a prayer.

He reached for the alb. Jehan held it out to him. For a moment their hands touched. Alf smiled. "My bulwark," he said. "Thank you, Jehan."

The novice bowed, smiling back; Alf drew the white robe over his head. There was comfort in this ritual of robing, each movement prescribed, each thought foreordained. For so long he had only served and watched; he had forgotten the quiet joy at the center of the rite.

One of the novices peered round the door. "Almost time," he said.

They were all without, the monks, the kings and their men, even Thea, schismatic Greek that she was. Her mind brushed Alf's for an instant, bright and strong.

The procession had taken shape while he paused. He moved into his place, walking slowly beneath the weight of his vestments.

As he passed Aylmer, the Bishop touched his arm. "Remember," he whispered. "'Thou art a priest forever, in the order of Melchisedec.'"

Forever.

He lifted his chin. The chant had begun, slow and deep. "*Requiem aeternam dona eis, Domine* . . . : Eternal rest grant unto them, O Lord, and let perpetual light shine upon them. . . ."

Morwin lay before the altar dais, as for three days he had lain with Alf as his constant companion. The procession moved slowly past him, Alf last of all, and divided, each man or boy taking his place as the ritual commanded.

Alf bowed low to the Abbot on his bier and lower still to the altar. In the silence after the antiphon, his voice was soft and pure. "I will go up to the altar of God."

"To God who gives joy to my youth," the acolytes responded.

He gathered all of his courage, and went up.

*   *   *   *   *

Richard watched him as he had watched on that first day in the camp by the lake. Then Alf had been only an acolyte; now he was the priest, Abbot-elect of St. Ruan's. Yet he looked the same, too fair to be human, rapt in the exaltation of the Mass.

As the rite continued, it seemed to the King that all light gathered about the slender figure on the altar. The priests about him, the novices moving about their duties, the chanting monks, faded to shadows. When he raised the Host, it blazed like a sun; his splendid voice rang forth: "*Hoc est enim corpus meum:* For this is my body."

Richard covered his eyes with his hands. Mass had always been a duty, and a dull one at that. But this was different. God, the God he had ignored or given only lip service, had entered into this place and shone through the priest, the sorcerer, the manslayer, soulless and deathless.

He is a priest, the King thought, too certain of it even to despair. *Aylmer will have him. Aylmer or the abbey. What a fool I was to think that I could ever make a lord of him!*

Looking up, he found Gwydion's gray eyes upon him. The Elvenking shook his head very slightly. *Wait*, his gaze said. *He has not chosen yet. Wait and see.*

At the height of his exaltation, Alf looked again upon the Light to which Morwin had gone; approached it and almost touched it. In that moment he felt again Morwin's presence, like a warm hand in his, a quick smile, a murmured word. *Well done, Alf. Oh, well done!*

The young face within the Light, the old one upon the bier, merged and became one. His voice lifted. "'May angels lead you to Paradise; at your coming, may the martyrs receive you, and lead you into the holy city of Jerusalem. May a choir of angels receive you, and with Lazarus, who was once a beggar, may you find eternal rest.'"

Strong monks took the bier upon their shoulders and paced forward. In a cloud of chanting and of incense they bore it through the chapel, down a long stair into the musty dark of the crypt. There they laid it down, the chanting muted now, the incense dimming the flicker of candles. With gentle hands they raised the Abbot's body and set it in a niche, among the bones and the rotting splendor of the abbots who had gone before him.

The chanting faded and died. Alf bent and marked the cold brow with the sign of the Cross, and kissed it gently. "Sleep well," he whispered.

He turned. The lights and the candles departed one by one, leaving Morwin to his long sleep.

Alf took off his vestments as reverently as he had put them on. No one spoke to him, not even Jehan who served him, for the light lingered still in his face. When at last he stood in his brown habit, Jehan glanced aside, intent upon his duties; Alf slipped away.

The Thorn of Ynys Witrin slept its sleep which was like death, its boughs heavy with snow as with blossoms in spring. Alf stood beneath it, brown as it was, crowned with white.

He laid his hand upon the gnarled trunk. The power glimmered in it as in the stone of Bowland, rising drowsily to touch his own—a warmth, a green silence. It no longer wished him ill, if indeed it ever had.

"Choices," Alf said to it. "So many choices. 'A priest forever.' I am; yet I'm so many other things besides. What shall I do? Shall I be the Lord Abbot? Can you endure that? Shall I be rather a soldier of God? An elven-knight, or a prince of Anglia? What shall I be? What can I be?"

The wind whispered in the branches, yet without words. The gray sky bent over him. High above him a hawk wheeled, crying.

He turned his face to it. It was no common hawk, merlin or kestrel, but a splendid bird, the hawk of princes, the peregrine. Even as he watched, it turned upon its great wings and sped away eastward.

His breath caught. An answer, after all, and so simple. "I forgot," he said. "Dear God, forgive me for being a fool. I forgot, that Abbot or priest or knight, I remain myself. Alfred. Alf. Not Sir or Lord or Father or Brother. Only Alf. Myself."

Himself—with all the world before him and choices without number, and freedom at last. Freedom to choose as he would.

A moment longer he hesitated. He was afraid. To choose, who had never chosen—what if he chose ill?

What if he did not choose at all?

All of St. Ruan's gathered in the hall for the Abbot's funeral feast. Even Brother Kyriell had left his post at the gate, freed for once from his duties.

But a lone figure stood under the arch, wrapped in a cloak, waiting.

Alf regarded her without surprise, as she regarded him. "You've chosen," she said.

He nodded.

She looked him over from cowled head to sandaled foot. "You're going away."

"To Jerusalem."

"Alone?"

He nodded again. "Morwin thought I'd find peace there. Or at least that the journey would show me how to accept myself for what I am."

"And the kings? The Bishop? The monks?"

"They all want me to be a great lord. But how can I be great or high or lordly, if I don't even know myself? I'll be Alfred now, and only Alfred. I think they'll understand."

"They'll try," she said.

There was a silence. Alf stared at his feet. "Tell Jehan. The books in my cell are for him. With my love. The ring with the moonstone in it and the gold bezant, I'm keeping; but all the rest of his gifts my lord Richard can dispose of as he wills. Aylmer must have my vestments that I wore in the Mass. And

Gwydion . . . tell him to look in the coffer in the Abbot's study. The altar cloth there is my gift to him. And Fara—Fara he must have again. Tell him."

"I'll tell everybody."

"The Brothers will have to elect someone else. I hope they choose Owein. He'd make good Abbot, better than I."

She said nothing.

"And for you," he said. "For you I have this." He took her face in his hands. Lightly, awkwardly, he kissed her.

He drew back. Her eyes were wide, all gold; he could not meet them. "Good-bye," he said. "God be with you."

Still she did not speak.

He shot the bolts and pushed open the postern. A thin cold wind danced about him, blowing from the east. He turned his face to it and his back to the abbey, and left the gate behind.

Thea stood for a long moment as he had left her. He did not look back with eyes or mind.

Where a woman had stood lay a crumpled dark cloak. A white hound ran down the long road.

Her four feet were swifter than his two, and lighter upon the snow. She drew level with him, leaped ahead of him, bounded about him.

He stopped. "Thea," he said. His voice was stern, cold.

Jehan was a fool, she said in her mind. *He asked if he could come. I'm not asking*. She trotted ahead a yard or two and paused, looking bright-eyed over her shoulder. *Well, little Brother? Are you coming?*

He drew breath as if to speak. All that he might have done or said raced through his mind. Thea watched it all with dancing eyes. Did he think that any man, even an elf-priest, could gainsay her?

Suddenly he laughed. "Not even a saint," he said.

She ran before him, and he followed her, striding to Jerusalem.

ANDRÉ NORTON

☐ 54738-1 THE CRYSTAL GRYPHON $2.95
   54739-X   Canada $3.50

☐ 48558-1 FORERUNNER $2.75

☐ 54747-0 FORERUNNER: THE SECOND $2.95
   54748-9 VENTURE   Canada $3.50

☐ 54736-5 GRYPHON'S EYRIE $2.95
   54737-3 (with A. C. Crispin)   Canada $3.50

☐ 54732-2 HERE ABIDE MONSTERS $2.95
   54733-0   Canada $3.50

☐ 54743-8 HOUSE OF SHADOWS $2.95
   54744-6 (with Phyllis Miller) Canada $3.50

☐ 54740-3 MAGIC IN ITHKAR (edited by
Andre Norton and Robert Adams) Trade $6.95
   54741-1   Canada $7.95

☐ 54745-4 MAGIC IN ITHKAR 2 (edited by
Norton and Adams)   Trade $6.95
   54746-2   Canada $7.95

☐ 54734-9 MAGIC IN ITHKAR 3 (edited by
Norton and Adams)   Trade $6.95
   54735-7   Canada $8.95

☐ 54727-6 MOON CALLED $2.95
   54728-4   Canada $3.50

☐ 54725-X WHEEL OF STARS $2.95
   54720-8   Canada $3.50

Buy them at your local bookstore or use this handy coupon:
Clip and mail this page with your order

TOR BOOKS—Reader Service Dept.
49 W. 24 Street, 9th Floor, New York, NY 10010

Please send me the book(s) I have checked above. I am enclosing
$_____ (please add $1.00 to cover postage and handling).
Send check or money order only—no cash or C.O.D.'s.

Mr./Mrs./Miss _____

Address _____

City _____ State/Zip _____

Please allow six weeks for delivery. Prices subject to change without notice.

FRED SABERHAGEN

☐ 55327-6 BERSERKER BASE $3.95
  55328-4 Canada $4.95

☐ 55322-5 BERSERKER: BLUE DEATH (Trade) $6.95
  55323-3 Canada $8.95

☐ 55318-7 THE BERSERKER THRONE $3.50
  55319-5 Canada $4.50

☐ 55312-8 THE BERSERKER WARS $3.50
  55313-6 Canada $4.50

☐ 48564-6 EARTH DESCENDED $2.95

☐ 55335-7 THE FIRST BOOK OF SWORDS $3.50
  55336-5 Canada $4.50

☐ 55331-4 THE SECOND BOOK OF SWORDS $3.50
  55332-2 Canada $4.50

☐ 55333-0 THE THIRD BOOK OF SWORDS $3.50
  55334-9 Canada $4.50

☐ 55309-8 THE MASK OF THE SUN $2.95
  55310-1 Canada $3.95

☐ 52550-7 AN OLD FRIEND OF THE FAMILY $3.50
  52551-5 Canada $4.50

☐ 55290-3 THE WATER OF THOUGHT $2.95
  55291-1 Canada $3.50

Buy them at your local bookstore or use this handy coupon:
Clip and mail this page with your order

ST. MARTIN'S/TOR BOOKS—Reader Service Dept.
175 Fifth Avenue, New York, NY 10010

Please send me the book(s) I have checked above. I am enclosing
$_____ (please add $1.00 to cover postage and handling).
Send check or money order only—no cash or C.O.D.'s.

Mr./Mrs./Miss _____

Address _____

City _____ State/Zip _____

Please allow six weeks for delivery. Prices subject to change
without notice.

HARRY HARRISON

☐	48505-0	A Transatlantic Tunnel, Hurrah!	$2.50
☐	48540-9	The Jupiter Plague	$2.95
☐	48565-4	Planet of the Damned	$2.95
☐	48557-3	Planet of No Return	$2.75
☐	48031-8	The QE2 Is Missing	$2.95
☐	48554-9	A Rebel in Time	$3.50